SEE ALSO MURDER

SEE ALSO MURDER

A MARJORIE TRUMAINE MYSTERY

LARRY D. SWEAZY

SEVENTH STREET BOOKS®
AN IMPRINT OF PROMETHEUS BOOKS
59 JOHN GLENN DRIVE • AMHERST, NY 14228
www.seventhstreetbooks.com

Published 2015 by Seventh Street Books®, an imprint of Prometheus Books

Based on the short story "See Also Murder," Amazon Shorts, 2006

Cover design by Jacqueline Nasso Cooke
Cover image © Shai_Halud/Shutterstock.com;
Nic Taylor/Mediabakery; Korionov/Shutterstock.com

Inquiries should be addressed to
Seventh Street Books
59 John Glenn Drive
Amherst, New York 14228
VOICE: 716–691–0133 • FAX: 716–691–0137
WWW.SEVENTHSTREETBOOKS.COM

19 18 17 16 15 • 5 4 3 2 1

Library of Congress Cataloging-in-Publication Data

Sweazy, Larry D.
    See also murder : a Marjorie Trumaine mystery / by Larry D. Sweazy.
        pages ; cm
    ISBN 978-1-63388-006-1 (paperback) — ISBN 978-1-63388-007-8 (ebook)
    I. Title.

PS3619.W438S44 2015
813'.6—dc23

2014047728

Printed in the United States of America

To Carla Hall, Patrick Kanouse,
Cheryl Lenser, and Ginny Bess Munroe.
Without your efforts and support,
I would not have had the opportunity to
discover that I was an indexer or developed
the skills and experience to write this book.
Thank you. You opened a door that changed my life.

"We started dying before the snow, and like the snow, we continued to fall."

—Louise Erdrich, *Tracks*

"She must think everything out for herself with an occasional question."

—Mary Petherbridge,
"Indexing as a Profession for Women,"
Good Housekeeping, 1923

CHAPTER 1

July 1964

I saw a plume of dust through the window over my desk, and something told me trouble was heading my way. We weren't expecting anyone—not that we got much company, and it was too far past planting season for it to be the new county extension agent coming to introduce himself.

I carefully marked the page proof I'd been staring at for an hour, put the lid on my shoe box full of index cards, and gave a thought to running a brush through my hair but decided I didn't have time.

Even from half a mile away, I recognized Sheriff Hilo Jenkins' battered pickup truck.

Hilo had seen me in worse shape than I was at the moment, and I knew this wasn't a social call or him checking in on Hank. The sheriff normally reserved those visits for Sundays, after church and a long nap. It tore Hilo up to see my husband bedridden, a tiny shell of the man he was before the accident, but Hilo always came anyway—rain, shine, or subzero temperatures. Sometimes, I thought, just to fill me in on the latest gossip circulating around town; to remind me that I was still alive and that there was more to my life than nursing Hank the best I could and writing indexes for books nobody in North Dakota would probably ever read.

I took my reading glasses off, stood up, stared at the pile of papers on my desk, the stack of blank index cards next to my Underwood typewriter, then at the pile of books on the floor, overflowing from the shelves. I was in the midst of writing an index to *The Forgotten Tribe of*

Africa and the Myth of Headhunter Civilizations by Sir Nigel Preston. I forced a smile. How odd was it that a farmer's wife in North Dakota would be responsible for such an important part of a book about head-hunters? Life, I had decided not too long after Hank's accident, sure takes some funny turns.

With a chill rising up my spine, even though it was midsummer, I slid out of my book-filled office—a spare bedroom that was once reserved for a child who never came—as quietly as I could.

I peeked in on Hank. I could see his chest rising and falling. He slept peacefully, taking his afternoon nap. Nightmares were reserved for the middle of the night.

By the time I got to the front porch, Hilo was stepping out of his truck.

Our dog, Shep, a six-year-old border collie, didn't bother to bark at Hilo's truck. The dog knew the sound of the sheriff's engine from a mile away. Instead, Shep circled around Hilo, trying his best to herd him along to get a reward for a job well done. Shep was a good farm dog, more Hank's than mine since the two of them had spent more time together, but Shep and I had come to an agreeable understanding since the change of our fates. We'd had to rely on each other more than we ever had; he needed to obey me as well as he had obeyed Hank. And for the most part, he did.

The sky was crystal clear, blue as a freshly polished sapphire. No clouds, a little breeze, songbirds celebrating in the distance. It was about as perfect a summer day as you could ask for. Perfect weather was a rare gem.

"Hey there, Marjorie." Hilo nodded and doffed his hat quickly, exposing a bald head with a few wiry white hairs poking out on the sides. Hilo had been the sheriff of Stark County for nearly thirty years.

"I would have made some lemonade had I known you were coming," I said, stopping at the edge of the porch.

"Sorry to barge in on you. How's Hank?"

"The same." To most everyone else, except Hilo, I always responded that Hank was getting better every day. My lie comforted them, made them feel useful. I always smiled and looked into their eyes a little longer than necessary, so they wouldn't press further. It worked about a quarter of the time.

Early in grouse season last year, Hank had slipped. The shotgun he was carrying had the safety off. He tumbled forward and the gun went off, spraying his face with bird shot, blinding him in both eyes. The blast stunned him but didn't knock him out. He staggered forward and slipped again, this time into a gopher hole. Unable to catch himself, he fell backward.

The fall was the worst part of the accident. Hank fell on a huge rock, fracturing a vertebra and snapping his spine. He couldn't move or see and he was alone, a trifecta of bad luck. It was only by pure chance that Hilo Jenkins found him before he died.

I had gotten worried and called Hilo. We met at Hank's truck and, with a few other deputies, started looking for him. I was grateful that I wasn't the one who found him. I could never have gotten that image out of my mind. Not that I hadn't seen some awful things since . . . but that was the end of one way of life and the beginning of another.

The gloom in our house seemed to extend to the rest of the world a month later when President Kennedy was shot in Dallas. I was sitting in the hospital room when Walter Cronkite made the announcement and wiped a tear from his eye. I was cried out by then. For us, the accident was the end of Hank how I knew him, how I could love him, replaced by a different Hank. One that preferred dying to living. He'd begged for death to take him a million times since *our* fateful day, since waking to find his life so altered, but the Grim Reaper had been stubborn, deaf to Hank's pleas and my guilt-ridden prayers. If there was a bright spot to the accident, it was the fact that Hank couldn't remember a thing about the fall, the pain, or the fear. His memory, like the rest of his body, had been perforated by holes that had yet to heal—and might never heal, as far as the doctors were concerned.

Hilo nodded again, his gaze lowered to the ground. "You got a minute to sit and talk, Marjorie?" There was a quiver in his voice that I'd never heard before. Not even on the day of Hank's accident.

"Sure," I said, not moving. "Is something the matter?"

"Why don't we just sit, Marjorie," Hilo said. He dug into his pocket, tossed Shep a treat, and nodded his head hard to the right, signaling the dog to leave him alone.

Shep was more a reader of people, hand motions and such, than a dog who obeyed words. Another sign that he was Hank's dog and not mine. Words were all Shep and I had. Hank used hand signals to communicate with the dog. I had never paid close enough attention to learn them all.

Shep took the treat, eased to the bottom of the steps after a quick pat on his thick-coated, black-and-white head, lay down, and enjoyed Hilo's gift of a half-dollar-sized bone from last night's round steak.

"I can put some coffee on," I said. Hilo was making me nervous.

"No, that's fine. Mighty nice of you, Marjorie, but really, I can't stay long. I just have a question or two for you. This is police business I'm here for."

Unsettled by the sheriff's surprise call and uneasiness, I shook my head and sat down on the wicker settee Hank had built for me on our first wedding anniversary. We'd watched many a sunset from that spot. It seemed like so long ago—when everything was fresh and new.

Hilo leaned against the house a few inches from the front door. A sliver of white paint peeled off the frame and floated to the floor. "There isn't an easy way to tell you this, but we found Erik Knudsen dead this morning."

I felt the air leave my chest. That was the last thing I expected to come out of Hilo's mouth. "An accident?" I wasn't sure where the words came from. An automatic response.

Hilo shook his head no. "Lida, too. They were murdered sometime during the night."

Before I could catch my breath, I asked how. It was the same question I'd asked when Hilo came to tell me he'd found Hank in the shape he was in.

You got accustomed to tragedy on the plains, isolated like we were. The Knudsens' farm was the next one over, ten minutes as the crow flies.

Dickinson was a half-an-hour drive for us in the summer, two hours in the winter, if not more. There was usually no time to flower anything up. I had learned how to get to the point quickly from my father. Some people found it to be an annoying trait, and I'd embarrassed myself on more than one occasion by opening my mouth before I thought things through, but I just couldn't help myself. I suppose I didn't want to change. Didn't see any reason to smooth things over since I spent most of my time with my nose buried in page proofs, writing indexes, tending to Hank, and seeing to the farm the best I could.

"You sure you want to hear this?" Hilo asked. He peered inside the open door, hoping, I suppose, to catch a glimpse of Hank sleeping.

"I'll hear it sooner or later. I'd rather hear it from you so the facts'll be straight."

I gripped the arm of the settee, fending off the urge to run and put a chicken in the oven. Then I chastised myself for running through a list of ingredients, for making sure I had enough of everything in my cupboard to deliver the comfort of a daily meal. I'd always made lists. They helped me stay organized, focused in chaos. I supposed that was one of the reasons I took to writing indexes as easily as I had. Lists came to me as naturally as breathing.

I searched for a way to relieve my own fear and discomfort. I was as human as everyone else was, and I wasn't sure how I felt about Hilo's revelation at that moment.

"All right," he said. "They had their throats slit while they were asleep in bed. No sign of a struggle. Probably didn't know what happened. They had the window open, so we figure whoever did it slipped in and out unseen."

"Peter and Jaeger?"

"Asleep in their own beds. Didn't hear a thing. Thought it was odd when their mother wasn't up cooking breakfast, so they went in and checked on them."

"And they found them." I closed my eyes. The chicken didn't seem to matter any longer.

Every memory I held dear of the Knudsens flooded my mind,

and overflowed silently out of my eyes. I wiped away my tears as Hilo nodded and looked away, out over the empty paddock that reached toward the Knudsens' farm. Purple Martins dived and careened over it, feeding on mosquitoes and other insects.

Shep looked up, finished with the treat, content to lie on the ground and watch over the farm. There was concern in the dog's amber colored eyes. Usually those eyes were focused, certain of their task, but now, the dog looked like he understood every word Hilo was saying. That didn't surprise me a bit. I'd seen that look in Shep's eyes before.

"They called me right away," Hilo continued. "I guess those boys are orphans now." He looked down sadly and kicked an imaginary bit of dust off the porch.

Hilo Jenkins knew more about injustice and the meanness human beings could inflict on one another than I ever would, but it was easy to see that he was shaken to the bone by what he'd found on his plate of duties this morning. I knew him well enough to know that sooner or later he was going to get angry—mad as hell—that there was a murderer wandering around loose in his county.

Someone had set an edge of uncertainty on every human being within a hundred-mile radius, had taken peace and comfort away with an act that destroyed, and had brought terror to Stark County under Hilo Jenkins' watch. He took things like that personal.

We were simple, hardworking people. Not murderers—killers who used sharp knives and evil ways to resolve their problems. At least that was the way it had been before the Knudsens met a death that no one could have ever imagined.

CHAPTER 2

Tragedy and neighbors came in all forms on the plains, and on the day Hank had his accident I had been blessed and cursed in one fell swoop.

It had seemed like the whole town had showed up to pitch in or take a closer look for themselves at our place, at our troubles. But it was the Knudsens who took charge of the farm. They had volunteered to plant the wheat crop in the spring—which they did—then tended to the pigs that would provide meat through the winter and chopped what firewood remained, all the jobs Hank was set to do but couldn't because he was laid up in the hospital in Dickinson.

Erik had supervised and Peter and Jaeger, two eager boys barely past their teenage years, had done most of the chores on our place after they finished work on their own farm. Lida had brought dinner for months after the accident became old news and everyone else had gotten on with their lives.

Peter and Jaeger became like sons to me. At first, I took little joy in watching them work the farm and keep it alive as if it were their own, but after a while, as I secured my routine of tending to Hank after he came home and writing indexes late into the night to keep some money coming in the door, I had found comfort in their continual presence. The boys were ghosts of Hank's youth and vigor that I could touch and smell. Wheat sprang up in the steps they left behind, shocks promising to pile high at harvest, like golden mounds offered to the deaf God who supposedly resided in the wide, blue sky above.

Now it was my turn to attend to *their* loss, to ease Peter and Jaeger's pain and offer whatever comfort I could. I could barely speak or look into Hilo's drooping eyes as the news reverberated inside my chest, rattling my heart in a way that made it difficult to breathe.

"We had to question both of them, you understand," Hilo said in a sheriff's tone. "Rule them out as suspects."

I had not even considered that Peter or Jaeger could be killers.

"But," Hilo continued, picking up the fleck of paint off the porch floor, then stuffing it into his pants pocket, "I'm pretty certain that they didn't have anything to do with it."

I sighed. Relieved.

"Certain, but not one hundred percent positive, you understand," he added.

Hilo reached into his other pocket and pulled out a small object, a piece of jewelry, and handed it to me. "This was in Erik's right hand. I was hoping you could tell me what it means."

Shep's curiosity was piqued, anticipating another treat. But this was no reward. I subtlety shook my head no with a quick glance to the object, and Shep looked away, back to the horizon, searching for coyotes—or whatever else lurked out there.

The sheriff placed the odd-looking medallion gently in my hand. The center was made of copper and was clean, not tarnished with ancient green flecks at all, so I was immediately curious about its age. In the shade of the bright afternoon sun, I could see an outline of a lightning bolt in the medallion, though it looked like it had been rubbed down by human touch over the years, telling me the amulet was old but cared for. Three runes rimmed the copper; each one had a main character—a wolf, a serpent, and the face of a harried and evil-looking woman. Squiggles of ancient writing circled the smooth edge.

"It's an amulet of some kind," I finally said, holding it out to Hilo. I felt hollow inside, knowing the amulet had been found in Erik Knudsen's cold, dead hand.

Hilo stood stiff, silently refusing to take the amulet. "You don't know what it means? What it says?"

"It looks like something from Norse mythology, which wouldn't be surprising coming from around here. I don't know the language.

My Aunt Gilda, my father's sister, had some old jewelry that had been passed down through the years that kind of looked like this. She traveled the world with her professor husband and collected some great trinkets, things related to our heritage."

The sheriff shifted his weight and looked down the lane that led out to the road. "Do you think you could figure out what it says? What it is? I don't mix well with those college-types in Dickinson, and I figured you'd be the best person to come to. You're the . . ."

I nodded, anticipating what Hilo was going to say.

". . . smartest person I know."

At that moment, my love for books seemed like a curse more than a blessing. Not long after we got Shep, about five years ago, we hit a rough patch on the farm. A drought hit the spring wheat, dropping the yield to an all-time low. The price per bushel was already down because of the bad economy of the late '50s, during the waning Eisenhower years, and it was forced even lower by the weather.

A confluence of events struck us hard. Hank had bought a new combine the year before, straining our budget even in the best of times. Knowing our situation was dire, the previous county extension agent, Lloyd Gustaffson, had brought me a packet of paperwork from the United States Department of Agriculture. Inside was a list of courses designed for farmers' wives to make extra money during the long winters. I was immediately fascinated by the idea of writing indexes.

It was a job that could be done from anywhere but took attention to detail, tenacity, an ability to meet deadlines, and a love of books and words—all of which I felt I wholly possessed. I was a compulsive list maker, punctual—I couldn't remember the last time I was late for *anything*—and a neat and tidy housekeeper by nature. If something was out of place, I noticed. I'd read compulsively since I was a little girl.

I took the correspondence course, learned how to pick out keywords and concepts from the densest text, how to format and type up an acceptable index, and how to solicit work from publishers far away in the dreamland of New York City.

Indexes, I learned from the course, were a garden of words neatly tended—weedy modifiers pulled and discarded—only the most important ideas left to grow in unknown minds. The index, my work, would provide sustenance to the world in a tiny, tiny way, but a helpful, meaningful way, nonetheless. The work made me feel useful, like I was helping make the world outside my own front door better. I had desperately needed to feel hopeful, especially in those early days after the accident when things went from bad to worse.

Never believing that I could actually make money from reading books and writing indexes, I mailed fifty letters of inquiry after successfully completing the USDA course, expecting nothing in return. To my surprise, I was hired almost immediately by a well-established publisher, H.P. Howard and Sons. Two weeks later I was winding my way through the tedious process of writing my very first index.

The extra money saw us through the drought and helped us get ahead on the payments for the combine—until Hank went hunting and came back on a stretcher.

Each book since had been a new adventure, and not only had I indexed books about Africa, but New Zealand, Russia, and nearly every European country. The topics ranged from history to religion, and included of course, headhunters. I knew I'd never go to any of those places, or ever use the information in casual conversation, but the world was larger for me because of my endeavor of writing indexes; a savior of my heart and sanity.

I'd always had the reputation of being "smart," of talking above peoples' heads. I knew my place and had long since tried to acquire the skill of restraining the exposure of my intelligence, even with Hilo. Most days, my secret garden of words was enough for me, but the sadness of it all was that I would've never had the opportunity to learn any of these things if it weren't for a turn in the weather and my husband's bad luck.

"I thought you might have some books around..." Hilo had stopped mid-sentence to reconsider his words. "I know you have a full plate with Hank *and* the farm to look after, Marjorie," he said. "And I hate to ask you such a thing, but I think it's important. That thing there is the only real clue I have. It might be nothing. Peter and Jaeger had never seen it before, but that don't mean it wasn't something that belonged to Erik or Lida. I just don't know why he was holding it, why the killer didn't take it, just left it there. Helps rule out burglary at the very least, I suppose, if there's any value to it."

"Hard to say," I said, studying it.

"Kind of ugly, ain't it?"

I nodded yes, then hesitated and listened for a stir of noise coming from Hank's room. Silence. "If you think it'll help you find out who killed Erik and Lida, I suppose I can look in to it."

"I think it might."

"I'll have to go into town, check some books at the library." I sighed inwardly. It meant that I would have to go see if my cousin, Raymond Hurtibese, still had my Aunt Gilda's jewelry. He might know something about this kind of thing or be able to send me to talk to the right person at the college, but that didn't mean I was happy about the idea. "I don't have anything around here that I think would be of any help," I offered to Hilo.

Hilo nodded, relaxed. "I'll send Ardith out to look after Hank while you're gone. You keep the amulet. I won't tell anybody you have it, and it's probably best if no one knows that I asked for your help. I won't be hard to find if you need me," he said.

Hilo edged away from the door, toward the steps. Shep stood up and wagged his tail. Hilo ignored the dog. "I appreciate this, Marjorie, I really do. This is the first murder around here in twenty-five years, and the last one was pretty easy to figure out."

"I remember." Benefield Frankels had shot his wife square in the forehead at a roadside motel for stepping out with another man. Hilo had secured his position as sheriff for as long as he wanted after he solved that crime. "I'll stop by and see Peter and Jaeger while I'm out," I said.

"I'm sure they'd like that." He was as fond of the Knudsens as I was. "But don't mention that you have the amulet."

I agreed silently with another slight nod.

Hilo pushed past Shep and slouched to the truck, his shoulders heavy, his steps less calculated and more unsure than I could ever remember. Shep made his way up onto the porch, and we stood there and watched Hilo drive away.

The dust plume lingered just like it had when Hilo had driven up, and the amulet felt cold in my hand. I tucked it into the front pocket of my housedress as quickly as I could, all the time visualizing Erik and Lida Knudsen, lying in a pool of blood in their marriage bed.

At least they went together, I heard a chorus of voices whisper inside my head. The vision was clear; a gathering of church women, hands clasped tightly together, shaking their heads over a pair of walnut caskets.

"That would be the only blessing," I said out loud to the wind, to the sky, and to the meadowlark that was standing sentinel on the fence post at the end of the lane.

CHAPTER 3

I went about my business in the kitchen, resisting the atrophy of grief. My heart ached and my muscles were full of tension as I imagined two wounded angels ascending to heaven much sooner than they, or anyone else, had anticipated.

I'd never been one to keep an eye out for a pervasive dark cloud of tragedy on the horizon, even when it lived and breathed in my own bed, but for the life of me, I couldn't believe that Erik and Lida Knudsen had left the world. I wanted to cry, but I couldn't find the recipe for tears. Not now, anyway. I was still embarrassed that I had let Hilo see tears roll down my cheeks.

The pile of manuscript pages on my desk called to me as I rolled out the pie dough, banging the table with excessive force each time I made a pass to smooth the glob of flour and water. Indexing would have to wait. There was no way I could concentrate on headhunters. No way I could face death of any kind, no matter how far away, with the news that Hilo had brought me.

I couldn't escape the present crisis in my own world at the moment, and I thought even Sir Nigel would have understood that—though I wasn't sure my editor, Richard Rothstein, would.

Deadlines for writing indexes for books were rigid, mostly unchangeable. The publishing date and manuscript due date to the printer were appointed months in advance. Writing the index was one of the last tasks in the book-publishing process, since the pagination had to be set in stone. I'd never missed a deadline—most times I was early—and that effort had provided me with a steady stream of indexing work since I had started with H.P. Howard and Sons.

I was three-quarters of the way through Sir Nigel's four-hundred-page book, and the index had to be in the mail to New York in two weeks.

Normally, that would have been enough time—barely, with everything else I had to do—for me to compile the index, combine all of the letters from my index cards into a typed first draft, then do a final red-letter edit and create a publishable index. But I had agreed to help Hilo, and I didn't know how much time that was going to take.

All I knew was that I was going to do everything I could to help find out what had happened to Erik and Lida. Deadlines be damned—even if it meant never writing an index again.

I spilled some flour on the floor at the thought of losing money and a publisher that I had worked hard to create a reputation with. I got the impression from my editor that once you missed a deadline, you'd never work for them again. I understood that, but I just couldn't face the pressure at that moment.

I needed every penny I could get to keep the farm going. Luckily, the weather over the last couple of years had been nearly perfect for growing wheat and silage, our two main crops, but Hank's doctor bills had started to stack up, offering a new threat to any security or buffer I could hope to create.

Shep was out doing whatever job he could find to do. The inside of the house was no place for a dog as far as Hank was concerned—with the exception of the depth of winter when Shep was welcome to warm himself in front of the fireplace. The services Shep provided to the farm were far too valuable to just leave him to fend for himself in a freezing, subzero wind.

Hank and I differed on that point, and on occasion I would let the dog in the house, out of Hank's line of sight, in the depth of summer or whenever I needed the company of another living, walking creature.

Ever the border collie, Shep was industrious, always working, always figuring something out. My guess was he was out trying to herd the spring chickens. At the very least, he'd keep the hawks away and be out from under my feet. I was in no mood to be herded.

To make matters—and my mood—worse, I'd boiled the cherries too long as I stared out the window, contemplating what to do next. I had to start over again, using my last good bunch of fresh fruit. Finally, after an hour, I managed to get two pies in the oven.

It was getting near dinner time, and it had been a while since I had checked on Hank. Sometimes he was so quiet that I nearly forget he was in the bed, lost in darkness, unable to do anything for himself but wish for his old life back. I imagined him out in the front barn, tearing apart an alternator and putting in a new set of bushings, but he was never there. I only went into that barn when I had to now.

Hank was staring at the ceiling with blank eyes when I entered the bedroom.

"Erik and Lida," he whispered.

"You heard?" I walked over to the window and started to close it.

"Don't."

I ignored Hank and closed the window anyway. "Hilo said somebody came in through Erik and Lida's window."

"I heard every word Hilo said. Leave it open." His voice was raspy and weak, but there was an authority to it that wouldn't ever disappear—not as long as Hank Trumaine was able to take a breath.

I froze and realized why Hank wanted the window left open. I knew if he were able he'd take his own life. He'd told me so more than once, begged me to do it for him—and hated and loved me just the same because I wouldn't. I couldn't kill a fly without feeling a week's worth of remorse.

I slid the window back up, then gently climbed onto the bed and hugged Hank as tears came to my eyes. His muscles had wasted away, and he was a shell of the man he once was. I longed for him to hold me, to make love to me, to protect me from the violence beyond our tiny bedroom. But he couldn't lift a finger, and at that moment neither could I.

A rush of tears flooded out. I had not cried so heavily since my mother died.

"I'm sorry," I said when I could.

"Erik and Lida were like family to you," Hank whispered. "Better than family. That lout of a cousin of yours has only shown his face on this farm once since we've been married, and then . . ." He trailed off, refusing to mention the incident that had happened on that visit.

I nodded, glad that he didn't continue on, then resisted the urge to tell Hank that I was happy Raymond had never visited us. The company of my cousin had always been contentious. Relieved, I rested my head gently on Hank's fragile chest, too tired to push away the tears that were determined to fall.

Hank's steady breathing was a small comfort, but a comfort nonetheless. His words echoed inside my head, and I remembered, even though I rarely needed reminding, why I fell in love with him in the first place.

He didn't say another word until I stopped crying. "I don't want you to leave," he whispered.

"Hilo asked. Ardith will be here. She knows how to care for you." Ardith Jenkins, along with Lida Knudsen, would come over when necessary if I had errands in town to run; doctors' appointments of my own, that kind of thing.

Hank was silent for a moment. "I've never thought about losing you. I couldn't bear it if something happened to you. You are . . . always, just here. What would I do without you?"

I understood. I had never thought about losing Hank either. We were both still relatively young, in our midthirties, with most of our lives still ahead of us when the accident had happened.

Tragedy, in any form, had always happened to other people, and neither of us had ever had to seriously consider our own mortality. How could we have? The farm wasn't exactly thriving, but we were making a living and were mostly healthy before Hank went hunting. Our only problem was conceiving a child—and we took great pleasure in trying. I loved feeling Hank's hot, hungry skin on top of mine, but our efforts had been a lost cause. I was barren. The one thing I had looked forward to my entire life—raising a child, boy or girl, it didn't matter—was not to be.

I married Hank Trumaine, my high school sweetheart, without a question in my heart. There were only twenty-two of us in the entire school, so the choices I had were few. I swear, though, even if I had lived in a big city instead of North Dakota, amongst a mass of people instead of a smattering, I still would've fallen in love with Hank Trumaine. I knew I was going to marry him in the sixth grade, but I didn't tell him that until our wedding night.

Hank was a gentle boy who loved the land more than anyone I had ever met. He grew up to be a thoughtful, hardworking man whose passion for farming could barely be contained inside his lanky body. The demand of the land and the hard work invigorated him. He saw hope instead of dread in storm clouds. He watched the ground come alive in the spring as if he were reading a good book, and he could tell you how the growing season was going to go just by the size of the wings on the mayflies.

The North Dakotan lilt to his voice was like the trill of a meadowlark. Lord, how I longed to hear him excited about something—a bluebell blooming in the back forty, a new litter of piglets—instead of the whispers and gasps that were so hard to understand now.

I'd been enrolled in my second year of college in Dickinson when Hank had asked me to marry him. My father had been none too happy. He'd had dreams for me and wanted me to be something other than a farmer's wife. He would have been over the moon if I had gone on to be a teacher, which is what I'd planned on becoming.

My father and I shared an insatiable love of knowledge and books, and as much as my father loved the land, his dream had been to break free of tradition. Instead of following in his own father's footsteps he had wanted to be an English teacher, more specifically a professor at the local college in Dickinson like his sister's husband. But he'd been bound to the family legacy as his father's only son. He was tied to the earth, to the simplicity of working the fields, and expressed deep disappointment when I made the choice to leave college and marry Hank to do the same thing.

I had never regretted my decision not to become a teacher, never been angry about my life, like my father was. I loved the plains, the beauty of wide open spaces, the constancy of the wind. I could never have left the farm—or North Dakota for that matter.

I understood the rhythms of the seasons: the ferocity of winter, the nervousness and hope of spring and the growing season, and the relief of the harvest. Books were my transport to the larger world, even though I'd castrated more hogs than I would like to admit, pulled weeds until my hands ached well into winter, and withstood the fickleness of North Dakota weather like every other farmer's wife I knew. Farm work was in my blood, but books had always been my first true love. They were my magic carpet ride to a normal life; my sanity.

As long as Hank Trumaine was standing at my side at the end of the day, I was perfectly content.

"Nothing is going to happen to me," I finally said to Hank. "I promise. Hilo just wants me to find out as much as I can about an amulet he found at Erik and Lida's. He thinks it's important, and I'm the only one that he trusts to make sense of it for him."

"I wouldn't expect you to say no to Hilo Jenkins." Hank's voice was barely audible, his strength failing, but there was no animosity toward Hilo. Hank loved Hilo; he respected him near as much as he had his own father.

I kissed Hank's forehead, then wiped away my tears with my apron. "I need to get you some dinner."

"Hopefully, you'll have better luck with that than you did with the pies."

I almost smiled, happy to see a flicker of his impish wit. Instead, I pulled myself out of the bed and stood there as Hank drifted off and returned to his dream world, where I'm sure he lived, farmed, walked, and hunted to his heart's content.

CHAPTER 4

Luckily, I didn't burn the pies. They came out perfect. I just hoped they tasted as good as they looked. Still in a daze, I puttered about the kitchen looking for a way to make a quick supper. I decided on salt pork sandwiches, beans, and a bit of wilted lettuce from the garden.

I grabbed a jar of beans from out of the cupboard, then stopped cold as the memory of my mother rushed at me with a force that almost knocked me off my feet. Unexpected tragedies do that to you, I think. Bring the past boiling to the top of the heap, a reminder of how to deal with loss and pain.

I had learned the alphabet, and then to read, under my mother's watchful eye as I arranged the spices in the cabinet next to the stove as a child: allspice, basil, cinnamon, followed by dill, and so on. I was four, maybe five, and my mother was the rightful queen of our kitchen, the kitchen I stood in now. They had left me the house after their deaths, and Hank and I had made it *our* home.

My mother was always glad to have me at her side, joyfully and subtly instilling her sense of order and love for good food in me with every move she made. She made lists, too, and would have scoffed at the idea of making side-money from such a skill.

Momma was a tall, stout woman, forever in a pure white apron with daisy appliques lined perfectly across the waist—the same one I wore every time I cooked. She'd been more than a capable cook, no matter the ingredients that were on hand.

In the lengthening days of March, when the wind still howled across the rolling plains, and the duck ponds were still frozen, she could conjure sugar cream pies and produce suppers that looked like feasts when there was just a dab of flour, cream, corn, and brisket stored in the larder.

"Now, Marjorie," my mother had said over and over again, "you have to plan for days when things are slim. You can't eat everything up at once. The larder might look endless in November, but when March comes along you're going to be mighty hungry if you've shown no amount of restraint." There was always a dose of Norwegian on the tip of her tongue. She had gone through Ellis Island with her sister and parents when she was four.

"Yes, ma'am, I'll remember that."

Farming in North Dakota had never been an easy way of life, and restraint was a necessary quality no matter the season. The winters were hard. The wind was so fierce at times you felt like it was going to tear your eyes out. A relentless scream of air raced forever across the flatlands, entered your head like a tapeworm, burrowing deep into your mind, allowing no silence, no peace, unless you knew how to make it for yourself.

To my father's pleasure, I'd found my peace in books, in worn library copies of Cather, Chekov, Dreiser, and whoever else I could grab from the mostly bare shelves. But I had wanted to be just like Momma, too, from the moment I could remember. I hadn't known then that dreams, no matter how simple, could vanish in the flick of an eye, or at the barrel-end of an old shotgun.

I took a deep breath and pushed the memory of my mother away. Even years later, I couldn't decide which was worse—losing my mother or losing my father.

They had both died of age-related illnesses: a heart attack and a stroke. We'd said our good-byes with tears even though we had watched and waited for death to arrive, had expected it like a cruel tax man's visit. There was no one to blame. It was just life running its normal course. Peter and Jaeger Knudsen had a different row to hoe.

The next morning, I slipped away from bed before the sun broke the horizon and made my way into the kitchen with memories of life and death still churning in my heart. I needed Hank more now than ever, and it was the two-legged, bright-eyed man who was my husband that I longed for the most—but could not have or rely on to protect me. I still couldn't comprehend that Erik and Lida Knudsen were dead. Murdered. Their throats slit. No matter what I did, the horrible images in my imagination would not go away.

I shook my head, trying to free my sorrowful thoughts. I managed to make myself a cup of coffee, then called Shep to the kitchen door for his breakfast. He came running like a train on schedule, wagging his tail and anxious for the day to start. "I wish I shared your enthusiasm," I said, as I sat his bowl on the stoop and then headed for my desk.

I stared at the pile of manuscript pages and avoided the temptation to start reading. Once I began to write an index, hours could slip away, and I knew I needed to get on with the task Hilo Jenkins had set upon me.

I put on my reading glasses, opened the top desk drawer, and pulled out the amulet.

I had long since given up the notion that objects could contain magic—Excalibur was just a sword and Arthur was just a man who would be king. But I couldn't help but feel the coldness of the amulet and wonder how it came to be in Erik Knudsen's dead hand. If it was delivered by magic, then it was a dark magic, an evil energy that I did not want seeping into my skin, into my own body.

I dropped the amulet on the floor and wished I had never allowed Hilo to leave it in my house. There was enough darkness there already.

I picked the amulet up, wrapped it in a piece of white linen, and put it in my purse along with my glasses. I hated to be without the glasses, but I could survive just fine; they just helped me see things up close, like words on an index card that sat in a typewriter.

Like it or not, I had given the sheriff my word, and I owed him what little I thought I could offer. I would, at the very least, find out as much about the amulet as I could, though I couldn't imagine that anything I found out would help bring the murderer to justice.

Hank coughed weakly. I couldn't ignore his discomfort, so I set about our normal routine. A quick bit of exercise—moving his legs and arms, circulating his blood—then some breakfast—oatmeal and coffee—and a quick sponge bath. Hank was quiet the whole time.

A soft breeze blew through the window, fluttering the curtains I'd made and hung when life seemed easier, full of possibilities. They were faded and fraying at the edges now.

I barely noticed breezes these days; they weren't much of a relief from the constant wind, but the smell of coming rain seeped into the bedroom along with the comforting trill of our resident meadowlarks. Evil had not crawled through my window during the night, and for that I was glad. I had relied on Shep to keep away any intruders or alert me if the need arose. A .22 rifle sat behind the bedroom door, and Hank's grouse shotgun was stuffed in the corner of the wardrobe in my office. I couldn't bear to see it on a daily basis, but it was there if I needed it.

I hadn't asked the dog to guard the house, to watch over Hank, but there was no need to. Many a morning, before the sun had broken the eastern horizon, the grass was smashed down under the bedroom window from where Shep had slept. He was already on his tasks, checking on the pigs and chickens. He'd quit trying to herd the biggest of the pigs, a productive sow who was nearly as smart as he was and had little tolerance of the dog's pushy ways. I wouldn't bet against Shep, but I thought he was on thin ice with that pig.

A coming storm didn't raise my spirits, and it didn't give me hope. I was fresh out of that, and I wasn't sure if I would really ever get it back. Not true hope. Not happy-ending kind of hope. Not in this lifetime anyway.

"You're leaving soon." Hank forced a smile.

"Yes," I said, putting the wash bowl away in the closet. "I won't be gone long."

"It will do you good."

"Maybe under better circumstances."

"We need the rain. Just like you need to be free of this house. You're at your best when you're helping someone else, Marjorie. You always were the strong one."

I leaned down and kissed his forehead as I heard Ardith Jenkins pull into the drive. Shep didn't bark at her car either.

"Be careful of the wind," Hank whispered.

His quick change of heart about me leaving was worrisome. Melancholy was more difficult to fight than bed sores, and I knew there was nothing that galled Hank Trumaine more than being one hundred percent dependent on me. Sometimes, I thought he wished I'd run off with another man so he would never have to hear the strain in my voice again.

I shook that thought out of my head and loaded up the two cherry pies in the old Studebaker pickup, forgoing the baked chicken because of the itinerary I had planned, then headed back to the porch to give Ardith a list of last minute instructions.

"Go on," Ardith said. She was a plump woman with perfect white hair and a happy face, remarkably free of wrinkles. Most women her age looked windblown, their skin eroded with deep crevices of grief or laughter. "I've watched after Hank Trumaine since he was knee-high to a grasshopper; I think I can handle him now. If I need something before you get back, I'll call Hilo."

"He's got his hands full right now."

"That he does, but he told me it was important for you to be able to take as much time as you need, and I'm in no mood to set my husband off on a tirade. He's usually not one to bring his work home, but these murders have got him on a sharp edge. I've never seen Hilo so moody in all my life."

"Me, either."

"Well, go on then. Don't worry about Hank. I don't need no list," she said, staring at the paper in my trembling hand.

"That's all I ever do is worry."

Ardith nodded, smiled a knowing smile, and waved me off. "Go."

I drove away, my eyes glued to the rearview mirror until the house was out of sight.

It was a thirty-minute drive to Dickinson, to the library, and I had already called my cousin Raymond at the university, to make sure he would be home for lunch.

Unfortunately, I had never written an index that dealt with Norse orthography, so I had no foundation of knowledge to draw off of when it came to the amulet. Raymond Hurtibese was one of my only hopes.

I had the windows down, the radio off, enjoying the breeze and the soft rain that was falling from the gray sky.

Perfect days in North Dakota were like finding a nugget of gold in the Missouri River; rare, uncommon, almost unbelievable. It had been so long since I had witnessed a calm day that stretched out into a week; I wasn't sure if I could enjoy myself if a day like that did dawn across the farm. Yesterday's news certainly darkened what could have been the start of such a stretch.

A few miles from town I saw a coyote wandering along the tree line. I took little notice of it, other than that the coyote had stopped and watched me pass by. Coyotes were commonplace on the plains, feared and hated by most people because of their sly nature. The Indians were convinced that they were shape-shifters, evil tricksters hiding under a coat of fur. I was convinced that they were nothing more than small canines—scavengers, always hungry, always on the search for food. I put little credence in the lore of the coyote.

I had enough real evil to consider on the road that lay ahead of me without allowing the supernatural or old folk tales to enter into the equation.

CHAPTER 5

Dickinson was the Stark County seat, home to about ten thousand people, and its largest employer was a small university founded in 1918. My cousin Raymond was an assistant professor of paleontology, and I was hoping he could direct me to a source that would help me decipher the writing on the amulet. Not that I thought it would solve the murders, but I was curious now, unable to think of much of anything else.

I passed the hospital where I'd spent hundreds of hours with Hank and McClandon's Funeral Home, a bright yellow Queen Anne mansion, where I was sure I would be visiting in the next day or two. The sight of both places only served to darken my mood and egg on my worry about Hank.

The Carnegie Library was off the main square, a block south of the courthouse. It was a two-story, yellow-brick building with a pair of limestone lions guarding the entrance. It looked like most of the libraries built with the philanthropist's money in the mid-1920s. My mother had first brought me to the library when I was six. I had gotten my very own library card when I was ten. Fierce, unrelenting winters were made bearable by the large stacks of books we carted home once a month.

I loved the smell of libraries, of books. It awakened the memory of all my senses and emotions. As I entered through the double doors, I tried to leave my emotions behind, to push away the visions of my childhood visits, the joys and sorrows of being by my mother's side, and then later, on my own, as I fought off the loneliness of sleeping next to Hank's motionless body.

I headed straight for the librarian's desk. I'd known Calla Eltmore, a tiny spindle of a woman with a brain like an encyclopedia, most all of my adult life. I had used her as a resource on countless indexing projects, and we had struck up a friendship that I valued more than I could ever say, based on our love of books and shared curiosities.

There have been times when I needed a synonym, an access point into the text that just didn't exist within the pages of the title I was working on—or that I could pull out of the air. I provided a sorely needed challenge for the woman on a regular basis, and her eyes lit up when she saw me walk through the doors. I usually called on the phone. My queries and our chats could last an hour or more, depending on my schedule and the subject I was interested in. Some days, she said, I was the only person she talked to other than Herbert Frakes, the janitor and all-around maintenance man who lurked around the library twenty-four hours a day.

Herbert lived in the basement, in a small room next to the boiler room. He'd been wounded on Omaha Beach and came back from the Big War a little shell-shocked. He hardly ever spoke to anyone other than Calla, but when he did it was always with a hard, blinkless stare to the floor and a twitch of the left shoulder.

There was no sign of Herbert when I walked in, but that wasn't unusual. No one else was in the library that I could see, and Calla was at her normal post, standing guard over her domain at the front desk.

"Well, Marjorie Trumaine, you're the last person I expected to see walk in here today," Calla said, pushing her glasses off her nose. They fell to a dangle, held by a gold chain that I was certain was permanently attached to the woman's wrinkled, craned neck.

I sighed and saw the front page of the *Dickinson Press* lying open next to the black rotary phone on the desk. The headline was simple: MURDER in big, bold, black letters. The story took up the entire front page, along with a family picture of the Knudsens and a bleak black-and-white picture of their simple wood frame house.

"You heard," I said.

Calla nodded. Her glasses chain jangled, echoing up to the ceiling over our heads. It sounded like a twinkling of crystals; an ethereal sound edged with normality. "Café was at full tilt with the news this morning. You look pale, honey; you all right?"

"I didn't sleep well."

"Don't imagine you did with such madness going on a farm over." Calla looked around, then looked me up and down, assessing my state of being in a way that was completely normal and acceptable. I was usually the caregiver. "Why don't you and me step out back and get us a bit of fresh air. Herb'll come get me if I'm needed here."

The library was quiet as a church the day after Christmas. The only noise I heard was a distant fan circulating air, and the only smell the comforting aroma of a thousand books or more. I shrugged my shoulders; I knew why Calla wanted to go outside. "Sure, why not," I said.

A sly smile flittered across Calla's face as she grabbed up her purse, a small black leather clutch that looked like it was as old and battered as Calla herself. She spun around, then stalked to the back door without looking to see if I was following.

I knew the way and trailed after the librarian dutifully. We had stood in the same spot, "grabbing a bit of air," more than once since I had started indexing books.

By the time I was out the door, Calla was digging in her clutch for a pack of Salems and her trusty Zippo lighter; she was standing under a little overhang, protected from the rain. It was nothing but a drizzle now, but the grayness hung overhead like a dirty sheet that wouldn't come clean.

Nothing held up in the North Dakota wind like a sturdy silver Zippo. Matches were a mere annoyance, especially when time was of the essence.

She looked up and offered me the green pack. It had been recently opened, the paper torn off neatly, like one would expect from Calla. There were only two cigarettes missing. I was sure they'd all be gone by the end of the day—Calla liked her fresh air.

I took a cigarette out of the pack and put the all-white stick of tobacco to my lips. Salems didn't have the tan filter like some cigarettes did. My dim red lipstick immediately marred the filter.

Calla produced the silver metal lighter, popped the lid, ignited a flame on the wick with a swipe of the thumb, then cupped it to keep the fire alive as she pushed the lighter toward the tip of my quivering cigarette.

I inhaled and felt the rush of menthol explode inside my lungs. It was a relief, and the familiar ritual with Calla helped to calm my nerves. I exhaled as she followed the same routine. Our smoke mixed against the gray sky, then dissipated like it had never existed.

"What did we ever do before we had cigarettes?" Calla said.

"Drank whiskey," I answered. It was a lie, the farthest thing from the truth. I couldn't remember the last time I'd had a drink of alcohol. Neither Hank nor I had ever imbibed on a regular basis, and I wasn't a regular cigarette smoker, either. Not like Calla. The tips of her fingers were yellowed with the stain of nicotine. I could take or leave cigarettes, walk away and not have one for a month. But I had to say they came in handy some days when I needed to take the edge off. Today was one of those times, but I hadn't had the chance, or thought, to stop and buy a pack.

Calla smiled, but let the expression fall away as quickly as it came on. "Why are you here, Marjorie? Kind of out of sync, you are, aye? I figured you'd be over to the Knudsens', or looking after Hank, not gallivanting around town dressed like you were going to church on the first Sunday of the Easter season."

She was right. I had on my low-heeled black shoes that I'd ordered from the Montgomery Ward's catalog, along with my second-best dress, a simple blue sleeveless dress that I'd sewn from a McCall's pattern: princess seaming in the bodice and a three-gore slim skirt that fell just to the knees. My hair was up, sprayed in place with enough Aqua Net to hold a bird's nest to a tree limb. Truth was, I didn't want Raymond to see any farm in me at all—even though I knew that was impossible. I didn't mix with the academics at the college any better than Hilo did.

I didn't know how much to tell her, but I needed her help—just like I would Raymond's. "I need to do some research."

"For an index?" She sounded perplexed. "You're working today?"

I'd always been a horrible liar. One cover-up led to another, until you couldn't remember what you'd said or where you'd started, so I did my best to just blurt out what was on my mind—but not this time. I wasn't supposed to tell anyone about the amulet, or that Hilo had asked me to help him, so I just stood there and stared silently at Calla.

She took a deep drag off her cigarette and studied my face for an eternity of moons. "All right," she finally said. "I figure you'll tell me when the time's right."

"I will. I just need to figure something out." It was my turn for a puff. For some reason, the cool menthol of the cigarette suddenly tasted foul, like cough syrup on a snowy day. It smelled like formaldehyde to me, and I couldn't help but think of embalming fluid being pumped into Lida Knudsen's decaying veins.

I reached over and stubbed the cigarette out on the brick wall. A shower of sparks fell to the ground and I watched them all disappear. Shooting stars at night, a life snuffed out. Or two lives. Everywhere I looked I saw and smelled death—even at the library; especially at the library. Shakespeare whispered from *Hamlet* underneath the whirl of the fan, "For in that sleep of death what dreams may come." And Twain taunted me with his admonishment, "The fear of death follows from the fear of life." Dead men always spoke to me on these grounds.

Calla kept smoking, never taking her eyes off of me.

"I need some information on Norse mythology and orthography. As much as you can find," I said.

The librarian exhaled a cloud of thin gray smoke and shook her head. "You're a basket of surprises, Marjorie Trumaine, I have to tell you that. I've just never met anyone like you." Calla put her cigarette out, secured her clutch under her arm, and added, "You know if you need anything, anything at all, all you have to do is call me. You know that, right? Not just an answer, but a shoulder?"

"I know. Thanks, Calla, I really appreciate it. This is difficult. It's good to know that you're here. I always know that you're here."

CHAPTER 6

It didn't take Calla long to collect a stack of books that I hoped would help me figure out what I was looking for. Most of the books were old, dusty, not touched in years, and from the non-Christian religion section—Norse mythology was 293 in the Dewey decimal system. The entire section totaled seven books. Calla always complained about lack of funding. If she had her way there'd be books stacked to the ceiling.

There was a point in my life when I knew a good chunk of the Dewey decimal system by heart. I had decided as a girl to learn it, and commit as much of it to memory as I could, so it would save me time in the library. Most of our visits had been quick stop-offs on the way back home from shopping, doctor appointments, or other reasons to be in town. There were long stretches in the winter that were spent solely on the farm, and all-day library visits were rare, almost unheard of. There was too much work to do at home. Besides, that kind of memory exercise came easy to me back then.

But lately, mostly since I had started indexing books, my long-term memory had changed. Reading to index a book was different than reading for pleasure or schoolwork. It was impossible not to retain some of the information that I read, but my eyes looked for keywords, and my mind searched for concepts, ideas, and opinions that might lead to a question that a reader might ask of the text, then look for an answer in the index.

The desire to digest every word in every book I read for enlightenment had gone to the wayside once reading became a profession. The irony was not lost on me. It was almost like I had to erase one book from my mind, forget about it the best I could, before starting to index another one.

When the opportunity to write more than one index at a time presented itself to me, the skill of compartmentalization became almost as important as my memory and writing abilities. It was managed chaos, especially when the subject matters were worlds apart, like they most often were. Imagine juggling organic chemistry and headhunters at the same time. I was glad I didn't have to at the moment, especially now that Norse mythology had been thrown into the mix.

My requests made Calla feel useful, and that in itself calmed me down and made me less worried about the fact that I didn't know the Dewey number for the Norse mythology books. I wasn't sure I ever did. It wasn't a subject that had ever interested me.

Calla brought me two more books, from the philology section— 498, for Scandinavian languages—so I could look into the orthography questions I had. She brought a few other books on antique jewelry and amulets, then left me alone without saying a word. I knew she'd come running if I called out for her.

I was glad that I wasn't allergic to dust, or the mold that grew inside old books and gave them that wonderful ancient, brittle, smell.

I had picked a small corner off of the fiction section to conduct my research. Everything I needed was there, and from my many visits to the library over the years I had surmised that it was the most isolated spot in the building.

Calla had made sure that I had a small desk with a comfortable, padded, straight-backed chair for my continuing research trips. A brass library lamp with an oblong green shade, along with the overhead fluorescents, offered enough light to read by without straining my eyes.

I'd brought along a notebook dedicated to the task Hilo had set out for me, and I settled into work. The smell of distant cigarettes lingered, then mixed with the odor from the old books, and I soon forgot about my brief sojourn outside with Calla. It had been extremely difficult not to include her, not to tell her the real reason for my quest of Norse knowledge.

I spent the next three hours searching through the books, using the index first, of course, looking for something that resembled the amulet.

It was difficult not to judge another indexer's work when that's what I did for a living, but I had little time to linger and critique a style different from my own—still, I saw usability issues right away: a string of ten or fifteen page locators that offered no information and forced me to look at each page under the heading. An argument for subheadings and sub-sub-headings could have easily been made, since I needed more time to use the first index I dove into because of the lack of detail in its structure.

Indexing work was most often not acknowledged in the front matter of the book, so offering a complaint was a matter of writing to the publisher, which of course would prove as useless as the string of non-specified locators. I was lucky; H.P. Howard and Sons always included my name as indexer in the front of each book that I worked on.

The first time that I saw my name in the front of a book, it had brought tears to my eyes and validated my work on the USDA course— my existence beyond the daily chores of the farm. I had thought it might be a little bit of immortality at the time; my name, my work, might outlive me. My toil at something viable, something that would last, offered an avenue to esteem that I had never considered before. It was the child I could never bear, my small offering to make the world a little better place. At the very least, I felt useful. It was possible that an index would outlive me, and that filled a hole in my heart in a small way. It was a surprise and a relief—a gift, though, that I could not give to Hank. It was only mine.

I closed the first book, went on to the next, and found some interesting information, but nothing that gave any clues to the origin of the piece of jewelry Hilo had taken from Erik Knudsen's hand.

From there, I determined the three runes that I had noticed when I held the amulet for the first time represented the children of Loki, a Norse giant who was the personification of evil. A trickster with far more power than any coyote that I would ever encounter.

The children were: the Fenris wolf, a giant wolf preordained to slay Odin; the Midgard serpent; and the goddess Hel, the ruler of the realm of the dead.

The engraving in the center had to be Thor, but there was no depiction of Loki or Odin. I could only assume that the writing on the edge described the meaning of the amulet—what it was for or what it was used to ward off. But that was just an assumption on my part. I knew nothing of the lore and rituals of the Old World, of the country of my mother's people. I didn't even have her accent, and if there were any family traditions that had been brought over, besides the food—lefse and rakfisk for starters—they'd been tossed away, replaced by traditions considered purely American.

Assimilation was as much a desire as a requirement in those days, especially during the war and after; the demand of patriotism extended all the way out to the desolate plains. Now, I needed to know some of my own heritage, and my knowledge of it came up short when I really needed it. It was frustrating.

A chill ran through my body as I read about Loki and his children. It seemed the giant hated the gods of Asgard. Loki had eventually arranged the murder of Balder, the god of light, son of Odin and Frigg.

So I had to wonder, had someone arranged to have Erik and Lida murdered? If so, why? And who would do such a thing? What did Balder have in common with the Knudsens? Or was there any connection at all?

I made a list of my questions, too, not just the information that I had gathered. I printed the list instead of writing it in cursive. My printing was exact, almost as a good as a draftsman's when I took the time, and almost immediately I started to see an index forming in front of my eyes. It was the subject, Erik and Lida Knudsen's murder, that left me feeling hollow and cold. I had never made a list, something resembling an index, that was so personal, even though I was starting to become fascinated by the research I was engaged in.

Balder, as it turned out, had been one of the most beautiful gods of Asgard, and his mother had sought desperately to protect him from harm by gathering oaths from all things in nature not to hurt him. But she'd neglected mistletoe. Loki had tricked the blind god, Hoder, Balder's brother, into throwing a piece of mistletoe, and Balder was killed by it. Thor had punished Loki for the murder by binding him in a fishing net, but the evil quest had not stopped there.

The prophecy of Ragnarök, the doom of the gods, told of a great battle after Loki freed himself, and with his children led the enemies of heaven into battle. After Ragnarök, and Loki's demise, it was foretold that Balder would return to heaven.

I made another list of the names and the relationships, then scanned quickly through the antique jewelry books. There was nothing there that compared to the amulet I carried. I'd come up short in that regard, just like I'd expected to.

Secretly, I'd hoped to get all of the information that I needed so I could cancel my visit with Raymond, but that was not to be. I still needed to go to the university to see him.

I slid the notebook into my purse and closed up all of the books.

I wasn't sure what all the lore and legends meant, or what any of the information had to do with Erik and Lida Knudsen. I wasn't even sure if the amulet had belonged to Erik, or if it was placed in his hand by the killer as a message. I kept coming back to that thought; it left me in a quandary. Why would a killer leave a calling card, something for the police to use to track him down? It made no sense to me. But then again, I was unaccustomed to the ways of the criminal mind and murder as a topic to consider.

My head swam with the myths of the Old World, and that confused me even more. In all the years that I had known the Knudsens, not once did they ever express a belief in the ways of their ancestors. Just the opposite. Erik had always his faith as a Christian man, a devout believer, who had attended church every Sunday.

My eyes began to burn, and I looked at my watch. Time had slipped away, and if I didn't leave right away I'd be late for my appointment with Raymond. He hated tardiness more than I did.

My reflexes told me to stand up, tell Calla good-bye, and exit the library as quickly as I could, but another sense told me to stay seated.

I felt a set of eyes staring at me, on the back of my neck, and I caught sight of the shadow of a man standing in wait as I arranged my things to leave.

I took a deep breath and looked over my shoulder. Herbert Frakes was staring at me from an odd vantage point, stuffed in an alcove like he had been sent there as a punishment.

I jumped with a start.

When I made eye contact with him, his left shoulder twitched and he looked to the floor, just like he always did. But the glance downward didn't last. Herbert stepped toward me, his arms to his side, his eyes—almost black in the shadows—focused straight on me.

Out of instinct, I stood and grabbed up my purse. The look in Herbert's eyes concerned me. My purse was the only weapon I had if I needed to defend myself. I had never felt threatened by the janitor's presence, but I did now.

"You startled me, Herbert," I said, in a little louder voice than normal, in hopes that Calla was within hearing range.

He stopped about four feet from me, lowered his head, and looked away. The twitch had stopped. "Sorry, Miss Marjorie, I didn't mean to scare you."

"It's okay." I relaxed a little bit and thought for a second that I might have been overreacting—but I still held a tight grip on my purse. I was on edge. Had been ever since Hilo had come to give me the bad news and left me with the amulet.

Herbert Frakes was a gentle soul shattered by the war. I felt a little ashamed of myself for thinking he might hurt me in the one place I was sure that we both felt safe.

"She had a cousin like me, you know?" Herbert said.

"Who had a cousin?"

"The dead one."

I was uncomfortable all over again. His tone was odd. I looked past Herbert, hoping to catch a glimpse of Calla, but I saw nothing but an empty desk at the front of the library. "Lida Knudsen?" I asked.

Herbert nodded his head yes.

"I didn't know that," I said. Which was true. Lida had never had reason to mention some errant cousin. We'd never talked much about our distant families.

"Was in my unit," Herbert said. "Hurt the same day as me. D-Day. We was green as a bushel of spring apples."

I nodded again. "You think he had something to do with what you read in the paper?" It was an assumption on my part. Truth was, I didn't know if Herbert could even read. I tried to think if I had ever seen him with a book, and I couldn't remember a time when I had. I was tempted to show Herbert the amulet, but I restrained myself. Hilo'd told me not to.

Herbert shrugged. "Don't know. He moved to St. Paul after we came back. Never seen or heard from him since." He never looked up from the floor. "Just thought you should know since you was looking for answers." He turned and started to walk away.

"Herbert?"

He stopped. "Yes, Miss Marjorie?"

"You should tell Hilo about him if you think it's important."

"Sheriff knows. They was best friends when they were boys," Herbert said, then looked up at me like he wanted to say something else but couldn't find the words.

Instead, he hurried off, leaving me standing there alone in a tomb of books with a bit of information that I didn't quite know how to organize.

CHAPTER 7

I left the library drained. I sat in the Studebaker and tried to gather my thoughts for a long minute; a minute that I didn't have to spare.

The sounds of Dickinson surrounded me, but the hustle and bustle of a city, even a small one, with a city bus stopping and going, car horns blaring, people walking by on the sidewalk engaged in conversations, could not drown out the pounding in my head. Black cars, white cars, old and new, big finned spaceship-inspired convertibles mixed in a blur, along with a mix of farm trucks on duty to serve up a chore. None of the vehicles mattered to me. In town, on a busy day in the grim daylight, I was invisible—not a lone human standing out in a field, feeling like I was the only person in the world with pain and more to do than I could handle.

I felt a heave in my chest, and before I knew it I was crying. Crying deeply for the second time since Hilo gave me the news about Erik and Lida's fate. My emotions were usually in check and held firm, but the murders seemed to be too much to bear. I hadn't cried this much in years. Not even when Hank had had his accident. There were things to do and no time to worry about what couldn't be done.

The murder of my friends was just too much to consider. How could anyone kill such sweet, gentle people in such a vicious way? No one deserved to die like that. No one. I couldn't conceive of such pure evil, of hate and rage so strong that it would lead someone to climb through an open bedroom window in the middle of the night and slash a sleeping person's throat.

I allowed myself another good cry. Maybe I would get it out of my system. Maybe it was more than the murders. I didn't know for sure. I just knew there was a feeling in the pit of my stomach that wouldn't go away but felt a little better every time I cried.

Caring for Hank on a daily basis had taken its toll, too. So had managing the intense deadlines that came along with indexing books, and the constant demand to juggle my literary duties with those of the farm. I was constantly battling between the authors and publishers I was contracted to please and deliver for, and the bank that held the mortgage on the farm and the note on the combine, on Hank's dream. At that moment, it was all just too much. I felt selfish. I didn't know what I was going to do if I lost Peter and Jaeger's help—a thought that had been at the very edge of acknowledgement. I had grown dependent on the help of the two Knudsen boys, but now they had their own worries, their own matters to be overwhelmed by. I sucked in a deep breath of air at the thought.

My mother, if she were still alive, would chastise me. Tell me to keep a stiff upper lip, a woman's work was never done . . . all of the clichés she constantly wore on her sleeve to help get her through the day. I had abided by them for a long time, but my restraint was weak, overrun by my fears, my weaknesses, and my own grief.

After a few minutes of sitting in the library parking lot blubbering like an unwound idiot, I took another deep breath. "You have to get through this," I said to myself out loud, then looked in the rearview mirror, wiped my eyes, straightened up my face and hair in the mirror, and put the truck in reverse.

When I pulled away, I noticed a green Chevy sedan sitting across the parking lot with the window down. I couldn't see the driver. His or her face was hidden behind a newspaper. It was odd, but not unheard of. A lot of people came and went from the library. It was most likely someone taking a break from work and seeking refuge in the shade of the towering oaks.

I looked away from the Chevy and headed toward my cousin's house with a gnawing feeling that I couldn't quite get a hold of—or let go of. It was one of those feelings like something was wrong. Of course, my mind turned toward home, to Hank. I'd never forgive myself if something happened to him and I wasn't there.

I stopped a short way down the street at the first telephone booth I came to.

It sat on the corner, just outside the Rexall Drugstore. I was going to be late to Raymond's the way it was, and a few extra seconds wasn't going to make any difference in my timing, or my cousin's mood, which I predicted was going to be foul and snarly even if I were on time.

A quick wind greeted me as I stepped out of the truck. I glanced upward, at the sky, to see the gray rain clouds finally trailing away. Clear blue sky was behind it, pushing the storm away with the force of a thousand bulldozers. If I had to bet, the roads would be dry by the time I got home, and any evidence of the morning rain would be gone.

I dropped a dime into a slot at the top of the payphone, a tall black rotary dial phone that'd had a heart engraved in it a long time ago. Rust had set in. I ignored the etching and dialed my home phone number.

Ardith picked up on the fourth ring. The phone was on a party line, and our ring was two longs followed by two shorts. "Hello," she said, "Trumaine residence."

"It's me, Ardith," I said.

"Marjorie, I didn't expect to hear from you till you got home. Is everything all right?"

"Yes. Of course. I just wanted to check on Hank."

"He's fine, Marjorie."

"You're sure?"

"Well," Ardith said, "he wanted to play hide and seek, but I told him that was entirely out of the question." There was a chuckle at the end of her words, and that made me smile briefly.

"All right, then," I said. "I was just worried."

"He won't let me close the window," Ardith answered. "Wind's fierce right now, but it doesn't seem to matter to him."

I sighed. "Leave it open," I said. "Shep'll look after him if the need comes—if you're worried about something more than dirt coming in."

"How'd you know?"

"We all are, Ardith. We all are." Silence fell between us, and the telephone line hissed and echoed as the wind jostled the lines between the phone booth and the farm. "You tell Hank I'll be home shortly," I finally said.

"Did you find out anything, Marjorie?"

"Not yet. I'm on my way to my cousin Raymond's house. I hope he'll have something to tell me." I glanced up and saw the taillights of a car blink red, slow down, then speed up and turn the corner, disappearing from my view. It was another green Chevy or the same one at the library, I wasn't sure.

"All right, you be careful then."

I didn't answer right away and stared after the car. It was probably just a coincidence, but I rarely saw green Chevy sedans, and I had already seen two of them—or one twice—in a short time.

My mind was trained to see patterns of information, but it was also trained to discard pieces of data that were irrelevant. Not everything in a text made its way into an index, nor did silly details belong in my consciousness at the moment.

"Are you still there, aye?" Ardith asked.

"Yes, yes," I said, focusing on the telephone. "I'll be careful." I hesitated before hanging up the line. I wished the receiver at home had a long cord on it so I could hear Hank breathing, talk to him for just a second, but that was an impossibility.

I made my way to the truck, taking notice of the wind as I did. It didn't seem any different than normal, but then again I was in town, and that always made a difference. There was more to deflect it here than there was out in the country.

Raymond Hurtibese lived on the Dickinson University campus in a small bungalow just across the street from the Student Union building, a huge limestone building that looked more like a giant mausoleum than a meeting place.

I hesitated on the walk up to the door of the well-kept cottage. Raymond and I weren't close; we only saw each other on festive occasions and at funerals. Our relationship was similar to that of my father and his sister's—distant at best and bound only by blood. We saw each other out of necessity rather than pleasure.

My father had had a great intellect but chose to live his life as a farmer, destined to wager his fortunes against the forces of nature rather than climb the academic ladder to tenure. His anger about his career choice was rarely visible, but it usually showed itself in the form of disappointment—aimed directly at me.

I'd indexed a book once that chronicled several Jewish families from Eastern Europe. The book was a marker of success since the immigrants, who had not been allowed to own farmland in their home countries, brought their garment-making skills with them to the new world. There was a market in New York City for high-quality clothing. But that wasn't the point. The next generation, the immigrants' children, were almost all doctors or lawyers, highly skilled professionals. They hadn't disappointed their parents like I had disappointed my father by marrying Hank.

Anyway, Raymond's mother, my Aunt Gilda, was a smart woman in her own right. She'd married well and seemed to make all of the right choices—a fact she never let my father forget. Raymond's father, my uncle, Walter Hurtibese, had been the Dean at Dickinson University until a few years before his death, and Aunt Gilda was the "good woman" behind her man, taking to the social aspects of university life like a hummingbird to a patch of red, nectar-heavy flowers. She'd pushed Raymond down the same path before she passed on herself, a few years after Raymond attained the position of assistant professor.

The other reason I hesitated on the walk to the door was the passing resemblance Raymond held to my father. There were enough ghosts in my mind, and I was less than enthusiastic to add another one.

Raymond opened the door before I knocked. He feigned a smile and said, "You're late."

I smiled back, fully expecting his disdain. "It's so good to see you, Raymond," I said. "I appreciate the time you've taken for me." I extended my hand for a handshake. There were no kisses or hugs on this side of the family. Offering an excuse would have only prolonged the situation, and I was intent on getting the information I needed as quickly as I could so I could leave and go home to my Hank.

Raymond shook my hand weakly. His palms were sweaty, and I recoiled immediately. He stood squarely in the doorway staring at me.

"May I come in?" I asked.

"Yes, of course." Raymond turned sideways in an exact manner so he was flat against the open door.

I took a deep breath and walked into the bungalow.

"Your call was a surprise, Cousin Marjorie," Raymond said. He wore tan cuffed slacks, a blue Oxford shirt, and highly shined black loafers. A few years older than myself, gray was starting to show in Raymond's thick head of wheat-brown hair. His beard was meticulously trimmed, and his dark brown eyes perused me from head to toe, judging my hand-sewn attire as unacceptable.

"I don't get away from the house much these days," I said.

"I imagine not. How did you manage to today?"

"Ardith Jenkins was kind enough to look after Hank," I said.

"The sheriff's wife?"

"Yes, we've been friends for eons."

Raymond stared at me curiously, then said, "Have a seat." My cousin swept his hand fully across his body as if he were allowing me into a forbidden kingdom.

I sat down in the closest chair I could see, a soft high-back leather chair that faced an impressive stone fireplace. The fireplace didn't look like it had ever been used. "I can't stay long."

Raymond sat down across from me in a matching chair. "Would you like some tea?"

"No, no thank you. There's no need to go to any trouble."

"It's no trouble, really."

I shook my head no, and opened my purse.

"Are you *still* writing those indexes?" he asked.

I had wrapped the amulet in linen and tucked it in a side pocket of my purse—in the spot I usually hid my cigarettes if I had any. Hank disapproved of my smoking. I knew I was breaking Hilo's warning not to show the jewelry to anyone, but I'd run into a brick wall. As much as Raymond annoyed me, I felt like I could trust him, though I had decided not to tell him everything—like where the amulet had come from and why I was really there.

I pulled the amulet out of my purse and began to unwrap it, all the while trying to ignore Raymond's tone concerning my indexing work.

I knew Raymond thought it was remarkable that a woman without a college degree could do such a job, coupled with the fact that my formal training as an indexer was certified by a correspondence course and administrated by the United States Department of Agriculture. He never failed to make his dismay well known.

"Yes," I said. "I'm currently working on a book by Sir Nigel Preston. Are you familiar with his work?"

"I can't say that I am."

"A study on headhunters. It's really fascinating. You should read it once it's published."

Raymond feigned another smile. "I have no interest in headhunters."

"I had no knowledge of the subject, either," I said. "But it is very well written, and I have found it to be a wonderful read."

"How can you pretend to index a book you know nothing about?"

My mouth went dry. Raymond had pulled me into a game already, and I was on defense. I should have known better. Instead of taking the bait and engaging in an academic argument defending my credentials, I held out the amulet for the taking.

How many indexers in the world were also experts on headhunters? My skill was the ability to parse information and answer all of the readers' questions, not write a treatise or text on the subject. Even if I had said such a thing, I would not have enlightened Raymond. I would have just dug myself in deeper.

"I was hoping you could tell me something about this," I said.

Raymond hesitated, eyed me directly, then took the amulet without a concession of defeat.

He examined the amulet with a close eye, gently turning it over from side to side. "Where did you get this?"

I didn't answer. "Do you know what it is?"

"Well," he said. "It's most definitely Norse. I can't quite say how old it is, but it looks authentic. The wolf is—"

"—Fenris," I said. "The serpent is Midgard, and the woman is the goddess Hel, the ruler of the realm of the dead. All of them are Loki's children. I'm assuming the figure in the center is Thor." I couldn't help showing off my knowledge of the myth and competing with Raymond. It was an old game.

Raymond eyed me carefully. "You've done some research."

"A little. I seem to remember that Aunt Gilda had a similar piece of jewelry. Or something like it. That's why I called you. I thought you might know something more than I could find at the library."

"I sold all of mother's things a long time ago. Most of it was costume jewelry. Junk. I don't remember the piece you're talking about," Raymond said, tapping his fingers on the table.

I didn't believe him, but it didn't seem worth pursuing at the moment.

Raymond stood up, a curious look on his face, and walked to an orderly bookshelf next to the fireplace, searched it quickly, and pulled out a worn, leather-bound book that was as thick as a brick. "You are aware that a piece like this was stolen from one of my colleagues not too long ago, aren't you?"

I shook my head no. "Is Sheriff Jenkins aware of that?"

"I'm sure that he is. Has he seen the amulet?" Raymond squinted his eyes, staring at me warily and clutching the book in his hands as if it were a weapon.

I wasn't going to answer Raymond, but I was miffed that Hilo hadn't told me about the theft, left me uninformed so that I looked like an idiot. I was miffed—the sin of omission was the same as a lie as far as I was concerned. It would be the first thing I asked Hilo the next time I saw him.

"Do you need money, Marjorie?" Raymond asked before I could answer his question about the amulet.

"Heavens, no. That's not why I'm here."

"I just thought, given your current situation, that times might be, um, desperate."

I curled my toes in my Sunday shoes so much that they hurt. I wasn't about to allow Raymond to see my anger. "If I were a thief, Raymond, would I come to you?"

"I wasn't suggesting that you were a thief, Marjorie."

"Bull crap, Raymond, that's exactly what you're suggesting, and you know it." The words popped out of my mouth before I could stop them.

Raymond flipped open the book, escaping my glare, ignoring my outburst. It was not the first time that he had been at the receiving end of the sharp end of my tongue. A distant smile flittered across his face. He loved getting under my skin. "I think you're absolutely right about Loki's children," he said.

"I can't find anything to decipher the writing on the edges," I said, reeling in my tone, glad the topic of Hilo's knowledge of the amulet had receded. Sometimes, it was just best to give Raymond a win and move on.

"I think you should talk to Professor Phineas Strand," he said, flipping through the pages. The amulet was tucked underneath the book, secure in his grasp. "He will be most interested in seeing this, especially if it is from the collection that was stolen."

"Does he live on campus?"

"Just around the corner."

"Are you friends?"

"Ah," Raymond said, ignoring my question about his relationship with the professor. He stared at a page in his book without a flinch of any kind. "It looks like it is for protection. Much like a St. Christopher's medal. Thor is the key to that. The chaining that weaves in and out of the runes was a common protective design."

"Protection from what?"

"Evil, of course."

I nodded. *It didn't work*, I thought. But I didn't think it had been in Erik Knudsen's possession for protection. At least, I hoped not.

"The Scandinavians brought this kind of thing with them when they immigrated," Raymond continued. "By then Christianity had pushed the myths into a category of sin. Believing in anything other than the word of God was heresy, but there were always those who were hesitant to rid themselves of the old stories, of the old ways of their ancestors, even if those beliefs and trinkets were held in secret.

"Protection amulets were plentiful in the early eighteen hundreds according to this text. Almost all of them featured Thor as a center-piece. There is much debate about the writing. Several scholars have tried to interpret amulets like this, but they all come up with something different. Unfortunately, many of the old traditions were passed on orally, leaving a lot of room for conjecture."

I could see my father's profile in Raymond's face, softened by the diffused light of the room. I knew curiosity when I saw it, but there was something else, an expression bound by a tightness of the lips and a spark in the eyes.

"Is that all you can tell me?" I asked.

"Yes, other than I will tell you that once you leave, I will be straight on the phone to Professor Strand."

I stood up and extended my hand. "I would do the same thing if I were in your shoes, Raymond. But you needn't worry; I'll go there myself and talk to him."

He stared at the amulet, tightened his grasp on it. I half expected him to run off with it, to play a game of keep away like I had seen him do so many times at family reunions when we were children.

I didn't budge and did not withdraw my hand until the amulet was securely in my possession. I wrapped it up in the linen, tucked it back in my purse, and headed for the door.

"The book?" I asked, before I walked outside. "What was the title?"

"Ah, Larrson's, *The Book of Norse Symbols*. A small printing. 1901. A first edition, I might add. I've had it in my collection for some time, but I've never cracked it open until now."

"The library didn't have it," I said, running through the titles in my mind that Calla had brought me. "How do you spell the last name?"

"No, I don't imagine they had it. Larrson with two Rs, but that shouldn't have mattered."

I was glad to step out into the fresh air. Raymond watched me leave, but said nothing further. Which was just as well as far as I was concerned. His lack of mention concerning Hank didn't surprise me, but it rubbed my craw.

I expected nothing less, though it would've been pleasant if a member of my own family expressed an interest or a hint of caring about Hank, but that was just wishful thinking.

The only thing I knew to do was flee Raymond's presence as fast as I could.

CHAPTER 8

I rang the doorbell on Professor Strand's door not two minutes after leaving Raymond's house. I could hear the phone already ringing inside. The stoop had dried from the rain, but the leaves of a potted geranium still bore water drops.

I hesitated to press the doorbell again after hearing the phone ring on persistently, but I felt I had no choice. I wanted to reach Professor Strand before Raymond did.

But in the end, it turned out that the professor was not at home. I stood at the door for another five minutes, listening impatiently to the phone screaming to be picked up. I should have asked Calla for a couple of cigarettes, or stopped and bought some of my own, but I hadn't. I could use some calming down. Raymond was as frustrating as ever, and if I had it to do all over again, I would never have shown up at his door in the first place.

From there I drove to the campus's administrator's office to find out if the professor was teaching a class. He wasn't, I was told by a snippy woman outside the dean's office. Professor Strand had a class scheduled later in the afternoon, and when I pressed I was told that no one in the office knew where the professor was, nor was it a concern.

It seemed that I had no choice but to wait for a couple of hours or to head back home. I decided to go home—with a couple of stops in between.

Once I got back in the truck, I sat there for a second, letting everything Raymond told me settle in. I reached in my purse, pulled out my notebook, and scribbled down some more notes: the name of the book Raymond had used and the fact that Hilo had not told me about the theft were my main topics.

Satisfied that I wouldn't forget anything, I drove off the university campus without looking back. My discomfort of the place had only been reinforced.

I stopped at the payphone outside the Rexall again, only this time I called Calla at the library. I knew I should have driven straight home, but I had another nagging feeling in my stomach, like I'd missed something this time, not so much that there was anything wrong.

As always, Calla answered the phone. "Library, how may I help you?"

"Hi, Calla, this is Marjorie. I need you to check on something for me."

"Sure thing, what do you need?"

"Can you check on a book, *The Book of Norse Symbols*, for me? The author's name is Larrson. Two Rs. I don't think you have it there. At least I didn't come across it earlier. Could you see if you've ever had it? What the publishing history is?"

"All right. Hold on, Marjorie."

I heard her put the receiver down and walk away, so I closed my eyes and tried to gather my thoughts, tried to justify why I was questioning my cousin's actions and words—other than it was normal, since I held him in such low esteem and didn't trust him at all.

The fact that Raymond had not allowed me to see the book he quoted did not surprise me. He just seemed especially guarded. I didn't want to think that he was involved in any of this, but he knew more about the amulet than I did. He knew that it might have been stolen when I didn't.

"Marjorie?"

"Yes?"

"I can't find anything on this title. It doesn't look like there's anything that's ever been published by a Larrson concerning Norse symbols, at least with the records that I have access to. Are you sure you gave me the correct information? Maybe it was with a small publisher and not listed."

"Yes, Calla, I'm absolutely sure the information is correct. Wait,

Raymond said it was published in 1901. He was very proud that it was a first edition, a rare book."

"That would explain it. My records only go back forty-one years. I'll call over to the university library and see what I can find out. Do you ever call them?"

"Only as a last resort," I said, more truthfully than I wanted to.

"They don't all look down their nose at everybody who's not like them, Marjorie. They appreciate curious people like yourself. The university is a vast resource that you shouldn't avoid."

I took a deep breath. Not only had I been chastised by mother's ghost and Raymond since I left home, now Calla had joined the fray. The day was going from bad to worse. "I'll keep that in mind, Calla. Would you be a dear and call them for me? I have a few more stops to make before going home to Hank."

The line hissed and crackled, and Calla remained silent for a long breath. "Sure, Marjorie, I can do that."

"Okay, thanks, I appreciate it." I was ready to hang up.

"Marjorie?" Calla said.

"Yes?"

"Did you say something to Herbert to upset him?"

"No. No, of course not. Not that I know of. Why?"

"I saw him talking to you, then went looking for him after you left, and I couldn't find him. He never leaves during the day without telling me, Marjorie."

I took a deep breath. "He wanted to tell me about Lida's cousin that he was in the war with. Herbert said he 'was just like him.' Do you know what that means?"

"No," Calla said. "Affected maybe? Shell-shocked? I don't know. All I know is that I'm a little worried about him. I always know where he is, and he always knows where I am."

"I'll keep an eye out for him as I drive out of town. If something comes up, call me at home. I'll be there in a little while."

"All right."

"Calla?" I said. It was my turn to ask a question.

"Yes?"

"You don't think Herbert has anything to do with the Knudsens' murders do you?"

Calla didn't answer straight away, but when she did, her tone had lost all of its warmth. "No. Herbert Frakes wouldn't hurt a fly. Goodbye, Marjorie."

With that, she hung up the phone. More like slammed it down and left the phone dead in my ear. All I could do was stare at the receiver with my mouth agape for the longest time.

I finally hung it up, straightened my shoulders, and pushed out of the phone booth intent on stopping by the police station to see if Hilo was there. I wanted to ask him if the amulet I had in my possession really had been stolen, and if so why in the heck hadn't he told me? But I stopped in my tracks.

The green Chevy sedan was parked across the street.

It was empty as far as I could tell. There was no sign of the newspaper reader anywhere, even though the car was parked in front of the Western Auto store. The big red letters on the front of the blonde brick building were usually a source of comfort; it was a place to go to first in search of a myriad of needs. It was more than an automobile parts store; Hank bought his shotgun and the .22 there, along with most of the tools he kept neatly in the garage section of the first barn. The other two barns were used for housing what animals we kept, equipment, and hay bale storage.

A tremor of fear rolled up my spine as I looked up and down 1st Avenue. Most of the cars and trucks I saw were subdued colors: blacks, grays, and dark green like our Studebaker truck. There were a few yellows and reds. One of those, a little red rear-engine Chevrolet Corvair drove by, sounding odd, drawing my attention for a second because of the puttering of the engine and the size of it, not the color. That car would've fit in one of our pig stalls; it looked like a death trap to me.

Hamish Martin's 1960 buttercup yellow Plymouth Fury convertible sat in front of his insurance office with the top up. The car drew attention wherever it went—just like Hamish, with his wide loud ties. Most folks in these parts were simple and modest in their tastes, but the modern world was getting more colorful and loud, so I figured there'd come a day when the insurance salesman's car would become normal, and the sedate black sedans of the past would become quaint.

Still, the green Chevy stood out—at least to me. I looked up and down the street again and saw nothing out of place, then chastised myself, again, for being paranoid, nervous.

But, I was on a unusual mission, and it had been a difficult afternoon. I had an odd, perhaps stolen, amulet in my purse. My cousin had left me unsettled, and he had given me a reason to question Hilo, a man that I had always trusted implicitly. Calla was upset with me because she couldn't find Herbert Frakes. Two of my closest friends had been murdered in a horrible, horrible way, and my heart was breaking for their two sons, who must have been lost in a way they had never counted on. I longed to see both of the boys and hold them as tight as possible.

Before I knew it, a tear streamed down my cheek. It was all too much. I should have told Hilo no. Taken the pies over to the Knudsens' place and given the boys as much comfort as possible, then gone home to Hank and buried myself in my work. That's what I always did when things went bad. Work. It was the salve for most of the wounds I had ever encountered.

The tears didn't stop. They just cascaded more readily—and for whatever the reason, it didn't bother me that I was standing on the sidewalk doing so. Any other day I would have been mortified.

I should have been home working. My deadline for Sir Nigel's book was getting closer every day, and I was in town on a fool's errand, engaged in something I was wholly unprepared for.

"Pull yourself together, Marjorie," I said to myself. "You're stronger than this." It was my mother's voice, urging me on. I knew that and wasn't the least bit angry about it.

I dug into my purse, pulled out my handkerchief, wiped my eyes, looked up and down the street one last time to see normal life pulsing all around me, then looked over to the green Chevy.

"You're just imagining things, Marjorie," I said in a whisper. "Go on, go home where you belong."

I took a deep breath, pulled myself together, and headed toward the truck, but just as I got to the door, I decided to make a quick detour into the Rexall.

I hurried inside the drugstore, looked around to see if there was anyone inside that I knew, then made my way to the counter.

I had visited the Rexall more since Hank's accident than I had in my entire life. Gregor Landdow was the pharmacist, and he'd been there since the dawn of time. I glanced over to the drug counter and saw him standing there like always, his head down, counting out pills or reading up on some newfangled cure that the doctors were touting. I didn't know how he kept up with it all. But he was one of the few people I knew who used and appreciated well-written indexes. He told me so every time I saw him.

The counter girl was new, and I was happy about that. I didn't know her or her family, and she didn't seem to recognize me. "May I help you?" she asked. She was probably just out of high school and looked bored to tears.

"A pack of Salems, please."

The girl was a little taller than me and wore bright red lipstick and dark eyeliner, and her hair looked like a beehive had been sat on top of her head. It looked like a lot of work to me.

"Just one?" she asked.

I nodded. "Yes."

She bent down, pulled a pack from underneath the counter, and handed it to me on the way up. I was sure her hair was going to tip over, but it didn't. "Twenty-seven cents, please," she said, as she punched the numbers into the cash register and hit a button that thrust the drawer open with a loud ding.

I looked around unconsciously, hoping that the ding hadn't drawn any attention. I dug into my change purse as quick as I could, found a quarter and two pennies, and handed them to her in as smooth an exchange as I could muster. I felt like a teenaged girl doing something wrong. I'm sure it showed on my face. I just wanted to get out of there as quick as I could.

I stuffed the cigarettes in the secret place in my purse, next to the amulet, and started to walk off.

"Don't you want your receipt, Mrs. Trumaine?" the counter girl said. The sound of my name stopped me in my tracks. I was halfway to the door. I turned around and took a second look at the girl. She still didn't look familiar. I must have known her family somehow. "Do I know you?"

The store was empty, with the exception of Gregor Landdow. He hadn't moved from his spot or bothered to look up.

The girl shrugged. "I'm Betty Walsh."

The Walsh name kind of rang a bell. The old folks had a farm out South Heart way that nearly stretched all the way to the Montana state line. But I thought the family had sold the place a while back. Maybe the kids had moved into town. That happened. Or they went on down the road to Bismarck or Fargo, sometimes to Minneapolis or Denver.

I shrugged. "I'm sorry," I said. I really wanted to be on my way, but I didn't want to be rude, and I was curious how she knew who I was. "I don't recognize you."

The girl nodded. "I used to date Jaeger Knudsen in high school. I was out to your place a couple of times. Mostly, I just sat in the truck while him and Peter baled hay, or unloaded it."

I nodded, looked at her closely, and tried to imagine her young face without makeup. "Yes, of course," I lied. I still couldn't place her. I doubted if Jaeger ever introduced her to me. He was the silent one of the two. Peter would prate on and on about the phase of the moon, the state of the weather, pork belly futures, whatever he'd put in his head that day. Truth be told, Peter was my favorite. He had a curious mind and loved to learn. Jaeger was always in a dark mood, it seemed, but was the harder worker of the two.

"We broke up about six months ago," Betty Walsh said. "He was *so* jealous, I could barely ask for the fella down at the Sunoco Station to check my oil."

"I'm sorry," I said, interrupting her. I needed to get home and she looked prepared to launch into a sordid tirade that I had no interest in hearing. "It was good to see you, dear." I turned to leave again.

No one had come into the Rexall since I had, and I was grateful for that.

"I was sorry to hear what happened to his parents," Betty said, stopping me again. "He fought with them all of the time."

I didn't take that too seriously, except she had made a point to bring it up. Teenage boys arguing with their parents was common. There was nothing unusual about that.

"I'm sure Jaeger is stricken," I said. "It's such a tragedy. They were both fine people."

Betty twirled a stray strand of hair that had fallen from the beehive. "If you say so."

I was about to ask her what she meant by that, but the bell over the door jingled, announcing someone coming in. I glanced over to see a hunched-over old man, intent on making his way to see Gregor Landdow. In a town of ten thousand it was impossible to know everyone.

"It was good to see you, Betty. I'm sure I'll see you at the funeral."

"Oh, I wouldn't miss it for the world, Mrs. Trumaine. Everyone in town'll be there," Betty Walsh said with a broad smile on her face.

CHAPTER 9

The green Chevy was gone when I walked back to my truck. I looked long and broad for it, but there was no sign of the car at all. I shook my head. I was being silly.

Now I had something else to consider, and that was the state of mind that I would find Peter and Jaeger in. Betty Walsh had watered a seed about Jaeger that certainly needed my attention, but Hilo had said that the boys weren't suspects in the murders of their parents, though he hadn't ruled them out completely.

I could barely bring myself to think ill of Jaeger, that the boy could actually do something as horrific as cutting his own mother's throat. He had been such a help on our farm, especially after Hank had become bedridden and unable to make the daily decisions around the farm that needed to be made.

Jaeger was a natural manager. He excelled at seeing things through to the end. Diligent and calculating, he was cut from a similar cloth as Hank. But Jaeger lacked patience and tact. He was demanding and hard, especially on Peter.

Betty Walsh was right. Jaeger had a quick temper. I had seen him fly off the handle frequently over the years, but I always marked that up to his youth, his inexperience.

The truth was, I knew very little about Jaeger's emotional life, his real relationship with his parents, or how he saw the world. He was a closed book, eager to take on a task, and a hard worker if I had ever seen one, but never very open about how he felt about things—even the weather or the future—unlike Peter and Hank, who were poets in their own ways. None of those things added up, at least in my mind, to point to Jaeger as a cold-blooded killer.

Just the thought of the boys and their sad situation left me feeling emptier than I already did. Somehow, that just seemed impossible. I was wrung out, my tear ducts fallow, but my stomach still churned with an uneasiness that was hard to place.

I decided to let Hilo do the police work, let him figure out if either of the boys needed to be looked at closer, even though I was still sour with him.

The shadow of doubt about Jaeger still lingered in my mind. I hoped I would be able to look him in the eye with love and comfort when I saw him next. With that thought, I put the truck into gear and headed toward the courthouse, where the sheriff's office was located. I was in a mind to give Hilo the amulet and be done with all of this murder business.

Nothing good had come from my trip into town. Just the opposite, really. Either I was upset with someone or they were upset with me. I had to wonder if there wasn't a black curse on the ugly Norse medallion. A dark wind had blown across my face from the moment I had looked up and spied Hilo pulling up our drive. I had been cold ever since Hilo had placed the amulet in my hand. I didn't like it in my presence at all, and after the day I'd had, I was pretty sure I didn't want the damned thing in my house, or in my possession, for another second.

I took a deep breath, tapped the steering wheel, and said, "Poppycock," without regard to anyone around me walking by, who might see me talking to myself. "It's just a necklace, a thing, Marjorie. You don't believe in that kind of stuff, in ancient evil, in objects that hold dark powers. Don't be silly."

But maybe I did believe in such things. Or, at the very least, maybe I was starting to.

The courthouse sat off of 3rd Street, and was built in the mid-1930s. Nineteen thirty-six or thirty-seven—I couldn't remember for sure, and I wasn't going to go look at the cornerstone to find out. I knew the building had been built toward the end of the Depression, and that was enough.

There'd been a huge building boom in Dickinson, in all of Stark County, during that time, offering men work—a chance to stay off of relief—by working for the WPA, the Works Progress Administration. My father called FDR's New Deal program the We Poke Along Society, and he avoided any charity like it was the plague. But I had found out years later, after his death, that he'd been no different than anyone else. When the chips were down, in the depths of the Depression, he'd taken relief, too, though just for a short while. He was a proud man, my father, and it must have galled him to no end to accept a handout. I was glad that I was very young, just born during that dark time. The Depression years were a vague, distant memory for me.

The courthouse looked like a four-story wedding cake, square instead of round, made of blonde brick and accented with limestone inlaid columns. I'd heard someone say it was Art Deco once—but I never thought it was garish like some of the pictures of the New York Art Deco buildings seemed to be. There was no silver, neon, or fancy flutes adorning the exterior of the courthouse anywhere that I could see. It was an understated building that sat on a couple of grassy acres, surrounded by a few pine trees and a thin copse of tall cottonwoods.

A quick spin through the parking lot around the back told me what I needed to know. Hilo wasn't there. His parking spot was empty. His pickup truck nowhere to be seen.

I thought about going in and talking to the dispatcher to see if I could find Hilo, but on second thought I decided I didn't want to bother him if he was busy with the investigation, so I drove away.

Once I got out on the main street that would take me out of Dickinson, I glanced over to my purse and thought about the cigarettes I had bought at the Rexall. I wouldn't have thought about them if they weren't there. That's the bad thing about having cigarettes around. But I was nervous, on edge, and uncomfortable. It was as good an excuse as any.

I passed by Luther Van's TV shop and noticed a few people standing in front of the big window that fronted the street. It was stacked full of flickering black-and-white televisions. There always seemed to be someone standing there watching those boxes—transfixed, mesmerized, lost to the world around them.

Hank and I didn't have a television. We hadn't seen the need. The radio was good enough for us, and from what we'd heard from our neighbors, primarily the Knudsens, TV reception was spotty, affected by the wind and weather unless you had a really good and tall antenna. Hank had said it'd be something else to monkey with, and we had enough things to occupy our time. He was right. But I think he was afraid of the outside world coming into the house in a bad way. Farming had enough ebbs and flows of good fortune and bad. Hank's fate was proof enough of that.

I looked away from the TV store, from the moths drawn to flame, opened my purse, and grabbed up the pack of Salems.

I watched the road as close as I could while I tore the silver foil from the right top corner of the pack. I tapped a cigarette out, let it fall into the lap of my dress, and put the pack back where it belonged.

The midday traffic thinned as I made my way out of town, making it easy enough to pop in the cigarette lighter in the dash and watch the road. I was just waiting for the businesses to thin out before I lit the cigarette. I didn't want anyone to see me smoking as I drove by.

I hadn't seen any sign of Herbert Frakes as I made my way out of town, but that didn't stop me from looking. I felt bad for upsetting the man, and Calla, too. She had never hung up on me before, and it was unsettling.

With that thought, I had never been so ready to leave Dickinson in my entire life.

I had the radio on to the local station, KDIX 1230 AM. I was hoping for some news about the murders, but Peg Graham and her "Women's Club of the Air" program was rattling on. I was in no mood to listen to how to make a perfect meringue—they always fell when I made them—so I flipped through the stations until I finally gave up and turned the darned thing off.

The lighter sprang out and announced that it was hot just as I crossed over the railroad tracks, leaving the business district behind me.

The gray weathered grain elevator towered on my right, and the flat land spread out before me, dotted with a few houses. I breathed a little easier at the familiar, and less populated, landscape.

The lighter glowed in a hot red circle, and the tobacco flamed up for a second when I pressed the Salem against it. I took a deep draw on the cigarette and felt the rush of smoke push into my lungs. I relaxed as I exhaled.

I popped the lighter back into the hole in the dash, looked ahead of me, straightened the truck up a bit, then looked into the rearview mirror.

The green Chevy was trailing me about a half a block behind.

I looked closer just to make sure I wasn't imagining what I thought I was seeing. I wasn't. It sure looked like the same car that I had seen around town all day—and on second glance, it was speeding toward me, coming up faster than it should have been, like it was trying to catch me.

I took a quick draw off the Salem, then tossed it into the open ashtray, leaving it to smolder. I exhaled smoke and punched down the accelerator at the same time.

The V8 engine hesitated and coughed. I feared the truck was going to die right then and there and leave me stranded with the car coming for me. I was suddenly afraid. I felt like a rabbit trying to outrun the shadow of a hawk.

Hank was always good at giving the truck a once over every spring and fall. Maintenance was important to him; he changed the points and plugs, drained the radiator, tightened the belts, whatever was needed so the truck wouldn't fail him when he needed it the most. I had to admit that I'd let the maintenance go, had never pestered Jaeger to take on that task, and now that I needed the power of the truck to propel me out of trouble, or at least give me a shot at outrunning the Chevy, it was lacking.

The engine finally caught, but with a loud complaint as I pushed the accelerator as hard as I could to the floor. My Sunday shoes weren't made for such things.

The Studebaker had never been spry, and the steering wheel shook like a washing machine out of balance as the truck lurched forward up to speed. I had seen a washing machine nearly dance across the floor at the Coin Laundromat one day when I'd stopped by just out of curiosity. Lida Knudsen had told me they'd got all new machines and replaced most of the wringer-washers like the ones we both had in our mud rooms.

The interior of the truck cab was thick with cigarette smoke and exhaust fumes. I didn't dare take my hands off the wheel to roll down the window the rest of the way to clear the air. Every time I looked into the rearview mirror, the Chevy was getting closer. It was less than a hundred feet behind me.

I couldn't make out any details, but it looked like there was only one person in the car; a man driving. The sun glared off the windshield, and I could only see a pair of dark-lens glasses on his face. Every other second I was looking at the road ahead of me.

The road stretched out in front of me for as far as the eye could see. The fields on both sides of me had been planted with winter wheat and were already cut. It wasn't odd to see barren fields this time of year; rather, it was one of the comforts of the cycle. But plain and simple, there was no place to run, and certainly no place to hide if the man in the green Chevy meant to do me harm.

You could see a storm rolling toward you from fifty miles away—or it seemed like you could. Or a storm moving out, like the one earlier in the day. Just like I had thought, there was no sign of the earlier precipitation. Prairie dogs and gophers were the only ones with the advantage of underground towns; there one minute, then gone the next because a sentinel alerted them to trouble. Smart little critters, those rodents. I admired them as much as I thought they were pests and dangerous. You could snap an ankle in an unseen hole—or make a man fall and discharge his shotgun accidently.

When I looked back again, the Chevy was nearly on my bumper.

I braced myself for impact.

I was certain he was going to ram into me.

I was so tense that if he hit me my arms would have snapped in two.

But the green Chevy's front bumper didn't touch the truck. At the very last second, the driver swerved over into the other lane, accelerated, and sped by me without so much as a nod.

I was shocked, relieved, and failed to gain a good look at the driver. Before I knew it, all I could see was the rear end of the car, the taillights blazing red, like flames coming out of the bottom of a rocket, in a hurry to leave this world.

CHAPTER 10

I pulled the truck over to the side of the road and shut off the engine. I was certain that my heart was going to jump out of my chest and keep on going, right down the road, chasing after that green Chevy.

It had disappeared from sight, leaving me on an open stretch of road that reached all the way to Montana and beyond.

I collapsed forward so my forehead rested on the steering wheel. It was the only thing holding me up, keeping me from slinking off the bench seat straight onto the floorboard. I would have stayed there forever if I hadn't had Hank to go home to.

Once the engine started to cool down, the pings and groans diminishing and riding on the constant breeze like the rest of the worldly noises, the comfort of the plains, of the aloneness of the land, started to return to me.

The distant trill of a meadowlark eased its way into my ear, and I digested it like hot chicken soup on a cold winter night. The persistent bubbling tones were a salve to a nightmare, a return to normalcy, to a world that I recognized.

I looked up out the windshield, and movement immediately caught my eye. It was another bird—the big flittering black and white wings of a magpie as it landed on a nearby fence post. Another comfort. The curious bird stared at my truck, at me, and then seemed to shrug, as if it didn't mind my presence at all.

I had already chastised myself enough, so there was no use adding more of a burden to the pile. Not only was I in over my head, I was out of my head. Lost. I was sure, even though I was unsettled with him, that Hilo hadn't known what he was asking of me when he'd handed me the amulet.

I needed to write everything down that I had learned and experienced while I was in town, but the truth of the matter was that it all probably would have been for naught. I wouldn't have been able to organize any of my thoughts if my life depended on it—and a moment ago it felt like it had.

The magpie suddenly lit into the air, and I settled back against the seat and looked forward into the nothingness; the wide blue sky against brown empty fields, edged with the greenness and wildflowers of a brief summer. Black-eyed Susan, blanket flower, and beardtongue caught my eye. For some reason it was the beardtongue that interested me the most—it was used by the Lakota as snakebite medicine—but added subtle color to what I was seeing. The flower was easily overlooked even though it was a powerful medicine. Everything looked like it was supposed to, but it sure didn't feel like the world I knew and loved anymore. I couldn't seem to fix anything.

I drew in a deep breath, grabbed up the smoldering cigarette from the ashtray, and took a less-than-enthusiastic puff. The taste had gone from minty cool to stale and tasteless. My tongue felt like sandpaper. My mouth was dry, and at that moment, all I wanted to do was go home, crawl into bed with Hank, and pull the covers up over my head.

But I couldn't do that. The pies on the passenger floorboard reminded me that I had one more stop to make. After everything I had experienced in Dickinson, I needed to find it in myself to be a good neighbor, and a better friend, and offer Peter and Jaeger whatever I could to help get them though the horrible tragedy that had befallen them.

I stubbed out the cigarette, closed the ashtray, then straightened up my hair the best I could. My face was a mess, so I touched up my makeup and lipstick as quick as I could.

I didn't want the boys to see me all a muss with straggly hairs and tear-stained cheeks. They needed to see strength and love, the same faces their parents had offered me in my time of need. I had to give the Knudsen boys hope, reassure them that somehow, someway, they would get through this and survive it. The landscape would be different, changed—they would have to learn how to walk all over again and be better for the experience. I had a twenty-minute drive to convince myself of that, because if I didn't believe it they wouldn't either.

There were times when being a good liar would have come in handy.

The Knudsen family had migrated from Minnesota a few years before the stock market crash in twenty-nine and the start of the Great Depression. Erik's father, Reeger, passed his farm on to his eldest son as was the custom, while the other three Knudsen boys were free to explore at their pleasure—which they all had. Two of them died in World War II, and the other was killed in an automobile accident after coming back from service in Japan.

Lida's family had been in North Dakota since the wagon train days, surviving and carving out a living as shopkeepers and sheep farmers. Lida had two brothers, farmers too, in Stark County, who were successful in their own right. By successful I mean they were able to hold onto their farms from year to year, but they were by no means wealthy. They were land rich and bank poor, as the saying went. As far as I knew, neither of Lida's brothers were in financial trouble of any kind, but they would, perhaps, be sources to talk to about the cousin Herbert Frakes spoke of, if the need arose. It was obvious that I wasn't going to be able to completely disconnect from the murders until the truth of it came out.

But, I thought, none of the Knudsens, including Erik and Lida, were the type to burden other people with their problems. I knew I would be the last person to know if they'd had any real problems—money-related or otherwise.

Erik and Lida were a happy and gregarious couple, involved in their church and community. They were good parents and the best neighbors I could have ever hoped to have. And as far as I knew, Peter and Jaeger had no aspirations other than to follow in their father's footsteps. They wanted nothing more than to be farmers, honorable men like Erik, like Hank, who loved the life they were fortunate enough to live.

Truth be told, I was a little scared that Raymond was somehow involved with the amulet. He'd gripped it like he wanted to run off with it. I didn't really want to think that he was involved in the murders. Raymond was a mean boy, but never physical, at least with me. I had no idea beyond that. It would have helped to clear my mind if Professor Strand had been home.

Raymond lived in a world I knew little about. Power and social standing were the farthest things from my mind as I went through my day, but it was obvious that appearances and possessions meant a lot to Raymond—just as they had to his mother.

I slowed as I approached the lane that led down to the Knudsens' house. I was constantly aware of the other vehicles on the road and on the lookout for the green Chevy. I had not seen hide nor hair of it. Truth was, only two cars had passed by me, and neither of them were green. One was black and the other was gray. No surprise there.

I downshifted and drove up the lane that led to the Knudsens' house with an unsettled feeling growing in the pit of my stomach. A voice screamed inside my head: Go home to Hank. He needs you.

But I didn't listen. Peter and Jaeger needed me too.

I expected the yard to be loaded with cars, with people milling about and wandering in and out with food.

Only Erik's five-year-old red International Harvester pickup sat next to the house. Parked next to it was a brown and tan county police car, the bubble on top dark, the windows rolled up. That was it. There were no other cars or trucks about. When Hank had got hurt there was a sea of Detroit steel in our front yard, every make and model of car and truck that you could think of.

The chill of the amulet returned to me, rising up and down my spine.

I knew Hilo wasn't standing guard at the Knudsens'. He refused to drive anything but his old, battered pickup. It was probably one of his deputies given the duty to ward off curiosity seekers.

The thought caught in my throat as I pulled next to the car and stopped . . . I could only hope the deputy wasn't Guy Reinhardt.

Like just about everybody else in Stark County who was similar in age, Guy Reinhardt and I had known each other for most of our lives. I knew some of his joys and tragedies, and he knew some of mine, but we were never friends.

We went to different high schools, but since there were only three in the entire county, our paths crossed often. Guy grew up in South Heart. He was a Cougar. I was a Midget—an odd name for a high school mascot in my mind, even now, but it had been that way since the early 1900s.

Sports weren't really important to me back then. According to most people, Hank included, I couldn't pull my nose out of a book long enough to know whether it was night or day. But everybody in the state knew who Guy Reinhardt was.

Guy had been a golden boy, an athlete who was gifted beyond belief. There seemed to be nothing that he didn't excel at: baseball, track and field, and basketball. Especially basketball. He still held the state record for the highest scoring in a single game as far as I knew. There was talk of him going professional, whispers of scouts visiting games once Guy started playing at the university—a big deal in North Dakota—which, of course, in the end came to naught.

A week before the pro draft, Guy had been out drinking with friends and celebrating. Before the night ended, two of those friends were dead, and Guy, who was the driver when the accident happened, suffered severe damage to his right leg. He was thrown from the car and run over by an oncoming truck.

All these years later, Guy still walked with a limp—a hindrance that hadn't prevented Hilo from giving him a job when nobody else would. Other than the limp, Guy was whole, but those who knew him when he was young, at his best, could see a faraway look forever pinned in his sky-blue eyes.

It was like Guy had been forever cursed with the wondering, the curiosity of the past, the constant questioning of himself—if life would have been different had he made a different decision so long ago. We all had our regrets. I imagined Hank thought the same thing, lying in his bed, staring at the ceiling, unable to flick a fly off his nose.

Being a deputy was a far cry from being a pro basketball player, traveling the world, money not a worry, rather than sitting behind the wheel of a police car, spending most days alone—while everyone who knew your story looked at you with a bit of pity, looked at you like you were a loser, an idiot for throwing away all of your God-given promise.

Guy Reinhardt and I shared in that. Shared in the looks of pity. As I sat there, still wondering if Guy Reinhardt was the deputy on duty, I realized again that Peter and Jaeger had joined our club. We were survivors of life's harshest moments, moments that had forced us to get on with our lives even though our hearts were torn to tatters. We were all actors hiding the pain; some of us were just better at it than others. It was no wonder actors were called tragedians.

"I thought I'd heard somebody pull up."

I stood up out of the Studebaker, a little surprised that my questioning had been on point: It *was* Guy Reinhardt whose task it was to look after Erik and Lida's land.

Guy had come out of Erik and Lida's house. He stood on the front porch and eyed me carefully. The tightness in his face relaxed when he saw the pies. I stopped at the fence post that separated the yard and the drive. The wind circled around my ankles and threatened to ruffle my dress, but I pressed the pies down to keep it from flying up.

"Good to see you, Marjorie," he said.

"Same to you, Guy."

"How's Hank?"

"No better, no worse." On this day, I didn't feel compelled to lie to Guy Reinhardt, but I let my woes stop there.

He nodded and looked at me knowingly. "That's a good thing, I suppose."

The late-afternoon sun caught Guy's blonde hair, highlighting a tinge of gray in his sideburns. His face was angular, tanned, and he still had the look of a man whose determined face could have perfectly graced a Wheaties box. He was as tall as a cornstalk, and age had been kind to him; his body was still lean and fit. Only his sad blue eyes and limp belied any past history that would have given a stranger any hint that Guy Reinhardt was less than fulfilled, standing in the doorway of a murder victim's home, dressed in a uniform that required a gun, instead of sneakers, gym shorts, and a crowd to cheer him on.

Guy stepped off the porch. "Probably be best if you let me take those pies there, Marjorie. Hilo doesn't want anybody to step inside until he's certain there's nothing else we need to look at. I been runnin' folks off all day."

"They were just doing what folks do," I said.

"This is different," Guy answered. His voice was hard and direct. I suppose I needed that reminder as much as anyone else.

I hadn't noticed the yellow tape that surrounded the front of the house, crisscrossing the front door, until that moment. I didn't think I could confront the idea that Erik and Lida were really dead, not home . . . that their farm was a crime scene.

"I was hoping to speak with Peter and Jaeger, if only for a moment," I said, balancing the pies in my hands and warding off the threat of the wind at the same time.

"They're supposed to be talking with Hilo down at the station."

"I just came from there. They weren't there. Neither was Hilo. At least his truck wasn't there."

"Then he wasn't there, either."

I nodded and was tempted to tell Guy about the green Chevy, but there was nothing to point to that was malicious or criminal. Just a pattern that I'd noticed that probably didn't mean a thing, that was probably just my imagination playing tricks on me.

"Well, my guess is they had some business to tend to at McClandon's Funeral Home," Guy said. "They'll be along shortly. It's got to be hard going through something like this. Hard to say where Hilo was. Seems a mite busy today, as you can imagine."

"I suppose so."

I realized I had mimicked Guy's earlier response when he flashed a quick smile to break the tension and sadness in the air.

Unconsciously, I glanced to his left hand, and realized it was minus a ring. I hesitated, but only briefly, before I asked how his wife, Ruth, was doing, if only to change the subject.

Guy's face tightened, and he looked away from me, out toward the barn, freshly painted red so it was easy to find in the winter. The profile of Guy's face was hard as stone and my question about Ruth affected his professional expression like a cloud crossing in front of the sun.

"Ruth's back with her family," he said.

"Oh, I'm sorry, I didn't know."

"No," he said. "I don't suppose you would."

Ruth Reinhardt was Guy's second wife. His first divorce caused the normal whispers, his second, if it came to that, would be downright scandalous. North Dakota women stayed true to their husbands through good and bad. I was no exception. But I was also not one to judge another marriage . . . or another man's pain, no matter how hard he was to live with.

Rumor had it that Guy had a hateful relationship with whiskey that had followed him from his university days to the present. But to me, it was just a rumor. I had never seen him drunk, nor had I ever smelled whiskey on his breath. I doubted Hilo would put up with behavior unbecoming an officer of the law no matter who he was, so I'd always put little credence in those rumors.

I knew little of Ruth, a short brunette with two children from a previous marriage, just enough to know that she came from a family with more than a fair share of drinkers, fighters, and secrets. Trouble and angst seem to be a magnet for some people. Maybe it was that that broke them apart. Either way, Guy Reinhardt's misfortune was none of my business.

There was just something about him that I couldn't shake, and finally, I realized what it was once the breeze kicked up again. The air was filled with his odor, with the sweetness of his masculinity. It totally overtook any evidence of the previous rain.

Guy's skin glistened, tanned from the sun, from hanging his arm out of the window of the police car. It was the smell of life, of a walking, healthy man that I was responding to like a giddy schoolgirl. It made no difference that he might be just as disabled on the inside as Hank was on the outside, Guy Reinhardt was an attractive man.

I blushed at the sudden realization that I was betraying my husband by responding to another man whose only intent was his duty and nothing more.

"It doesn't matter," Guy said.

I pushed the pies toward him. "Make sure Peter and Jaeger get these."

Guy almost dropped one of the pies. By the time he regained his balance, I was in the Studebaker sliding the key into the ignition.

The truck's engine roared to life and I backed up as quick as I could, spun the tires, and kicked up a dust storm that rained pellets of gravel thirty feet behind me. I could barely see Guy shaking his head in dismay as I pulled out onto the lane and sped toward home.

CHAPTER 11

I had never been so glad to pull onto my own land in my entire life.

The midafternoon light was bright, intense as the sun beat down from the sky like a spotlight directed at the rooftop of our simple wind-beaten house. It needed a fresh coat of paint, but like the maintenance on the truck, I hadn't had the heart to ask Peter and Jaeger for any more of their time. Maybe next summer, once things settled down . . .

My stomach growled with hunger, and I realized that I'd passed up lunch while I was in Dickinson; I rarely missed a trip to the Ivanhoe for some of the best sandwich bread to be found anywhere in North Dakota, or beyond I guess. I wouldn't know for sure since I'd never crossed the state line outside of a couple of quick trips west, into Montana.

The Salems had staved off any real hunger, which I guess was one of the reasons why some women smoked them in the first place. It kept them thin and attractive and replaced the habit of eating the hearty meals we cooked for our husbands before sending them out the door to do a hard day's work. I suppose that had been a reason for me, too, but since Hank didn't like me smoking, especially since the accident, I'd taken to hiding from him when I did.

I hoped Ardith would join me for a quick sandwich and a cup of coffee before she left. Her car, a ten-year-old black Ford sedan, sat right where she had parked it.

I was halfway down the drive when Shep suddenly appeared, running out from behind the first barn, a streak of black and white, head and body low to the ground, barking at the Studebaker like he'd never seen the truck in his life. It wasn't a hello bark, or at least the normal bark that the diligent border collie usually offered me when I returned home from town.

The dog ran straight at the truck like he was going to nip the tires. I couldn't recall a time when Shep had tried to herd me while driving the truck. It was like he was trying to drive me away, force me to turn around and leave. I'd seen him attempt the same thing on Wally Howard, on occasion, when Wally'd had to deliver a box to the door; usually page proofs from New York.

At the very least, I had expected Shep to be happy to see me. It was rare that I was away from the house, from Hank, for so long.

"Silly dog," I said out the window. "Go on, get out of the way before I run you over." The thought of hurting Shep caused a tremor of fear to ripple all the way from my heart to the tips of my fingers.

My tone was obviously too light. It didn't deter Shep at all. My words just seemed to infuriate him. He barked his fool head off even louder, then lunged at the front tire, biting at it so close that it truly scared me. I stopped the truck right then and there.

As soon as the tires quit rolling, Shep circled around the truck, barking continually, ears back, an unusually aggressive snarl on his upturned lip. Something had set him off, and I didn't like it.

There had never been any question that one of Shep's jobs was to keep a lookout, be a guard dog of sorts, but his quarry was mostly foxes and coyote. His real job was to keep the chickens safe since we'd long ago given up on sheep, even though he thought his job was to keep the chickens in order. If I wasn't paying any attention, he'd keep them trapped in the corner of the pen for half a day. Shep would have made a great indexer if he were a human being.

Up until a day ago, there had been no reason to hold onto any fear at all about strangers coming onto the land. Most farm folks, or those in town as far as that went, had never locked their doors in their entire life.

I shut the engine off and sat in the truck for a long second, eyeing everything in sight. Nothing seemed out of place except Shep's behavior. But even that could be explained away. Border collies were an overprotective, obsessive breed, and sometimes it didn't take much to set them off. Timing was everything; a move, a look, a word spoken the wrong way could trigger a sort of madness that required a stern but gentle hand to quell. I had seen Shep act like this before, but it had been a long time ago—back before Hank stepped into that damned gopher hole. It was usually only Hank who could calm the dog down, but I knew it would be up to me this time around.

The rain and gloom of the morning was just a memory; the only remnant was the softness of the ground, but the wind would dry it out pretty quickly unless it rained again real soon. I had no idea what the forecast was; I'd been preoccupied with the task Hilo had straddled me with and everything that had happened since.

I knew that I'd been distracted, but I couldn't see a thing that wasn't where it was supposed to be, a reason for Shep's uncertain fit—except a repetitive banging that slowly drew my attention to it. I could barely hear the sound underneath Shep's constant barking.

I looked over to the house.

The screen door was banging in the wind. Open. Closed. Hit the jamb. Back again. The wind wasn't fierce, not by North Dakota standards by any means, but it was strong. Strong enough to push a storm to the east, then come through an open window, snake through the house, and rattle a door so it banged consistently like the echo of a heartbeat.

I froze for a second, looked at the swinging door, then back down to Shep. He was trying to keep me from going inside the house.

Hank . . . my mouth went dry.

Without thinking through my options, I jumped out of the truck and my heel instantly sank about a quarter of an inch into the soft dirt drive, enough to cause my balance to waver.

I wasn't used to wearing heels—especially when I wasn't thinking. The pitiful fear that had bubbled up in the pit of my stomach replaced any hunger I thought I might've had. I lurched sideways and caught myself against the Studebaker's door.

Shep dropped into a crouch, barked one last time, and gave me that long amber-eyed border collie stare. He was trying his best to stop me, but nothing could. My heart raced and matched the bang of the screen door.

"Stop it!" I shouted at Shep, then offered a hard glare of my own in return.

He ignored me and barked again. *Stubborn dog.*

I pushed off from the door, pulled my foot out of the shoe, and left it behind as I hurried to the house with a one-shoed limp.

The wind met me head on. It seemed to want to keep me out of the house, too. I must have looked drunk, but as far as I could tell there wasn't another human being around for miles.

I didn't care if there was.

"Hank!" I yelled out as I made my way to the door.

No answer. Just Shep's bark riding on the wind like an alarm that wouldn't shut off. He was behind me, and I expected to feel a pinch of canine teeth on the back of my heel any second.

"Ardith!"

Again, no answer. *Crap. Shit. Damn.* Panic. She should have come to the door as soon as Shep started barking, as soon as I pulled into the drive. *Where was she?*

I didn't hesitate when I reached the stoop. I burst through the door, not afraid, at least for my own wellbeing, but determined to find both Hank and Ardith and numbed by adrenaline since neither one of them had answered me.

My eyes searched the path to the bedroom and saw nothing out of place. Nothing but the black receiver dangling from the cord, down the wall.

It was silent inside the house. There was no busy signal on the party line. Most likely someone, probably Burlene Standish, was yelling at us to hang up so they could make a call—or listening in to see if she could tell what was going on in my house.

"Ardith? Hank?" I yelled out again as I pushed through the kitchen, praying the whole time. *Please let them be all right. Please . . .*

"In here." It was Hank's voice. I was so relieved to hear him that I nearly broke into tears.

I stumbled into the bedroom, kicking the other shoe off. It hit the wall with a boom "Are you all right?" I asked, in between panting breaths.

"No."

I blinked, cleared my eyes, and saw that Hank's face was pale, his forehead dotted with perspiration. He was covered up to the neck with a thin white sheet, but that wasn't unusual; I usually always covered him when he napped. Pneumonia was one of our biggest fears, which was another reason why I was opposed to leaving the window open. I glanced over and saw that Ardith had compromised with Hank. The window was only open about six inches—enough, though, for the wind to make its way in and bring a hint of after-rain-coolness on its push.

I nodded as I took in Hank's condition. There was a wet spot just below his waist. He'd soiled himself, something he hated more than living this way itself.

"Where's Ardith?" I asked.

"I don't know."

Shep had stopped just outside the bedroom door. The dog didn't relax. He crouched and stared at me—or Hank, I really couldn't tell which—still trying to pen us in.

"What do you mean you don't know?" I said. "What's happened, Hank?"

He looked stricken, his eyes hardened by the strain of trying to get out of bed. I knew he wanted to be up, in charge, taking care of things, but that was impossible. It never stopped him from trying, though. He had been trying to move since the day he had taken the fall.

"Breathe easy," I offered. His throat dried out when he was upset and made it difficult to swallow.

Hank blinked hard, and I knew that to be a nod. "The phone rang. I heard Ardith pick it up. First thing she did was yell at Burlene to get off the line and mind her own gall-darned business." His voice was scratchy, like sandpaper.

I moved to the nightstand and put a glass of water with a straw in it to his lips. He drank right away, wetting his throat, and blinked again when he was done.

"Oh my," I said.

"Ardith has never had any patience with busybodies."

"I know, but . . ." *I'll have to talk to her*, I finished thinking. I didn't care to be on bad terms with the neighbors, even though I agreed with Ardith. Burlene Standish was a tongue-wagger with no regard to who she hurt with her repeated—and most often embellished—tales of other peoples' woes.

"I think it was New York," Hank said. He stared at me, knowing I'd be on edge right away at the news that my editor had called and I hadn't been there to answer.

He was right. I could hardly bear the thought of missing a call from Richard Rothstein. It was either a request for more work, or there was a problem with Sir Nigel's headhunter book. Either way, it was a call that I didn't want to miss.

"What happened to Ardith?" I said, not lingering on the call.

"I don't know," Hank said. "I heard her ask the person on the other end of the line to hang on, then Shep barked and she padded out the door. She never came back. After a few long minutes, I called after her, but she never answered me, Marjorie. She just disappeared and never came back."

"How long ago was that?" I was stone cold frozen in my spot at the end of the bed. Shep was transfixed on me. I'm sure we both looked like statues.

"Over an hour, maybe longer. I don't know. I lose track. You know that. Minutes are like hours when I'm here alone."

"You've been here by yourself for that long?" I snapped.

"I'm fine. Just worried. I think you ought to call Hilo."

I shook my head. "I'm going to find Ardith after I get you cleaned up."

"I've been here this long. If you're gonna go, then go now. I'm fine. It's not like her, Marjie. It's not like Ardith at all to walk out and not come back when I called out for her."

I started to argue with Hank. I wasn't about to leave him there in his own filth. But he was right. It wasn't like Ardith Jenkins at all to leave him alone. She loved Hank. She always had. He was like the son she'd never had.

I nodded and turned to go out the door, but Hank's voice stopped me. "Marjie," he said, with as much authority and concern as he could muster.

"Yes?"

"I think you best take the .22 rifle with you."

CHAPTER 12

I thought long and hard about leaving Shep with Hank, but I knew I'd feel better if he was with me. I'd always looked to the dog for comfort far more than I ever had for protection, but in that moment, he was all I had to defend the farm from the unknown, other than the rifle behind the bedroom door.

My bones ached with fear and dread. There was nothing that I could think of that would pull Ardith Jenkins away from caring for Hank. Nothing. But I couldn't allow myself to imagine her fate any more than I could imagine the moment that Erik and Lida Knudsen had met their own deaths. . . . I just couldn't. I loved Ardith, and the thought of her leaving Hank riled me in a way that would border on a forgiveness that could never be granted. Unless something had happened to her. Then I would blame myself for leaving her on the farm, alone, in the first place.

Hank didn't have to tell me twice to grab the Remington .22 from behind the door. It was a light rifle, five pounds at the most, and looked like a slightly smaller version of the classic Winchester '73, the rifle that had tamed the west. Truth was I was a better pie maker than a marksman.

Hank had taught me most everything I knew about guns—the two in the house—but I'd had little practice when it came to shooting. Guns, hunting, and chasing off coyotes had always been the provenance of the men in my life: my father, Hank, Peter, and Jaeger. I had never known a situation when a gun had to be taken up for protection, to ward something evil off the land. It was a madness never considered, something beyond a raccoon stricken with distemper or an old dog that needed put out of its misery.

My eyes glanced down to the safety, a push-pull pin that was closed. As I picked up the rifle, I opened the chamber by pressing the safety off with my thumb. The .22 was fully loaded, seventeen cartridges plus one in the chamber, ready to go; death in my hands, fear in my heart.

"You sure you shouldn't call Hilo?" Hank asked. A wheeze in his chest echoed inside the small bedroom and danced off the walls with another warning, another dread.

It stopped me in my tracks. "Are you all right?" The smell of soured urine filled the air, and it was all I could do to not pull off the sheets, not allow Hank to lay in the wet bed any longer. There was a closet full of freshly bleached sheets just outside the door.

"All right as I can be," he said. "It should be me goin' out there to find Ardith, not you."

Hank's loss of mobility was a deep wound, but this wasn't the time to console him. He knew that as well as I did, but I wouldn't expect any less of him. I wanted him to be the one to go find Ardith, too.

"I need to go," I said. "Come on, Shep."

I had heard that wheeze in Hank's chest before, and as much as it concerned me, it was the least of my worries at the moment. Ardith needed me more. I was sure of it.

"Marjie," Hank called out.

I stopped again just at the threshold of the bedroom door. "Yes?" Shep followed my actions and did what I did. He stopped and never took his eyes off me.

"If you have to shoot, shoot for the head. That rifle won't kill a man with a shot anywhere else 'less you get lucky and put it through his heart. Even then, I'd shoot till he dropped. Jus' keep a pullin' the lever and the trigger till the bullets are all gone."

It was cold, hard advice, and my hand trembled against the smooth wood stock of the rifle. All I could do was nod. I didn't know if I could kill a man. I hoped to never find out what I would do if the chips were down, if I had to consider the choice of someone's life I cared about over a stranger set on doing them harm—or harm to me. I just didn't know what I would do.

I pushed out of the bedroom with a different set of eyes, leaving the stench of lingering sickness behind me, and walking toward an abyss of darkness conjured only by my imagination. I was glad Guy Reinhardt had kept me from entering the Knudsens' house. I didn't want to know what murder smelled like, though I had a good idea.

There seemed to be shadows everywhere I looked. The cabinets in the kitchen cast an undue darkness onto the clean-as-a-whistle floor and dappled it with a saucer-shaped gloom from the dishes that rested in the drainer, air drying.

Whatever had taken Ardith's attention out of the house had come after she'd fed Hank his lunch. I was grateful for that, even though I felt horrible for leaving him.

I didn't linger or allow my thoughts to slow me. I made my way past the telephone, the dangling receiver, ignored the notepad on the counter, and found myself at the front door, slowing with hesitation.

I looked back over my shoulder at the notepad and stopped. My eyes had perused Ardith's writing on the paper as I'd passed, and I knew by heart, even without my reading glasses on, the number she'd written down: 212-555-0408. It *was* Richard Rothstein's phone number. He would be greatly annoyed that I hadn't returned his call immediately, but that would have to wait, too.

My personal life—Ardith's life—were more important than any back-of-the-book index I could ever imagine, even the one Gregor Landdow used at the Rexall.

I sucked in a deep breath and walked out of the false sense of security I felt inside my house. "Come on, Shep. Where's Ardith? Let's go find Ardith."

He didn't answer me. Instead, the dog followed after me, then bolted around me once I was fully outside. He circled me three times, then came to a frozen stance about ten feet in front of me.

It was a game, a silly border collie game that I was in no mood to play, but I stopped, too. "Stop it," I said. "Just stop it this instance, Shep. This isn't the time."

Shep's ears stood fully erect and pointed straight up to the waning sun. There were no clouds, and late afternoon would soon become evening, then night. As warm as it was, the darkness would bring a chill with it; good sleeping weather with the windows open if there was a reason not to be afraid.

I looked away from Shep's beguiling eyes, to the ground below me, hoping to see a sign, a trail, something that would lead me to Ardith straight away.

There was nothing but grass that was in need of being cut. If it had been trampled down an hour before, the resilient blades of hearty greenness had already stood back up, reached up to the sky in praise to the sun, leaving no sign of disturbance or human touch.

I turned slowly in a circle, imitating Shep in my own way, for my own purposes, cradling the .22, the forestock in my left hand, the index finger of my right hand on the trigger.

I traversed in and out of the wind, ignoring the specks of dirt that kicked up from the drive and sprayed my face.

The morning rain had done little to tame the sandy grains. They were most likely dried ten seconds after the rain quit falling from the sky, caressed as they were by the rush of the constant movement of air.

If the wind ceased, it was like someone had quit talking. A murmur gone. Wisdom silenced. Stillness was alien on the prairie, more noticeable, more foreboding than almost any storm, the exception being the ones that you could see coming at you from miles away; black walls of rain and thunder, mad power unleashed. There was no place to hide from those storms except in the cellar. Silence wasn't nearly as dangerous.

I saw nothing unusual in the perfect radius of my turn. The farm looked like it always had, everything in its place, weathered a bit, neglect settling in from the lack of attention from the overseer, the man who had loved everything about the land that was once his responsibility.

All that was missing was Ardith Jenkins.

CHAPTER 13

I drew in a deep breath, settled my finger on the trigger of the rifle, and watched the ground for potential pitfalls. I knew the reality of an accident—the result of losing focus for just one second—all too well.

The grass under my feet was dry and offered little concern. In the rush to get to Hank, I had lost my shoes, and had thought little of putting them, or any others, back on as I left the house.

After brief consideration, I knew where I was going to look first after I called out.

There was absolutely no sign that anything mischievous had occurred in my absence. The murders on the nearby farm had touched me, set me on edge, and heightened my fears. But in reality, Ardith was of the age where anything could have happened to her that had prevented her return to Hank. A heart attack or stroke could have just as easily struck her down as anything else. The question was—what had pulled Ardith's attention away from the phone in the first place? She knew how important my New York calls were.

"Ardith!" I called out. "Are you here?" My words caught on the wind, whistled upward, and disappeared east just as quickly as they had come out of my mouth. "Ardith, please . . ."

No answer. All I could hear was my own heartbeat, a little louder than normal.

"Come on, Shep," I said, as I padded over to the cellar doors.

I didn't bother to look over my shoulder to see if the dog obeyed my request. I knew he would, eventually, when he thought it was his idea. There was no question that Shep was Hank's dog through and through.

I stopped at the bumpy cement lip that jutted out into the grass just before the double wood doors. They were slanted against the house, and the steps down into the cellar were steep. I hesitated. The cellar wasn't one of my favorite places. Never had been. I had screamed like a banshee at the first clap of thunder as a little girl, anticipating an undetermined amount of time in the spider-mouse-monster-infested hole in the ground.

Unfortunately, root cellars, storm cellars, basements, whatever, were a necessity in North Dakota. Spring was ripe with tornadoes, hail storms, and a hundred other natural occurrences that could cause a person harm. The cellar was the first place to run to seek safety when trouble showed itself. But that didn't mean I had to like going down into it.

I released my finger off the trigger and eased the .22 into my left hand. I really wished I had put on a pair of shoes. Any shoes. But I hadn't, and I needed to look and make sure that Ardith wasn't down in the cellar, waiting for trouble to pass, for somebody to come for her.

I lifted the right door and let it fall over onto the ground. It thudded, and dust from the inside of the door leapt into the air, looking very much like a dirty brown cloud.

Cobwebs, spider webs, and detritus of undetermined origins awaited my trip down the steps. It had been a while since I had swept them clean.

I immediately looked for any sign of human passage and didn't see any. That didn't mean I didn't have to go down and have a look. I did; I just didn't want to.

I steeled my courage, pushed all of my horrible childhood memories as far away as I could, and stepped down onto the first step. It creaked under my weight, "Ardith," I called out, "are you down here? Please be down here."

I didn't expect an answer, and I didn't get one.

All I had to do was get to the bottom of the steps, just to the edge of darkness, and my fear of the darkness would be alleviated. An eighteen-inch silver Stanley flashlight awaited my touch, sitting in the same spot for as many years as I had been on this earth, and probably more, though it was most likely a whale-oil hurricane lamp before that.

I walked downward, cautiously, pushing cobwebs out of my way, easing each bare foot down on the cruddy steps as gently as I could. I would scream bloody murder if my skin touched something furry, slimy, or moving.

The smell of rot and old, black air assaulted my nose, and I caught myself holding my breath as I counted down the steps. Three more to go.

"Anyone here?" I said. I had cradled the .22 back to its original position, my index finger on the trigger.

I stepped down on the last step. *Olly Olly oxen free.*

The flashlight was to my right, just where it was supposed to be.

I situated my grip on the rifle again, grabbed up the silver torch and turned it on, fully expecting light to banish the darkness, and hoping like hell to see Ardith Jenkins sitting on the floor waiting for me. Neither happened.

I felt a pair of eyes on the back of my neck and looked over my shoulder. Shep stared down at me, standing firmly on the lip.

"That's all right, Shep. You stay right there." I tapped the flashlight gently against the wall and it flickered dimly. The batteries needed to be replaced. I was lucky they hadn't busted at the seams, leaked acid inside the tube, and ruined the flashlight. I tapped it again, and a soft white beam shot upward. Along with the waning afternoon sun, the light would be enough to see the entirety of the cellar.

I balanced the flashlight in one hand and the .22 in the other. If the need to defend myself quickly arose, I was a bumble of inexperience; I'd probably drop the gun.

I was comfortable reading books, breaking down their structure into understandable, digestible bites, not looking for an errant friend under questionable circumstances and worrying about shooting someone in the head.

The beam of light shook in my nervous hand and flickered as I swept it across the cellar. My eyes knew what was there, what to look for. Still, I was cautious as my glance fell across garden tools, empty insecticide cans, boxes of canned vegetables, moth-eaten blankets, and gallons of water jugs kept in case bad weather—or something worse— forced us to stay below ground for days instead of hours.

The something worse was a horror beyond imagination, beyond even the most destructive storms: a nuclear missile attack from the Soviets. The Red Threat. The Cold War. An unseen menace always in the news. Death and immediate destruction a constant worry, a never-ending threat.

Air Force men had been negotiating leases on farmland all over the northern apron of North Dakota and preparing to build a vast network of missile silos, deep launch pads, to defend the nation from such an attack. Hank and Erik Knudsen had told them no, sent them packing, but that was last year when the crops looked good and all was well with them both. The threat of a nuclear winter looked a little differently now, and so did a monthly lease check from the United States government.

As far as I knew, all of the leases had been negotiated, but I wasn't entirely sure of that. I had ignored the event, the presence of the Air Force men, as much as I could.

I sighed. There was no sign of Ardith in the cellar. I did, however, catch sight of Hank's knee-high black rubber mud boots. They sure would beat walking around barefoot, so I made my way to them as carefully as I could, turned them upside down, and tapped them out. A dead grasshopper fell out of the right one. I started at the sight of it, then found a rag to wipe them both out, once I was sure nothing living had taken up residence inside them.

The boots were a little big, but I could navigate in them, and that was all that mattered. No more worry about a mouse or a rat running over the top of my foot.

The flashlight flickered off on its own, and I tapped it on the wall again, but it was no use. It was dead. The light from the door led me out of the cellar, and I was happy to be standing on solid ground.

Shep had waited for me. He circled me again, then crouched ten feet in front of me, freezing in midrun. I just shook my head and ignored the game. "Where were you at when I came home?" I said aloud, studying him.

Shep settled to the ground and tilted his head at me. *Silly humans; I can't talk*—that must have been what he was thinking, what the expression on his intelligent border collie face suggested he was thinking.

I closed my eyes and thought back to driving in from the Knudsens'. Shep had come out from behind the first barn in a rage.

I looked up to the house, hoped Hank was all right, then made my way to the barn. The boots squeaked as I went, and there was no way I was ever going to sneak up on anyone.

Shep followed after me, staying close enough to my heels to nip at them if he wanted to, if I wasn't going the way he thought I should. At least I had rubber boots on.

Fresh air felt good on my face; a relief from the stench of the cellar. "Ardith, are you there?" I called out as I rounded the side of the barn.

No answer. Just the wind, the pant of the dog behind me, and the bang of the screen door in the distance.

I slowed as I noticed a tall stretch of needlegrass knocked down alongside the garage. The grass had yet to spring up from traffic of some type. It could have been knocked down from Shep running out to greet me, but I gripped the .22 tighter and eased my finger against the trigger with the surety of needed pressure. A flick would have fired off a round. My hand was suddenly sweaty.

I bent around the corner of the barn with a peek, then stepped around a rusted old mower and nearly lost my breath.

I blinked to make sure I was seeing what I thought I was seeing: Ardith Jenkins propped up against the back wall of the garage, her head titled forward, down, the front of her dress covered in blood.

Her throat had been slit. Slit just like Erik and Lida's. Her eyes were wide open, and her skin was as pale as freshly fallen snow.

I couldn't force a scream from my lips. It was stuck deep in my chest. I turned to run, to go back to Hank, to call for help, but something caught my eye. Something that registered in my mind, something that I knew that I had to see.

It wasn't an amulet like had been left behind at the Knudsens', but a piece of greenery; not grass, not any wildflower seen at this time of year, but I was certain I knew what the greenery was. I had seen the plant before. At Christmas. Stood underneath it as tradition called for.

It was mistletoe. Someone had left mistletoe in Ardith Jenkins' dead hand.

CHAPTER 14

I pulled myself out of bed early, before the sun peaked over the eastern horizon, before the most punctual bird whistled its first tune of the day. It had always been that way; long before I started taking index work to make ends meet, I was rising before the sun. Life on the farm, at certain times of the year, was a twenty-four-hour-a-day, seven-day-a-week operation. It was another commonality that I had discovered that farming shared with the publishing business. Deadlines had to be met no matter the weather or the prevailing circumstances in one's life. There was no union, no labor laws to offer protection or job security. Indexing was a work-for-hire situation, and the publishing cycle had to continue on, uninterrupted, or the job—from the publisher—was lost, and no one wanted that. Including me.

The house was quiet, dark with the exception of the dim lamp burning on my desk. There was no wind; it had vanished soon after the onset of darkness. It was like everything and everyone had retreated from the world and hunkered down somewhere far away. Even the moon seemed to hide, nearly invisible in its new phase.

Most of the time that kind of stillness was reserved for winter. The silence at night, when two-foot drifts pushed up against the door and the stars seemed too cold to sparkle. Desperate isolation could drive a person to madness, convince them that no one else on the planet existed, that they were all alone. If only that were the case.

I could barely process the chaos, the confusion, the sadness that had occurred after I'd discovered Ardith's dead body behind the first barn. Flashing lights, a rush of police, firemen, newspaper men, all followed by a parade of onlookers, gawkers, and rubberneckers driving by the house as slow as they could. Word had gotten out fast. Hank's accident had only been a primer for the reaction to bad news. Folks were curious, afraid. I couldn't blame them, but that didn't mean I liked the idea of our farm being the object of all of that attention. The trail of cars continued late into the night, then finally trickled down to nothing not long after midnight.

Watching Hilo collapse at the sight of his beloved wife was too much. There was nothing I could do for him anymore than there was anything he could do for me on that fateful day when he'd found Hank, barely alive, changed forever. But still here, unlike Ardith.

I was sure Hilo would have traded places with me in a heartbeat to have Ardith's voice, encouragement, and wisdom to draw off of even if her body was only a shell. Hank would have traded places with Ardith, too. I was as sure of that as night had fallen. The look on Hank's face when I told him what was happening said everything. He wished it was him that the killer had come after. He wished he was dead. Not Ardith. Dear, sweet Ardith. He whimpered, then turned away . . . toward the crack of the open window.

I had retreated to the house after seeing Hilo collapse, tried to compose myself, get on with the normal steps of the evening. I bathed a quieter-than-normal Hank, fixed his dinner, which neither of us could touch, and finally attempted to sleep once everyone had left us to ourselves on our blood-marred land. Everyone but the deputy parked at the end of the drive. He was our lone protector, our shield until daylight came again, and the curiosity and madness started all over again.

If I had slept a wink, it was lost on me. I felt like I had been awake for days, numb and delirious, but still strapped with duties, chores that saw no end. There was no hope for rest anytime soon. So, in the middle of the night, I had found my way back to my desk, my sanctuary of sanity, my safe place in all of the storms in my life. The one place where I could leave this world and venture happily, eagerly, and curiously into another.

Books had always been my escape from the daily toil of my simple prairie life. Mother said that reading, both fiction and non-fiction, strengthened empathy, a necessary quality for a happy and productive life. I had never argued with that idea. But at that moment, I was having a difficult time finding feelings that I had in common with a headhunter tribe in Africa.

I had tried to return Richard Rothstein's call, but by the time I got around to it, by the time I could compose myself and speak intelligently, the offices in New York were closed. Any dire publishing emergency would have to wait until morning—New York time. I was counting the seconds with a dry mouth.

I had tried over and over again to focus on the page proofs that were laid out on the desk before me, the same ones, in the same place, as when Hilo had come out to tell me about Lida and Erik. It seemed like an eternity ago.

Hank was no worry. The last time I had peeked in on him, his eyes were closed, his chest rising and falling with regularity. Whether or not he was truly asleep was another question.

The house was as safe as the house could be; it creaked, cracked, and settled in the middle of the night even though the foundation was seventy-five years old. The .22 was within reach, and Shep had settled in at my feet. I had overridden the No Dog in the House rule, and as far as I was concerned Shep could stay inside with us as long as he wanted to, as long as I needed him to.

Every time I looked down at the dog, he was staring at the door, waiting, it seemed, to lunge at the first thing, or person, who pushed inside who wasn't supposed to.

And the deputy, our watchman, none other than Guy Reinhardt, made regular rounds and patrolled the house every half hour. I watched for the orange glow of his cigarette out the window to make sure he was still there, still awake, on the job. All the while, I pushed away the temptation to join him for a cigarette myself. He had a job to do, and so did I.

I knew I was as comfortable as I could be, all things considered, so I put my reading glasses on and tried to relax into my work by reading the same paragraph of *The Forgotten Tribe of Africa and the Myth of Headhunter Civilizations* over and over again:

The Igbo people spoke various Igboid languages and dialects. The languages formed a cluster, a common link with other, nearby tribes. Mutual intelligibility between the Izii–Ikwo–Ezaa–Mgbo languages could be distinguished only on a closely-listened-to basis. The Igboid languages included the Ekpeye as well as the Igbo, a branch of the Volta-Niger language family. The Igbo were one of the largest ethnic groups of people in Africa; thus, the core Igboid language was widely spoken.

Passages like this took me about as far away from my little farm in rural North Dakota as I could go: A thousand miles from the fact that one of my dearest friends had been murdered a few yards from where I sat, while I had been out on a wild-goose chase, looking for information concerning a silly Norse amulet. Except, that amulet didn't seem so silly as the day had come to a close and events unfolded like they had. Still, I couldn't process any of what I was reading. My mind was not a machine that I could turn on and off.

I had not forgotten about the mistletoe left in Ardith's hand, but the significance of it was lost on me. I would have to revisit the notes I made at the library. The truth of the matter was I didn't want to know what the sprig of festive greenery meant. I wasn't sure if it meant anything at all. I was done playing detective, and I meant to tell Hilo just that and return the amulet the next time I saw him in decent enough shape for him to comprehend what I was saying. He would have to find someone smarter, more capable, more mobile than I was able to be. As far as I was concerned, Hilo could call on my cousin Raymond to take that job, or Professor Strand, if he could get him to answer his telephone.

I sighed out loud, drawing Shep's attention briefly, then pushed back from the desk, tossed my reading glasses on the open book—frustrated even more than I had been when I sat down.

Any indexer with the lowest amount of skill would've had no trouble determining the keywords or arranging terms in a discernable order from the passage that I was stuck on. All I had done was stare at the words until they were nothing more than a blur—languages, dialects, Ekpeye, Volta-Niger language family—and found myself unable to commit to any of them, to define the appropriate sorting criteria, or rank the term selection in its importance. Main entry or subentry? I wasn't sure I could decide. I had lost my confidence, or I was just too tired to make a decision. I didn't know what my problem was—or didn't want to face it.

My Underwood typewriter sat silent; waiting. The words were nothing more than marks and hashes floating in a murky white paper-based stew, mixed in with other, more important ideas, concepts, and feelings that seemed foreign and familiar at the same time.

I had accepted Ardith's help so I could run off to town, and the unthinkable had happened. A nightmare on top of another nightmare was beyond my comprehension. I didn't know if I was ever going to be able to get the image of Ardith's lifeless, bloody body out of my mind.

I knew deep in my heart that there was no way I could have foreseen what was to come, that my decision bore no fault, ill-intent, or lack of concern. Plain and simple, Ardith's death was not my fault. I had been told that over and over again, but I didn't believe it. Not yet. I wasn't sure that I ever would believe it, no matter who said so.

And then there was Hilo. I had been trying to help him, and in doing so, my absence had hurt him in a way I could never have imagined. His life was forever changed.

How could I ever leave Hank in anyone's care again and not worry if they were in the same kind of danger Ardith faced? I couldn't ask anyone to do such a thing. Our life was changed, too, even more so than it had been when Erik and Lida had been murdered.

I glanced over to the shoebox of index cards I'd written up since starting Sir Nigel's book, flipped through the letters, and stopped when I got to G. Just as I thought. I hadn't put a main topic entry in the index for Guilt.

Instead of getting up, quitting, and walking away from my desk, I felt compelled to stay, to work out an idea I had considered on the way home from town.

I put my glasses back on, and slid a fresh piece of typing paper into the Underwood, forgoing my normal routine of creating entries on individual index cards. The work I had in mind wasn't about the head-hunter book, even though Lord knew it should have been. It was about clearing my mind, organizing the words that danced in my head relent-lessly, refusing to go away. If I vanquished them, then maybe I could get on with the real work at hand, facing the Sir Nigel deadline, doing the indexing work that needed to be done, and dealing with whatever it was that Richard Rothstein had found so important to call about.

I had never written a personal index before, but it was the only thing I knew to do:

A

Amulet
    found in Erik Knudsen's hand. *See also* murder
    Norse mythology. *See also* Norse mythology
    theft of
Ardith Jenkins
    death of. *See also* murder
    married to Sheriff Hilo Jenkins
    mistletoe in hand
Asgard, gods of

I stopped typing, and realized that I needed my notes from the library in front of me if I was going to write a proper index, if I was going to purge the words from my mind. There was no sign of my purse, and as I thought back, retraced my path since I'd returned to the farm, I realized that I had left it in the truck. Not only was the notebook in my purse, but so was the amulet that Hilo had entrusted to my care.

I panicked at the thought that I'd let the amulet out of my sight. I knew nothing of its financial value, only that it was an object of value in a murder investigation. On top of everything else, I was concerned that the amulet was safe—safe just so I could return it to Hilo.

"You stay, Shep," I said, as I got up from the desk. The dog looked up at me and made no move to follow after me. "Good. Watch over Hank."

I left my office with the rifle in hand and eased past the bedroom door. Hank was in the same position I'd last seen him, still asleep, or resting with his eyes closed. He didn't seem to notice as I passed.

I hesitated at the door, questioned whether it was wise to go outside in the middle of the night, then forced myself to suck in a deep breath and rely on Guy Reinhardt and the .22. If that wasn't enough, then I was in big trouble.

The cool night air greeted me as I stepped out on the stoop. I glanced to the county police car, saw Guy's silhouette, then padded to the Studebaker in my bare feet.

I opened the door easily, as quietly as I could, and sighed with relief as I saw my purse sitting on the seat where I'd left it. I grabbed the purse like it was a piece of stolen gold, and hustled through the contents. Even in the dark of night, I could see the white linen that I'd wrapped the amulet in. "Thank goodness," I whispered out loud.

"That you, Marjorie?"

I started at the voice, dropped the purse, and spun around, the rifle firmly in my left hand but pointed at the ground.

"Lord, Guy Reinhardt, you scared the bejesus out of me."

"Didn't mean too, Marjorie, just heard footsteps."

"You've got good ears."

"Been told that." He flashed a smile that lit up underneath the black, star-filled sky, then faded away just as quickly, settling into a straight jaw that looked more official than proud.

I could smell cigarette smoke on him, and my desire for a Salem amplified. "I forgot something in my purse," I said. I realized then that I was standing before Guy in my nightclothes, a thin cotton shift cut just above my knees with a raggedy housecoat thrown over the top. I was embarrassed, but not as uncomfortable as I would have been without the housecoat.

"I best get inside," I said.

"Probably a little late to be out and about, all things considered, Marjorie."

"You don't think they're still around do you?"

"Who?" Guy asked.

"The killer," I said. "Ardith's killer. The person that did this horrible thing."

"Hope not. But if they are. If they come back, you don't have nothin' to worry about, Marjorie. I'm as good a shot in the county as there is."

"That makes me feel better. I best go in." I grabbed up my purse, turned to go back to the house, but stopped about ten feet away from Guy. "Would you like some coffee? It wouldn't take much to put a pot on, seeing that you've been sitting here all night. It's the least I can do. I don't think I'll be sleeping much any time soon."

"Sure, Marjorie, that'd be mighty kind of you. Mighty kind of you."

CHAPTER 15

I waited for the cast iron percolator to come to a rest. The smell of freshly brewed coffee filled the kitchen, and for a brief, fleeting moment, everything felt normal. Coffee was a staple, the first pot to be on the stove no matter the season. It warmed the house and put everything on an even keel, at least most of the time.

I was too unsettled to work, too unfocused. I knew that kind of mental weakness couldn't last, that my deadline ticked away with cold disregard to my emotional or physical state, but I just couldn't clear my mind enough to concentrate on the dense text concerning headhunters. Maybe when things settled down, if that were possible.

I'd considered asking Richard Rothstein for an extension on my deadline, explaining my situation to him when we spoke. I had never done that before, and just the consideration of missing a deadline seemed fraught with peril. The truth was, I was going to need my indexing income more than ever if Peter and Jaeger couldn't help with the farm any longer. I'd have to hire out the chores and pay far more than the Knudsen boys had ever charged us. Any potential profit from the upcoming crop would be lost, and that would just be another crack in a foundation teetering on collapse. We still carried debt on the mortgage and from the bad stretch we'd suffered before Hank's accident. Sometimes, all I could pay was the interest on the loans we carried.

I poured two cups of coffee, fought off the peckish feeling in my stomach, and headed to the back door. Shep followed after me. "You stay, boy. Bark if you need me."

I was convinced that the border collie was the most intelligent dog in the world, but I knew in my heart of hearts that he didn't understand

the English language any more than I understood any of the Igboid languages. But I hoped he would bark if Hank needed me, if something
bad showed itself out of my sight.

Shep did what I asked of him and sat, wagged his tail, and watched
me navigate out the door holding two cups of steaming coffee. At least
the kitchen floor was going to get swept.

The air had remained cool since I was out before, but it wasn't cold.
It was too early in the year for that, though it wouldn't be long before
the first snowflake fell. September would push in on us in a blink, and
we'd be left wondering where the summer went. Only this one, as it
was going, would not be soon forgotten. Most folks would be ready for
winter if all the sadness would go away that the summer had brought.
At least in winter, you could track a cat—or a killer.

I'd made sure my housecoat was buttoned all of the way to the top,
and I'd slipped on a pair of closed-toe house slippers that Hank had
bought for me from the Woolworth's in Bismarck ages ago. The last
thing I needed to do was come down with a cold.

I had only thought for a second that I was being forward, presuming
Guy Reinhardt would want coffee, that he didn't have a Thermos of his
own in the police car, but we were both in the middle of unusual circumstances, and I was glad he'd accepted my offer. Truth was, I think
I needed someone to talk to as much as anything, and waking Hank
hadn't seemed like a good idea. I was surprised that sleep had come to
him at all.

I hadn't forgotten how Guy had made me feel at the Knudsens', but
that seemed even more foolish now; unimportant, like an eighth grade
girl would feel—which was a long, long time ago, when life was much,
much simpler. My emotions were out of control, that's all there was to
it. I could never be attracted to a man like Guy Reinhardt.

The sky looked like the inside of an oven turned off to cool. Alu-
minum foil stars poked in and out all over the roof of it, dotting the
blackness with little bits of silver light, of life pulsing somewhere
distant. There was no sign of the Northern Lights, and I was glad of
that. The early people—the settlers, pioneers, my parents' people—

were convinced that the wavering ribbons of colors in the night sky foretold the end of the world, and I wasn't so sure that they were wrong. It felt like the end of the world for all of us, even without a flicker of the weird and unsettling lights.

The county police car was pointed grill out toward the road. Guy sat on the hood, smoking a cigarette, watching for anything that moved. From a distance, it would have been easy to mistake the glowing tip of his cigarette for a meteor falling from the sky as he casually tapped his ash to the ground.

I wasn't trying to be quiet this time. It would have been almost impossible anyway on the dry drive with hard-soled slippers on my feet. I was having a hard time keeping my balance, trying not to spill any of the coffee.

Guy turned back to me as I approached from the rear of the car, a newer model Ford, painted in two tones of brown, one light, one dark. Starlight reflected off the bubble on the roof. He coughed and tried to cup the cigarette in the palm of his hand to hide it.

"It's all right," I said, coming to a stop next to him. "Smoking doesn't bother me." I offered him one of the steaming coffee mugs.

Guy took the mug with his other hand and kept the cigarette partially hidden the best he could. "We're not supposed to smoke in front of folks while we're in uniform. Hilo's not too fond of smoking, anyway, you know?"

"Him and Hank both, but I doubt Hilo would mind." I sipped the black coffee. I'd made it a little stronger than normal. I wasn't blind to the fact that I had a long day ahead of me, and I knew it had already been an even longer day for Guy Reinhardt. He had already been on shift before I called the police, holding down the fort at the Knudsens'. He'd been the first to arrive after the call had gone out about Ardith.

"I suppose you're right, Marjorie." Guy's shoulders relaxed, and he slid off the hood of the Ford, easily balancing the coffee in one hand and the cigarette in the other. "Hank sleeping?"

I nodded and looked up at him—Guy still had a basketball player build, and probably always would—then I looked over my shoulder to the house, wind-beaten white, but enough to stand out in the darkness. I had left the lamp burning on my desk. It was the only light on in the house. "He's sleeping, thanks. Hard to tell sometimes."

"I suppose so, Marjorie. It's a hard row to hoe you've got here. Even without all of the troubles of late."

I didn't know quite what to say to that. Guy was right, of course, but allowing our troubles to stop us, to become a burden to someone else, well, it just wasn't our way. Never had been, even when I was a little girl. I was a Hoagler before I was a Trumaine. Mother and Father were stiff-upper-lip kind of people. Don't complain. Forge ahead. Clean up your own mess so other folks didn't have to walk through it. Hank was the same way. Quiet, accommodating, always demanding that we keep our problems to ourselves. Maybe it was just how prairie people were, I couldn't say for sure since I'd known no other way of life.

Instead of agreeing, I reached into the front pocket of my house-dress and pulled out the pack of Salems I'd bought at the Rexall. "You don't mind, do you?"

"I didn't know you smoked, Marjorie."

Guy seemed to enjoy saying my name. There was a lilt to it, that familiar Nor' Dakota accent. Perhaps Sir Nigel's book should have been about us. I might have learned something useful, something that could inform me every day. Prairie tribes instead of myths about headhunters.

I shrugged. "Hank doesn't like it that I smoke—his mother died of cancer—and I understand, but it calms my nerves. Helps me to think straight when things are all jumbled."

"Like now?"

"Like now," I said. I sat the cup of coffee on the wide front bumper of the Ford and pulled a cigarette from the pack. Before I could reach for the matchbook Betty Walsh had given me with my change at the Rexall, Guy flipped opened a Zippo and produced a steady flame.

I wasn't surprised. It was the gentlemanly thing to do—light a woman's cigarette. But it was an act of chivalry, and I was grateful for it. Hank had been like that, the kind man who always opened the truck door for me, made sure I walked into a restaurant first on the special occasion when we didn't eat at home. Simple things. I missed those simple things the most.

I drew in on the cigarette, bringing it easily to life. I leaned back, exhaled, and watched as the glow of the Zippo's flame vanished as quickly as it had appeared. This felt different—but similar—from the smoke I'd shared with Calla behind the library. We both needed an escape.

Guy's stoic face lost its glow, but I didn't look away from him. He had weathered his own difficulties, and cigarettes seemed to offer him the same salvation that they did me. I couldn't imagine any other reason that he would smoke, especially considering that he had once been the most talented athlete in the county. I guess even athletes succumbed to the pressures of time and age.

Guy settled back on the hood, the cigarette in one hand, the cup in the other. "That's a fine cup of coffee, there, Marjorie."

I relaxed, too, against the corner of the front fender, standing directly in front of the dark double-headlights of the police car. I followed Guy's gaze, toward the horizon, to a thin ribbon of gray hope that had broken into sight, unannounced by birds or any other voices in the sky, like wind or thunder.

The unsettling silence had remained throughout the night. The cool summer air was still, almost like it was too heavy to move.

"Thanks." I took another sip of coffee and stared at the first sign of the coming day. I was more than ready to walk on the earth in the daylight, to be able to see for as far as the eye could see without worry about what was coming, or what was hiding in the shadows. "What do you think this is all about, Guy? These murders." I remembered not to mention the amulet, since Hilo had told me not to. But I wondered what Guy knew of it, what the rest of the men in the department knew. Was the amulet just a secret between Hilo and me? I had to think that it was, but I would have been relieved if he had mentioned it.

I couldn't help myself from asking the question. The only reason Guy was at the farm was because someone had murdered Ardith. The last time he had been around was the day everyone else had shown up for Hank.

"Can't rightly say, Marjorie. I can tell you this, though, I never expected to see such meanness and violence in all of my life, not even with this badge on my chest. People around these parts just aren't like this. Nothing could hurt so bad as to lash out like I've seen in the last couple of days. I mean, I've been angry, said things I sure wish't I could take back, but I can't conceive of a matter when a knife to the throat is the only solution." Guy glanced at me quickly, then looked down to the ground. "My apologies, Marjorie. I shouldn't speak of such things. This has to be difficult for you."

"Harder for Hilo, I would imagine."

"There is that. Not sure that I'd be able to come back from such a thing, if it was me." Guy drew on his own cigarette then. It was the last puff. He pinched the burning orange tip of tobacco off the butt, and let it fall to the ground; Lilliputian fireworks, distant falling stars snuffed out with a heavy grind with the toe of his recently polished black boot. He field-stripped the butt, and dropped the filter and what was left of the cigarette into his pants pocket.

Guy stared hard at the horizon, and his words hung in the air. I heard something that I wasn't quite sure of. Maybe it was ambition, a desire to step into Hilo's place if the opportunity arose, or something else, a sadness or regret that I could never know.

My father, engaged in his own lifelong battle for his place in life, had once said to me, "There are two kinds of men in this world, Marjorie. Ambitious ones and ones with ambition. One's to be avoided and the other's to be encouraged." I'm not sure why I remembered that at that moment, maybe it was the look in Guy's eyes, maybe it was the way he said my name. I just wasn't sure. But I knew I'd seen that look before.

Guy didn't seem to me to be the kind of man who would take advantage of someone else's tragedy, but then again, he had been a star basketball player when we were young, and he had to be competitive and aggressive to achieve that kind of praise and skill. Age didn't always erase those kind of traits. Sometimes, the disappointments that came along the way were nothing more than fertilizer, causing the ambitions to grow in an ugly, out of control way. Me and everyone else in Stark County knew Guy Reinhardt had had his fair share of disappointments.

"I've known Hilo a lot of years," I said. "He's one of the strongest, most dependable people I've ever met. But you may be right. This might just be enough to bring him to his knees, get the best of him."

"I hope you're wrong, Marjorie. I sure hope you're wrong."

The mix of coffee and cigarettes put a foul taste in my mouth. I wasn't used to the combination so early in the day. I pinched the fire off my Salem, then hesitated before I ground it out with my rubber-soled house slipper. Guy noticed, stepped over, and took care of it for me.

"Can't be too careful, Marjorie," he said. Grassfires were another nightmare; a spark brought to flame by an easy wind could destroy the year's crop and a hundred-year-old farm in one fell swoop. We'd both seen it happen more than once.

"Thank you," I offered, as I watched him pick up the butt, perform the same stripping operation, then stuff it into his pocket with his own.

When Guy straightened back up, he fixated on the horizon for a long second. "Be a lot of comin' and goin' around here today. You up for that, Marjorie?"

"I suppose I have to be, don't I?"

"I suppose you do." He hesitated, then looked me in the eye. His gaze cut through the early gray dawn like a hot knife to butter. "State Police'll take over. Hilo can't handle this. Three murders in a matter of days, all so close together. They're gonna look at you and Hank awful close, Marjorie."

Guy's words bounced around inside of my head and nearly took me off my feet. "What do you mean, 'look at us close,' Guy? Hank and I haven't done anything wrong."

"Don't matter, Marjorie. They have to do their jobs. I just wanted you to know what was coming your way. Everybody's a suspect, Marjorie, everybody. At least till they've been cleared, alibis and such checked. Even you and Hank. You're a suspect as much as anybody else."

CHAPTER 16

I stared at the telephone. I didn't want to touch the black receiver, hear the crackle of the live line on the other end, but there was no avoiding the call to New York that I had to make.

My indexing income was just like some farmers' royalty payments from the oil wells that teeter-tottered unattended in their fields. Hank had always chased the oil and gas men off, afraid the pumps would foul the water and the land.

My payments weren't royalties. It was a one-time payment. The author saw royalties from the publisher, I supposed, but I never did. I saw no long-term benefits from writing indexes. If I wanted to make more money, I had to take more work, or go out and find it—and that wasn't as simple as it sounded. It wasn't like publishers put help-wanted ads for indexers in the back of the Dickinson, North Dakota, newspaper.

My fingers tingled as I looked up at the clock on the wall. There was a two-hour time difference between New York City and North Dakota. I had waited as long as I could; otherwise, I risked getting a call back from Richard Rothstein, and I was positive that call would not be pleasant.

Not that any call is ever pleasant. Even on the occasions when I had spoken to Mr. Rothstein for normal business purposes, he had been curt, quick to speak, and bordered on being rude; the kind of rudeness never seen or heard in this part of the country.

I understood that things were different, faster paced, on the East Coast than they were on the prairie, and I'd had to adjust my sensitivities when I dealt with anyone in the New York offices, but I never ever looked forward to talking to any of them. It was like they spoke a different language.

I picked up the receiver reluctantly and listened before I dialed the 212 exchange.

There was a distant hum, which was normal most of the time, but the hum echoed, reverberated with distant, unidentifiable sounds, and that meant someone else was on the line, waiting, or getting ready to make a call. I listened for a couple of extra seconds to make sure that wasn't the case, that I wasn't stepping on someone else's conversation or intention.

The sound continued. Hum, hiss, distant voices. A television turned down low.

"Is that you Burlene Standish?" I demanded, frustrated. I was in no mood for eavesdroppers, all things considered. I wanted this call over with, and the traffic on the road out front had already picked up.

A steady line of curious folks drove by the house as slow as they could, turned around in the field just beyond the end of the yard, then drove back by again. They pointed grimly at the first barn. I'd had enough morbid curiosity to suit me for a lifetime, but I knew there was nothing I could do about any of it.

Burlene didn't answer me. Whoever it was on the other end of the line cupped their hand over the bottom receiver a little tighter. The echo diminished, but it didn't disappear completely. I knew her ways. It wasn't like this was the first time she had listened in on my conversations. Hardly.

"I know you're still there, Burlene," I hissed. I could barely contain my anger. Rage was as foreign to me as finding a dead body on my property, but I recognized them both—and they made me equally afraid.

Funny thing was, I wouldn't have recognized Burlene Standish if she was standing next to me at the checkout at the Red Owl grocery store. Her husband, Miller—Mills to most folks—scowled at everyone when they mispronounced his name by accident or on purpose, and called him Miles. He'd worked as a butcher at the Red Owl for as long as I could remember, so come to think of it, I doubt she'd be there at all. Miller most likely took home all of the groceries.

I wasn't sure why, but I'd heard Burlene had always been sickly, a shut-in if there ever was one, so I supposed her sources of entertainment and human interaction were limited. Television should have kept her occupied. Still, being elderly and lonely didn't give her the right to be a class A nibnose. *Damn party lines.* That's what I thought. I needed some privacy to deal with the things that had presented themselves in my life.

I heard a whisper on the other end of the phone, but I didn't understand the words, couldn't hear them clearly. "What?" I snapped. "Look, I've got important business to attend to, Burlene, so if you've got something to say to me, then speak up, and get on with it." I might just need more coffee, since I hadn't slept well and had spent longer talking to Guy Reinhardt than I should have. Maybe she needed to make a call, but I doubted it.

"I heard something, Marjorie," the quivering old woman's voice said just above the former whisper. It *was* Burlene, there was no mistaking her wobbly voice. I wanted to continue to be mad, but any anger I felt disappeared once her words settled in my mind, confronted my rage with consideration of the timing of her bad habit of listening in on other peoples' business.

"What do you mean you heard something?"

I remembered the telephone dangling when I had come home from town. Ardith had been on the phone, taking a message from Richard Rothstein, when something had drawn her away. Burlene had been listening to the whole thing. Most likely, she had heard Ardith's last words. I shivered at the realization.

"I heard something," she repeated. It sounded like Burlene was afraid, had just seen a ghost, or someone lurking outside her window. I imagined her cowering behind a plastic-covered davenport.

Click. Hiss. The line was open, and Burlene was gone, but that didn't stop me. "What did you hear, Burlene? Damn it, what did you hear?"

Silence. No answer. Just the rustle of the wind from outside my own house. I stared at the phone, frustrated. How could Burlene do that, say something like that, then hang up? It was mean and frightening at the same time.

"You all right, Marjie?" Hank called out.

"I'm fine," I answered back, cupping the mouthpiece myself, just in case someone else had picked up.

"You were yelling," he said.

My fingers trembled on the phone. I exhaled deeply. "I'm fine, Hank," I called back to him. "It was just Burlene Standish on the line."

"Sad busybody she is."

"It's fine, Hank, don't worry about it."

The window was open, and an easy morning breeze fluttered the curtains. The hem was starting to unravel, but mending was low on my list at that moment.

It was going to be a warm day, there was no mistaking that, but it wasn't uncomfortable yet. Perspiration beaded up on my forehead, and my heart beat like I'd just run from the third barn to the house without stopping.

"If you say so," Hank said. His struggle to speak reverberated through the house, though my veins. I stared at the bedroom door and let Hank's voice fall away without offering a response.

I tried to push away what Burlene had said, but I couldn't get it out of my mind. She had heard something. But what? A scream? A gunshot? If she had heard something, wouldn't Hank have heard something, too? What had he said? *I heard her ask the person on the other end of the line to hang on, then Shep barked and she padded out the door. She never came back.*

My mouth went dry all over again. Hank hadn't said a word about hearing something other than Shep barking. *Could that have been what Burlene had heard?* There was no way to know. Not at that moment.

I exhaled deeply again and chided myself silently. *Now you're questioning Hank? What's next, Marjorie? What the heck are you doing? He's never lied to you in all of the years you've known him, and you've never lied to him. What the heck are you doing?*

I shook my head, listened again to make sure the line was clear, licked my lips, swallowed hard to moisten my throat, then dialed Richard Rothstein's number. I had to get on with it. There was more at stake than I could imagine.

The rotary dial snapped back with a loud clack, hard plastic hitting hard plastic, and I waited for the other end to start ringing. I breathed deep, thoughtful breaths, preparing myself the best I could.

It took half a second and the line buzzed with a ring on the other end. The miracle of technology never failed to amaze me: Invisible pictures flew through the air, caught a metal antenna, and danced on glass screens all over the world. Voices in real time, traveling over a thousand miles of wires, networks, switches, from one telephone to another, all in a matter of seconds. The president wanted to put men on the moon within a decade. I didn't question a bit that that could happen.

A receptionist picked up on the second ring. "H.P. Howard and Sons. How may I direct your call?"

Each time I called the office—which was rare—it sounded like a different receptionist. The publisher was either difficult to work for, or much larger than I had ever imagined. I had only seen a picture of the skyscraper the offices were located in, and that building might as well have been on another planet. I had never seen a skyscraper in my life.

"Richard Rothstein, please," I said, trying to steel my voice, shoving any nervousness away that may have been there, doing my best to forget the state that Burlene Standish had put me in.

"One moment." The woman's voice was distant, and it sounded like she had a clothes pin attached to her nose. The speed of her words was not lost on me. Every time I called New York I had to listen extra close. They spoke so fast, along with the sway of the wires, and it was all I could do to keep up.

A click, then another ring. The whole time I was also listening for Burlene Standish, or someone else, to come onto the party line. So far, I was pretty sure I was alone. I was grateful for that. There was no way I would admonish anyone while I was on the line with an editor.

"Richard Rothstein." He always sounded rushed, overwhelmed, angry.

"Mr. Rothstein, this is Marjorie Trumaine returning your call."

Silence. The lines buzzed between North Dakota and New York City. My words echoed, and I wondered if my accent sounded as odd to him as his did to me?

"Trumaine?" Richard Rothstein finally said, like we had never spoken before.

"I'm working on the Nigel Preston title . . . Headhunters."

He cut me off. "Oh, the indexer. Right. Sorry, a lot of balls to juggle here. That was yesterday."

"I understand."

"There's a problem."

My heart sank. I was hoping for good news, not bad. There'd been way too much bad news to process. I wasn't sure how I would handle any more. Quit? Fight back? *Calm down, Marjorie. Listen. It's your job. Don't assume the worst.*

"I received some corrections and new material from Sir Nigel," Richard Rothstein continued. "He's been on safari and out of touch for far too long. I was worried about him, all things considered. I'd be wary of those people. It might be his head on a stick next. Anyway, the pages are on the way to you. I airmailed them yesterday. They should be there tomorrow."

"Corrections? New material?" I asked trying to hide the dread in my voice. "I'm a good ways through the book, Mr. Rothstein."

"The pages rewrapped from the beginning of the book. Sir Nigel discovered some holes in his research, and we couldn't let it slide. This is an important book for us, Miss Trumaine. The pagination had to be changed. There was no avoiding it. I'm sure you've handled situations like this before."

Rewrap was a nightmare to an indexer. All of the page numbers had changed, meaning the work I'd already done was useless. The thought of it boiled my blood. I was a missus, too, not a miss. I wanted to correct him, but I didn't. "I understand, but . . ."

He cut me off again. "We have to have the index as soon as possible. Our date with the printer is set, and we cannot miss that delivery by an hour. Do you understand? This does not change the deadline. It is imperative that you understand this."

"I'll have to compare the pages sentence by sentence, word by word, for that matter. It's a very tedious process, and adds more time to an already dense text," I blurted out. I was mad all over again. Why should I have to work harder just because Sir Nigel wanted to make changes to the book at the last minute?

"That's why we hired you, Miss Trumaine. You come highly recommended by other editors in the house. We don't want to tarnish that reputation now, do we? We have to have the index by deadline, regardless of the circumstances. Am I clear? It's an important book for us. This could be a prize winner. That would be a nice feather in your cap."

I exhaled, bit my tongue. It was obvious that I had no choice other than to throw my hands up in the air. But I couldn't do that. We needed the money, and I needed the stream of work that came from H.P. Howard and Sons to continue. I knew a threat when I heard one.

"I'll do my best, Mr. Rothstein," I said.

"I need more than that. I need your excellence." He paused, like he was writing something down. "Well, I'm sorry about this Miss Trumaine, but it happens, as you must know."

"Yes, of course," I said. "There won't be any more changes will there?"

"I can't guarantee that. Nothing is written in stone until the book goes to press. You should know that."

I didn't say anything right away. "Yes, of course, I understand," I finally said.

"Is there anything else?" Richard Rothstein asked.

"It's just that . . ."

"All right, I'll call again if anything comes up." And with that, he hung up. Richard Rothstein hung up without a decent good-bye or thank you.

All I could do was stand back and stare at the telephone. I hadn't realized how hard I was gripping the receiver. My fingers were red. I gritted my teeth and slammed the handset onto its hook. It echoed like thunder inside the house, like a storm had invaded all the walls and windows, and a dark rain cloud had permanently affixed itself over my head, threatening to rain at any second.

It was all I could do not to scream out loud. Instead, I hurried out of the house with tears welling in my eyes, just in time to see a green Chevrolet sedan slowing down and pulling into our drive.

CHAPTER 17

Guy Reinhardt had left just after the sun had come up, relieved by another deputy, Duke Parsons, an old-timer that I hardly knew at all, at least personally.

Duke looked like he had been sitting behind the steering wheel of a police car all of his life. He was short and squat and kind of resembled a blood-engorged tick. He wobbled when he walked, and I always thought he was going to fall over and roll away. He smelled like lard that had been left in an iron skillet too long, but from what I'd heard you'd be a dense fool to underestimate him. He could run faster than anyone thought and shoot straighter than an arrow—better than anyone else in the department. I'd never seen proof of those assertions—but I was glad that it was Duke sitting in front of my house. He would protect me from the green Chevy—if he could get out of the car.

My vision was blurry, and I blinked to make sure I was seeing what I thought I saw. I hadn't invited tears to my eyes, but I was sure that's what was fiddling with my sight.

I couldn't remember being so upset in my life. Richard Rothstein had just sent me over the edge and put more on my shoulders than I thought I could handle. But I had no choice but to face the present—and that came with an extra helping of fear. I wiped my eyes clear and steeled myself all over again.

There was no question that the Chevrolet was the same one I'd seen around town, the one that had sped around me on my way home. I was positive of it. The color was unusual, lighter than any other Chevrolet that I could recall seeing. Maybe it was new for the model year? I didn't know and I didn't care. I just wanted to know why it was on my land.

I was tempted to turn right around, go back in the house, and get Hank's shotgun. But Duke Parsons's presence kept my feet firmly planted on the stoop.

The green car stopped next to the brown and tan Ford for a second, then drove straight up to the house. If there were any words exchanged, they were deaf to me—but Duke Parson had obviously given them permission to proceed forward.

There was a single person in the car, a man with dark sunglasses on, just like the green Chevy that I had seen at the library and had zipped by me on the way home. I couldn't make out much more than that, until he came to a stop and stood up out of the car.

I didn't know whether to be afraid or concerned. I think I was both, if that were possible.

"Miss Trumaine?" the man said, after pulling a jacket out of the seat of the car. He removed the sunglasses, exposing white streaks on both sides of his tanned face. He was obviously outside a lot.

A leather briefcase occupied his left hand. It barely had a mar on it. The man, though he could barely be called that since he had a boyish face, looked freshly scrubbed. Taller than normal, but not as tall as Guy Reinhardt. He was half a head shorter, but built similar, like a tall stalk of ironweed instead of corn. His hair was dark—at first glance it was black—with flecks of auburn dark red in it and recently cut. The sun reflected off of the skin around his ears.

He wore a heavily starched white shirt, a thin black necktie, tan slacks, and a pair of Red Wing boots that looked like they'd never seen a dollop of polish on them; they were far more worn than he appeared to be. His jacket was the same color as his pants and had some kind of patch over the pocket on the right side, but I couldn't make out the emblem.

Nothing that I saw suggested that I should be afraid, but I glanced out to the brown and tan car just to reassure myself that Duke was watching over me. He was.

"Missus," I said, correcting the man as harshly as I had wanted to correct Richard Rothstein when he'd called me miss, too. I crossed my arms across my chest as tight as I could.

"I beg your pardon, Mrs. Trumaine." He stopped five feet from me. Our eyes were nearly on the same plane, even though I was standing on the stoop. "I understand I need to speak to you since . . ." The words fell off, and the young man looked down to the ground, to the top of his boots.

"Since Hank is indisposed?" I said.

"Yes, I suppose so. I heard about his accident. It must be difficult."

I ignored the comment. I didn't know who this man was, and I certainly wasn't going to acknowledge any of my troubles to him. "What's this about?"

"Oh, I'm sorry," he said, then reached around to his back pocket and pulled his wallet out as quickly as one of those gunfighters on TV pulled out a six-shooter. His actions were distinct, like his joints caught an extra-second longer than anyone else's. It was almost like he was arthritic, but he was far too young for that kind of affliction.

I jumped at the move but tried to hold myself together the best I could as he handed me a card. I read the simple type quickly and had to force my mind not to try and categorize the information it held. It said: CURTIS HENDERSON—STARK COUNTY EXTENSION AGENT

So, this was Lloyd Gustaffson's replacement? A youngster, green behind the ears, who looked like he'd just graduated from college?

I wondered what wonderful advice he thought he could bring me about the operation of the farm, the state of the soil, the roots to my wheat, on a day like this? I was in no mood for an agronomy lesson. Not today. If ever. Conversations about dirt bored me stiff, even though my indexing job wasn't working out too well. Books were making my life crazier, more pressured and stressful than I could have ever imagined they would. Maybe I needed to reconsider my priorities. . . . Life as a farmer's wife had to be simpler.

I looked up at Curtis Henderson and nodded. I had to say I was a little relieved. Truth be told, I'd half expected him to be a newspaper reporter, maybe one from Bismarck or Fargo. I figured news of the three murders, in two days, had spread across the state like wildfire.

The new extension agent stepped forward and offered his right hand for a handshake. "Curtis Henderson, ma'am. I'm happy to make your acquaintance."

I sighed, accepted my position as a farmer's wife, a proxy for Hank in more ways than I had ever counted on, and offered him my hand. He looked at me with great surprise as my grip equaled his. I never saw the necessity of demurring to a man, especially under "difficult" circumstances. "Nice to meet you, Mr. Henderson," I said.

He withdrew his hand. "You have a good handshake."

"Thank you," I said with a little bit of pride. I needed every complement I could find to help buoy me in the storm I was in the midst of. "You have big boots to fill. Lloyd Gustaffson was the closest thing to a magician, psychiatrist, and financial analyst any of us had ever met. He changed my life."

"I've heard that," Henderson said. He stepped back, but continued to face me directly. He had good posture, square shoulders. He was confident in himself. I liked that, and I was already starting to relax. There was nothing nefarious about the green Chevy at all. He was new in town. That had to be it. One less thing to worry about.

"I've spent some time with Mr. Gustaffson," Henderson continued. "He's filled me in the best he could on most of the local farms. But I understand circumstances have changed drastically in the last few days for folks around here."

I'd kept my place on the stoop, but my arms weren't quite as tight as they had been when the agent had first stepped out of the car. "You could say that. This really isn't a good time," I said, looking past Henderson as a couple of pickup trucks downshifted out on the road and slowed down as they passed.

"I understand; I really do. I just wanted to stop by and introduce myself," he said.

"It's good to know there's someone in Lloyd's place," I said. I glanced down at the briefcase. I was sure Henderson didn't have a Welcome Wagon package in it. He had business on his mind and in his face. There was no mistaking that, regardless of what he said. "I'll tell Hank you came by," I said.

"I'd really like to introduce myself to him."

"It's not a good time, Mr. Henderson," I said, staring directly into his wheat-brown eyes. "Our dear friend was found killed behind the barn yesterday, and the Knudsens . . ."

Henderson nodded and interrupted me. "I'm aware of the terrible tragedies that have occurred in the county, Mrs. Trumaine, but it is imperative that I speak with your husband."

I was none too amused to be cut off again, this time on my own front stoop. "You can speak to me about anything concerning the farm, Mr. Henderson. There is nothing that I don't know about our operations, our finances. I've paid the bills since Hank hasn't been able. I know that our circumstances are not the best they could be."

Henderson looked down to his boots again, then back up to me quickly. "Lloyd Gustaffson said I should only speak to Hank about this one thing, ma'am, and I took that as a directive, a certainty. This is business, ma'am. I'm only here in a consulting capacity. I think it's best if I speak to Hank," he insisted.

I shook my head back and forth, trying to understand and fight off the anger that was rising from deep inside of me at the same time. I couldn't do both. Any understanding I had was lost, and the anger quickly won over.

I stepped down off the stoop and didn't stop until I was toe-to-toe with Curtis Henderson. He smelled like Old Spice, citrus on the wind, an odor out of place and nearly unidentifiable. "There is nothing that I don't know about this farm," I repeated, my jaw set hard. I had to restrain my right index finger from rising upward and wagging in the young man's face. "I make all of the decisions that need made. Do you understand me? Hank is incapable of handling the pressures that the farm brings right now. He is an invalid." I stopped, but it was too late. That word, a word I had sworn to never utter, escaped my lips, funneled its way through Henderson's ears, then rode on the wind, over the barn, until it vanished. But there was an echo of it in my own ears, in my own mind, in my heart as it broke all over again with the reality that was inside the house, lying in my bed.

Henderson said nothing, just stared at me with a look of concern that I wasn't sure was real. It almost looked condescending. Like he wanted to say what he really thought but didn't dare to. Smart boy.

I lowered my head. "It is all Hank Trumaine can do to eat, to do his exercises so he doesn't die of bed sores, and do everything he can to keep himself sane, Mr. Henderson. The business of daily life is too much for him. If there's anything dire or urgent concerning this farm, you will have to speak to me, and then I will decide if it is something Hank can contribute to, can handle. Do I make myself clear, young man?"

I eyed the new extension agent as directly and with as much confidence as I could. I might not have ever had children, but when it came to protecting the ones I loved, I sure knew how to do that.

Nobody was going to push by me and upset Hank any more than he was already. Losing the Knudsens had been a big blow, but losing Ardith had knocked him down. I had never seen Hank so depressed, distant, and forlorn.

Curtis Henderson nodded and gripped the briefcase a little tighter. "I'm sorry to have bothered you, ma'am. I'll come back when Hank is having a better day." He started back toward the car.

"There will be no better days for Hank, Mr. Henderson. What don't you understand about that?"

"I'm sorry, Mrs. Trumaine. My condolences concerning your loss. I'm sorry to have bothered you." And with that, the young Curtis Henderson turned around, walked steadily to his green Chevrolet, got in, and drove away.

Filled with nothing but frustration, fear, and curiosity, I watched as the car disappeared down the road.

CHAPTER 18

Shep greeted me when I returned to the inside of the house. The dog knew better than to jump up on me, but he did anyway. Once he was on his hind legs, Shep stretched upward as gently as he could and put his paws on my chest with equal pressure. He stared up at me with his amber eyes, intense and unflinching. The forbidden act stopped me in my tracks, surprised me, and I started to admonish him, but I couldn't. I stepped backward until I was flush with the closed front door and let it—and Shep—hold me up. I hadn't realized that I was crying.

The dog didn't linger. The jump was like a quick hello, or an attempt to save me from falling over an unseen cliff. He dropped to the floor and sat before me, offering a nervous wag of the tail. If Shep could have spoken English, or Igbo for that matter, I'm sure he would have said, "Calm down. Stop. Take a breath. Don't do anything you'll regret. Sheep get eaten by wolves. Chickens scurry out into the road and get run over. Don't. I'm telling you just don't—stop." But it wasn't Shep's voice. It was my own, bouncing around inside my head like a .22 bullet would; not forceful enough to break through bone, but with enough momentum to slice through the brain, doing all the damage it could before it stopped. I wasn't sure I could make everything I was thinking or feeling go away.

How could things ever be normal again?

"It's all right, Shep," I whispered. I knew he was doing nothing more than holding me at bay, just doing what border collies were bred to do, even though I was rarely in need of herding, at least in my opinion. His timing was prescient, but that was nothing unusual. Shep thrived on the anticipation of what came next. He knew I was heading straight to Hank. He knew I needed to be stopped. So he broke the jumping rule. He saved me a second or two that I might regret for the rest of my life.

Herding was all right as long as he stopped there with his working dog behavior. Nipping wasn't allowed either, not on human ankles or any other part of the body, any more than jumping up was. I was sure that I would've had a completely different reaction if the dog had put his teeth to my skin.

I already felt like the sanctity of my home had been violated by some dark force, a killer that had possibly lured Ardith out to the first barn and left an indelible mark on the ground forever. Regardless of the weeds or flowers that grew there in the future, I would forever see a pool of blood and a sprig of mistletoe in an outstretched pale white hand.

Get ahold of yourself, Marjorie. Days'll be worse than this once winter sets in. It was my mother's voice working in concert with Shep to calm me down. Some days that's all I had to listen to, ghosts and dogs, made-up voices inside my head.

I might have been better off if I'd taken a second job waitressing at the Ivanhoe so I could talk to real, live, human beings every once in a while, instead of taking up indexing. But it was a fit for me. I got paid to read books. I hadn't counted on the double dose of isolation sending me to the edge of sanity.

"Who was that you were talking with, Marjie?" Hank called out. His voice was raspy, the volume low, barely audible over the breeze cutting through the house. But I knew his words, could have anticipated his question just as easily as Shep had known the future of my path when I'd stalked back inside the house. Not only was I Hank's caretaker, but I was his eyes and legs, too—he was as much a creature of habit as the dog was; as much as I was.

I wiped the tears from my eyes and took the deep breath that the dog had encouraged me to. "The new county extension agent come to introduce himself," I called out.

Silence. Long enough for me to straighten my dress and get myself together as much as I could.

I ran my hands over my windblown hair and patted it back in place. I was about to step to the right of Shep, but he knew that before I did and jumped from his sit to a stand, blocking my way again.

"Got timing like Hamish Martin," Hank answered. He was right, of course. Hamish Martin was the local property and casualty insurance agent and drove the yellow convertible I had seen in town in front of his office. Hamish always showed up after a catastrophe of some kind or other, trying to sell you more insurance coverage than you would ever need. Hank always said he was a land shark and could smell blood, or a tornado, from a thousand miles away. I thought he was a buffoon and never allowed myself to be in a room alone with him.

I stopped and stared down at Shep. I couldn't be mad at the dog, even though I wanted to be. "He was young, just out of college," I answered back. The force of my mood pushed my voice toward the bedroom. I did my best to hide the emotions I was battling. "I don't think he was from around here. Never seen him before."

The clock over my desk ticked loudly and echoed throughout the house. The day had already gotten away from me. I had so much to do; I didn't know where to start.

I pushed past Shep, even though he had scrambled to block me. "Stay!" I yelled at him.

The dog's ears retracted instantly and he dropped to the floor, finally submitting to my tone and glare.

"What's the matter?" Hank said.

"Shep's underfoot, that's all."

I was at the bedroom door in the blink of an eye. Hank was just where I left him, unmoved like always, his cloudy eyes staring upward at the ceiling. He had lost weight since the accident, and his profile had withered just like the rest of him. Some days, I hardly recognized him. All I had was a voice and the memory of a strapping man busting out the door every morning to take on the land and the weather. He might as well have been a ghost himself.

"Dog like that doesn't need to be in the house, Marjie. Just leads to problems. I told you that."

"Somebody needs to keep an eye on you."

"I'm not going anywhere."

"Says you." A flinch at the crest of his cheek; a remote smile from one of the few muscles that would still respond, consciously or unconsciously, to Hank's command or feeling.

I stood in the doorway, stared at Hank, and let the silence settle back inside the house. I knew we weren't alone. Duke Parsons sat guarding the drive. Gawkers still drove up and down the road, looking, I supposed, for some sign, some clue, that the worst of this storm was over. At least, I hoped that's what they were looking for. I know I was.

"He wanted to talk to you," I said, my voice straight and direct as a new fence row.

"What about?"

"Wouldn't say but wouldn't budge either when I pushed him and told him I could deal with whatever it was he wanted to talk about."

"You know how it is out here, Marjie." Hank's words had some weight to them. Just enough of a push to realize what he was saying was true.

"You men have a secret language?"

"Something like that."

"This farm's different."

"Maybe he thinks you got enough to shoulder. He talked to Lloyd?"

"Said he did."

Hank's eyelids fluttered easily. It was his casual nod. "Then he knows all of our old troubles along with the new. Don't suppose he has much experience at talking with someone who found a dead body on their land. Boy was most likely nervous, Marjie. I wouldn't take it personal if I was you."

I stared at Hank, then to the open window. The curtains pushed in and out like the house was breathing. I had made the curtains not long after we had gotten married.

"You're not keeping anything from me, are you, Hank?" I tried to keep the words even, with any doubt, anger, or fear, hidden.

Hank turned his head to me fifteen degrees. It was nearly his limit of movement, and took all of the energy and focus he could muster. "Why would I do that?"

I shrugged my shoulders and didn't answer. I knew Hank could not see my reaction, not physically, anyway, but he knew me well enough to know what had just happened. Hank and Shep had a lot in common when it came to reading people, exercising anticipation.

"Burlene Standish said she heard something, Hank. I'm confused is all. Confused and concerned."

"Heard what?"

"She didn't say."

"I told you what happened. I didn't hear anything."

"You're sure?"

"As sure as it's summer and there aren't enough hours in the day to get ready for winter. I heard Ardith put the phone down and walk out the door. That's it. Nothing else. You're going to trust that busybody over me? She could have heard anything—on anybody's line, not just ours. What's the matter with you, Marjie?"

It was my turn to nod. Hank was right. Burlene could have heard anything. There might have been somebody else with an open receiver. It happened all of the time. "I'm tired, Hank. Just tired and numb. It's a lot to take in."

"New York didn't help much."

"You heard that, too?"

"Of course I did." Hank paused, straightened his head back, so his blank eyes stared upward to the ceiling. "You don't have to do that work, Marjie. It'll all pan out without you burnin' the candle at both ends. Take a day or two. Do the things you need to. Make them wait for once, make them see your life has value to it, too."

"I wish I could, Hank. I wish I could."

CHAPTER 19

I stared at the pile of page proofs on my desk and came to the slow realization that I had more time than I thought I did. What had seemed like a burden, more work, more pressure from Richard Rothstein, was actually a small gift if I chose to see it that way.

In all of the comings and goings of the last two days, in all of the sadness, confusion, and terror, it hadn't dawned on me that my indexing work had ground to a complete stop. The pagination had changed, and it would be a day before the Air Mail box would arrive from New York with a set of new page proofs inside. It would be fruitless to move on, to mine the pages on my desk for keywords and concepts and commit them to an index card in wait of compilation. I *could* go ahead and do that, type up the entries anyway, but then I would have to go back and insert the correct page numbers one index card at a time. It seemed like planting the same field twice to me.

I had the break that I desperately needed, but I knew it would come with a cost. The delay would eat into the deadline that was forbidden to move, and I would have to burn the midnight oil to make up the time lost once the pages showed up on my doorstep.

I sighed at the thought. Honestly, I was in no frame of mind to direct readers to the cause and religion of casual decapitation. Under normal circumstances, I would have been thrilled for the opportunity to learn something so exotic, something I never would have encountered if it wasn't for the job I had taken on. When it came to that, to the learning, the immersion in another culture, the joy of being inside a text, the mind of a distant, brilliant man, there was nothing better. It wasn't about money, or a combine payment, or Hank's condition. It was about surviving and growing, seeing the world a little differently in a bleak landscape.

There was no way to know what the next few days held in store, but there were certainties that I knew I would have to deal with. The chores of the farm would still be a demand, as would be the continual complexities of caring for Hank. Those duties hadn't stopped, and they wouldn't for the foreseeable future. And then there were visitations and funerals to attend, food to carry to Hilo's house like I had to the Knudsens'—all without the help of Lida or Ardith. Somehow, I had to figure out how to get everything done I needed to, which was normal, but this was the most extreme time I could ever remember. I constantly craved a cigarette.

I sank into my chair as the weight of my life returned to my thoughts. Indexing a headhunter book seemed easy and irrelevant in comparison to my reality, especially when I considered the potential loss of Peter and Jaeger's labor and the fact that I still had the Norse amulet in my possession.

It was my opinion that that ugly thing had started all of this madness. I would always rue the day that I looked up and saw Hilo turn into our drive with that insidious relic in his pocket, ready to hand it off to me because I was "the smartest person" he knew. That felt like a curse more than ever now.

I sighed again, louder than the last time, drawing Shep's attention to me. He was lying between me and the door of my office, had done so on his own, and I was grateful for that even though I didn't know whether the dog was holding me at bay or protecting me. I hoped it was a little of both.

The office window was open. I was tempted to lock up the whole house, seal it like a jail cell so it was impossible to get into, or out of, for that matter. But I needed the fresh air, the promise of a normal, lazy summer day.

The sky was cloudless and the temperature was comfortable, lacking any humidity at all. Even the insects seemed to be in a dull mood, buzzing softly, allowing the breeze to propel them from one flower to the next in the garden that grew perennially underneath the window. I loved the sweet, innocent fragrance of lilies of the valley.

I had allowed myself to be momentarily lulled into a moment of laziness, but the truth was that I was still afraid of what could come through the window next. The .22 was within an arm's reach, and so was the realization that someone determined to get inside the house would find a way to do so no matter how tight the house was locked up or protected by one of Stark County's finest deputies. I needed a bit of normalcy even though I knew it was just a blue sky fantasy. An unknown darkness had settled on this tiny slice of North Dakota, and I didn't figure it was going anywhere any time soon.

Shep settled back down as my sigh vanished. I stared at my desk and decided I needed to get on with it. Just as I reached up to close the lid on the shoebox that housed my collection of index cards from the headhunter book, a powerful gust of wind pushed up against the house, then snaked inside of it with a certain amount of arrogance that I found annoying. It was like the wind was mocking me, showing me that it, or anything, could waltz through my house any time it wanted. I felt violated, even though for most of my life the presence of the wind was so benign and ubiquitous that I barely noticed it.

The gust was so strong that the shingles on the roof rattled and echoed loudly, almost like a train had derailed and fell from the sky. Shep jumped to his feet and looked upward warily. His black and white fur flipped and rolled in the waves of strong air, and I reached for the page proofs, for a spiral of flying index cards, but it was too late. They exploded upward and scattered, then rode the current straight out of the window.

"Damn it." I stood up and watched the pages disappear. It was not a catastrophe. More pages were coming. But I panicked at the thought of losing any of the index cards. It would be easier to adjust page numbers I had recorded than to start from scratch.

I rushed out of the room with more purpose than I'd had all morning. A quick glance to Hank as I passed the door told me he was awake, but quiet. He said nothing as I made my way outside.

A few of the pages caught a thermal. They circled upward on the edge of an invisible twister and out of reach. I let them go. I was more interested in saving the cards. Luckily, they were heavier and didn't go as far.

I found the first one settled on top of the lilies of the valley. The wind pushed the sweetness of the bell-shaped flowers upward as I grabbed the card before it launched again on another gust. The aroma gave me no comfort or pleasure.

The card was an E with the main heading "Europe." The subheading was "Celtic Gaels, headhunting practiced by, 156. *See also* the Ulster Cycle."

I studied the index card for a second and tried to think back to the text in Sir Nigel's book. If I remembered right the Celts mounted heads of their enemies on their chariots as a practice of tradition rather than a religious practice.

Shep was at my feet, the wind swirled around me, and for some reason, at that moment, I wondered if there had been any headhunting done by the Vikings, by the Norse gods, for any reason at all. I hadn't considered a link between the amulet and the book I was indexing, but maybe, just maybe, the key to the motive of the killings was staring me right in the face and I just didn't know it. It really didn't make any sense, but at this point anything was possible.

I'd have to search through the text a little closer to see if Sir Nigel had provided me with the information I needed. If not, I could phone Calla at the library and have her check the resources there. Beyond that, I'd be left with calling Raymond, or the university library, and that was something I didn't want to do. Not now. Not ever, really. Asking Raymond for more help was like taking a bitter medicine for an ailment I didn't have. Same with using the university library. I didn't like the attitude there, the snobby reception I'd always received from them. Maybe it was my perception, my insecurity due to the lack of a college degree, but right now was no time to climb an emotional mountain and eat crow—although I would if I had to.

I tucked the index card into my dress pocket, then went after the rest of them like a child chasing an errant kite.

I looked up after scooping a couple of cards off the ground just in time to see Duke Parsons staring at me, shaking his head from side to side with a look on his face that suggested I was the silliest thing he'd ever bore witness to.

After collecting all of the index cards I could find, I caught up with the morning chores. I fed and watered the chickens and pigs, checked the larder for an alternative to the cherries, since I'd ruined one bunch and used the last of the harvest to make a pie for Peter and Jaeger. If the rhubarb was ready, I'd use that—a nice patch of it grew at the back of the house. I knew rhubarb pie wasn't Hilo's favorite anyway. He'd eat it if it was mixed with strawberries, but I didn't have those, either. I had little choice, since leaving to pick up ingredients was out of the question. I thought for a minute and settled on lefse, a potato flatbread that was buttered and sprinkled with sugar and cinnamon, and a staple on the holiday table. I had just enough cream and was certain of the rest of the ingredients—and I knew the Norwegian treat was one of Hilo's favorite things.

From there I tended to Hank. Got him his morning bath and shave, rolled him and checked for bed sores, then proceeded with his exercises. He was quiet and distant, and I didn't push. Losing the Knudsens and Ardith so close together and in such a horrible manner, was enough to stagger a healthy man, and even more a man in Hank's condition. I let him be, and considered his silence as grief. When I left the room, his face was turned toward the window and he barely offered me a word of any kind. Even though it was as beautiful a day as one could ask for, the gray gloom of recent events continued to affect us both. I felt like I was walking in glue.

Once I was finally free for a moment, I considered what was left for me to do. Calling Hilo seemed out of the question; this was no time to return the amulet to him. I was left with my thought process, with the personal index I had started writing to put my mind in order.

I considered it for a moment, then decided the best thing I could do was call the library and clear my mind of the possibilities of Norse headhunters, or why an act of murder might have been committed. I was stuck on the thought of motive, because that seemed lacking to me. The only thing that tied the three murders together was the amulet, and only then because of the mistletoe left in Ardith's hand. The murderer had connected them himself, left a calling card—one that seemed important—and one only I would recognize as a link to the amulet and the tale it told.

CHAPTER 20

I picked up the phone and listened for Burlene Standish before I dialed the library's number. The line was dim and normal, but I proceeded cautiously, listening with every turn of the rotor for someone to come on and interrupt me—or listen in.

Calla picked up on the second ring. "Library." I was relieved to hear her voice. It was almost as if life was normal and everything was as it was supposed to be. For a brief second, anyway. Not long enough.

"Calla, Marjorie. Do you have a second?" Silence answered me back. Silence and the crackle of the line. It lasted for what seemed like an eternity but was maybe only fifteen or twenty seconds. "Calla, are you there?"

"I'm here," she finally said. Her voice was sharp, annoyed. I imagined her face drawn in, the lines around her lips as deep as a Badlands' canyon.

I hadn't talked to her since leaving town yesterday. A lot had happened since then. I wasn't sure she'd heard about Ardith, since there was no hint of compassion to be found in her voice at all.

"Is this a bad time, Calla?"

"What can I do for you, Marjorie?" The question was impersonal, businesslike.

I drew in a deep breath. "Did you find Herbert?"

A breath in, a hesitation, then, "Yes, thank you very much. He was down at the Wild Pony, thanks to you. Do you know how long it's been since a shot of whiskey has touched that man's lips? Now he has to start all over again, and I don't know that he has it in him. The fights he has fought, Marjorie. You just don't know. No one does."

I was taken aback and hardly knew what to say. "I didn't mean to upset him, Calla," I whispered, then turned away from the bedroom just in case Hank was straining an ear my way. "He came to me to tell me about Lida's cousin, I didn't seek him out. I wouldn't have troubled him with anything concerning the Knudsens, you have to know that. Everybody understands how fragile Herbert is."

"He's not fragile. He's wounded and he's never recovered."

"I beg your pardon."

"You should be more aware of your words, Marjorie. You know better. You of all people."

There was nothing I could say to that. Calla was right. In normal times I might of thought about what I had to say, how it might affect someone—the key word there was *might*. But these weren't normal times, and I wasn't myself. I was numb from the inside out.

"Well," Calla continued, "whatever you said to him set him off on a fine bender, the likes of which I've not seen in years, that's all I know. Your snooping around was the last thing he needed."

"You heard about Ardith?" I really wanted to scream, *"I wasn't snooping!"* But I restrained myself.

"I did. Of course, I did. Do you think something like that would go unheard of in this town? It's awful, just awful. Everybody was afraid before, but now they're really, really scared. Even the sheriff's wife wasn't safe. How can we sleep at night?" The edge fell off of Calla's voice, but it wasn't too far away. "Hank all right?" she asked after a long second of silence.

I nodded, bit my lip. The realization that he'd had no way to defend himself when the killer was on our land had already been examined in my mind a million times, but I hadn't been able to settle the fact that I left him in the first place. I had left Hank and Ardith to face some vile monster on their own. I shuddered at the thought of what would have happened if I had been home when the killer came calling. "He's fine. Hank's as fine as Hank can be. He's fine," I said.

Calla knew it was a lie, but she didn't press. "That's good to hear. You call to find out about Herbert, or is there something else, Marjorie?" The sharp edge on the side of her tongue was back.

"I am concerned about Herbert, Calla. How could I not be? I know what he means to the library, to you." There had always been speculation that Calla and Herbert were more than coworkers, that they were romantically involved, but I had never broached the subject with her and she'd never offered. I thought she was affectionate toward Herbert and looked out for him like a big sister might. If there was anything else between them, then it was none of my business, simple as that.

"Of course, you are," Calla said. "But there's something else isn't there?"

"Yes." She knew me too well.

"I figured as much. What is it? What do you really want, Marjorie?"

I recoiled from the telephone. I didn't like Calla Eltmore's tone. I didn't like it one bit. In all of the years I had known her, she had always reserved her snippiness for other people, usually out of earshot, but sometimes not. She could make the smartest person feel stupid with just a glare. A sharp comment could melt a child. She ran the library like it was a ship and she was the captain born to the right. I had always accepted that the library was Calla's domain, expected it, really, but I was upset enough already, I didn't need one of my only remaining confidants to abandon me. I needed the empathetic Calla, not the hardnosed biddy everyone else thought she was.

Truth was, I'd never thought it would be my turn to endure Calla's spiteful tongue. We were friends, colleagues in an odd sense. Our jobs were similar and required the same kind of organized mind, the same kind of curiosity. Calla Eltmore was an intellectual mother to me. She'd directed me to Chaucer and Chekov and warned me off Wilkie Collins and Edgar Allan Poe. I'd ignored that warning of "vulgar writing," as Calla had called it, choosing instead to find out for myself what kind of writer Poe and Collins were. But our bond had been broken somehow, in an unintentional way that I struggled to understand.

"Maybe it's not as important as I thought," I said, reconsidering my query about Norse headhunters. "I can call back, Calla. Everybody's on eggshells right now. I just thought if you had a minute, you could look something up for me, that's all. It's not that important."

"Don't call me back, just ask me now. Is it a reference question?"

"Yes," I said, with another nod. "I'm just curious if there's any . . ." I paused, knowing what I was about to ask would sound strange, even to Calla. "Any headhunters mentioned or represented in Norse mythology?"

The telephone line hissed and buzzed. "Headhunters?" Calla asked. "You're serious?"

"Yes, completely."

"I'll have to check on this, Marjorie." A hint of familiar curiosity and normalcy returned to her voice for a brief second. "I wasn't expecting that. Why does this concern you, if you don't mind my asking?"

"The book I'm indexing isn't clear, and I'd like my cross references to be accurate," I lied.

I wasn't going to tell her that I was in search of a motive for the killings. The question sounded outlandish even to me, and I wasn't really sure I would find a motive in the book I was working on. It was a stretch, and I knew it.

"It might take me some time," Calla said. "Are you going to be around home?"

"I'm not going anywhere," I answered.

"All right, I'll call you when I find something."

"Thank you, Calla. I really appreciate it."

"I have to do my job, regardless of how I feel about things."

"Please tell Herbert I'm sorry."

"Tell him yourself. You can just tell him that yourself. If he's not here, I'm sure you'll be able to find him at the Wild Pony," Calla Eltmore barked, then the line went dead, dead as it had been when I picked it up. All I could do was shake my head and hang up.

I made my way back to my desk. It was my safe place when the world turned dark. Or it had been. All I had to do was look past my bookshelves, out the window, to the first barn, and the image of Ardith Jenkins' dead, bloody body appeared in my mind.

It had been one thing to hold the amulet in my hand and imagine it settled in Erik Knudsen's stiff dead hand, but to see Ardith murdered in cold blood on my own property—well, that was unimaginable, something I knew I would never be able to forget or recover from.

I looked away from the window, stood up from my desk, and took in the work that awaited me.

The page proofs were stacked and rubber-banded together so they wouldn't fly off. They waited to be replaced, to be used as a foundation for the pagination change. The shoe box was closed up, bound with a well-used piece of twine. My dictionary was closed, and the typewriter sat empty, void of paper. All that remained on my desk was a single document held down by a rock from the yard; my own personal index. The one I had started to create to clear my mind. It wasn't complete either and waited as a repository of my thoughts. I knew there was a clue there somewhere—somewhere in the knowledge I'd collected and the events that had occurred. I just couldn't see it, couldn't see the why and the who. Motive and killer.

It was a job that I was less than qualified for, but Hilo Jenkins had set me on that path, and now he was indisposed, more grief stricken than I could imagine.

I felt like finding the killer was up to me now.

I just had no idea how on earth I was going to be able to do that.

CHAPTER 21

I glanced out the window just to make sure that Duke Parsons was still parked out front. I was relieved to see that the deputy was sitting in the car, his arm anchored out the window, a fresh cigarette dangling from his stubby hand. The wind pushed away the steady stream of smoke as soon as it touched it.

A magpie sat on the fencepost, looking out over the barren road. The tragedy-seeking traffic had died down to a trickle, much to my relief.

I had no idea how long we'd have protection from the county sheriff's department. I hoped a police car would be parked in the drive until the killer was caught, but I wouldn't express that to Hilo and inflict my worry on him. He had enough to deal with.

But I had no desire to stay on the farm with just Hank and me there. If the sheriff's wife couldn't fend off a killer, how would I be able to? Just the thought gave me a January shiver. *Could you kill a man if you had to? If you had no other choice, Marjorie? What would you do?* I didn't know how to answer those questions. I hoped I would never have to find out.

Regardless of what came, the fact was that Duke was still out there—watching, waiting, directing traffic, and protecting us the best he could—and that gave me a small dose of comfort. Of course, it was still daylight. Any false sense of security I felt would disappear once the sun fell from the sky, even if it was Guy Reinhardt who came to relieve Duke.

I settled back down in front of my desk and grabbed the index I'd started earlier. I needed my notes, too, since I really didn't expect the quest I'd sent Calla off on to pay off, to provide a real motive for the murders. I was deluding myself if I really expected an answer to be found in some obscure book. Still, I thought the idea of headhunting was worth checking out. It might help me to assign motive.

But at that moment, my mind turned back to mistletoe.

I had only made one entry in the murder index under the main entry, concerning the plant.

Ardith Jenkins: mistletoe found in hand.

The winter-inspired shiver I'd experienced earlier returned and didn't leave as quickly as the last one. I could hardly comprehend the reality that Ardith was really dead.

The mistletoe was far more viable as a clue than my curiosity about headhunting. I figured that hunch was a dead end, or at the very least, it would tell me whether the Norse people participated in the practice of decapitation for religious reasons or just as an act of war. Maybe that would help. The mistletoe, however, was real, left by the killer—I supposed—on purpose, as a message, as a link to the Knudsen murders. That was clear. It was also clear that the message, the mistletoe, was left for me, or for someone who understood the symbols and origin of the amulet left behind at the previous murder.

Did the killer know I had the amulet? If so, how? Only Hilo knew, and he'd sworn me to secrecy. A swear that I'd easily kept—with one exception: Raymond. It was all something to consider.

But I also had to consider the opposite, that the killer didn't know that I had possession of the deadly jewelry. It would mean the message wasn't for me. Then, I had to wonder, who was it for?

There was no way that the mistletoe could have floated through the air and landed in Ardith's hand by accident. It's a plant that, to my knowledge, that didn't grow in North Dakota. I was certain that it was placed there with intention, and that someone had to go to some trouble to get a live sprig, since it couldn't be found growing along the side of the road.

The origin of the plant was something to consider, but more important was the origin of the amulet. If the amulet was stolen from Professor Strand, then he would most certainly know the story of Loki and Balder. He would know all of the characters associated in the mythological murder plot, and he would understand the meaning. Surely, the professor knew more about the thing than I had discovered in my small amount of research. If that were the case, then Strand would understand the significance of the mistletoe, too. But he had not been home when I'd left Raymond's cottage to go see him, and I had failed to try and contact him since. A lot had happened to keep me occupied. I had also been unable to speak with Hilo and tell him of my findings, as muddled and inconclusive as they were.

Maybe, I thought, staring at the short, incomplete, index, *maybe, I need to talk to Duke or Guy.* I nodded. It was a good idea, especially if I didn't get a chance to speak with Hilo if the appropriate opportunity presented itself. I was sure that Hilo Jenkins was grief stricken. He and Ardith had been married since the dawn of time. But I was more comfortable with talking to Guy than I was with Duke. Duke seemed like a decent guardian, but Guy seemed more inclined to go after someone. Maybe it was his ambition, that innate desire to keep moving. Truth was, I trusted Guy more than I did Duke. Probably because I knew more about Guy. Duke was just a man in a uniform doing his job. Guy Reinhardt had a sad story attached to him. One that made him likeable to me.

I sighed out loud again.

Shep had followed me back into the room after my conversation with Calla and had situated himself between the desk and the door. It was quickly becoming his normal spot.

The dog took no notice of my sigh. Maybe he was getting accustomed to hearing my release of frustration. Or maybe he was listening to Hank and not paying any attention to me. It was a possibility.

Mistletoe. My mind went back to mistletoe. Why did someone leave mistletoe in Ardith's hand? I dug into my notes to reorient myself with the myth that was imprinted on the amulet. Balder was killed by mistletoe. I made an index entry:

B

Balder
  god of light
  killed by mistletoe
  second son of Odin. *See also* Loki; Odin

It was the mistletoe that I was stuck on, so I perused the story, my notes, a little closer.

Balder had started to dream of his death, so his mother, Frigg, traveled the earth to obtain an oath from every object, living and dead, not to do harm to her son—but she overlooked mistletoe. So Frigg failed to protect Balder and left a door open for harm to come to him.

Did that mean something? Did the protective quality of the amulet fail to keep Erik and Lida alive? If it was stolen and placed in their hands, that didn't make sense. But if it was Erik's—or Lida's— then the amulet's placement might have meant something significant. But what?

Was the mistletoe an afterthought? Or something more? Loki tricked Frigg by wearing a disguise and asked Frigg directly what could harm Balder—and she told him. *She told him, but she didn't know it was Loki that she was speaking to.*

So, I had to wonder, was there somebody here in Dickinson, somebody that knew Erik, Lida, and Ardith, and who was presenting themselves to be someone other than who they really were? Maybe wearing a disguise, looking for a weakness?

I made another entry, only this one under V:

Vulnerabilities. *See* mistletoe

But what was at stake here? Why did Erik and Lida need protection? From who, or what? None of it made any sense to me. All I knew was that the mistletoe was a weapon, fashioned into a dart during a game and given to Hoder, Balder's blind twin brother, by Loki and used to kill the God of Light innocently. Loki didn't kill Balder. Not physically. But he knew what he was doing. Hoder was innocent—but he was a killer.

I had completely allowed myself to become consumed again by the stories in Norse mythology. But I had to wonder . . . had Ardith's killer been tricked, too? Tricked into killing her without knowing what he—or she, for that matter—was really doing?

It was something to consider. It was a logical explanation for the mistletoe. But if the killer didn't put it in Ardith's hand, who did? I wasn't sure that I would ever know.

And I had to wonder one last thing: What if the green sprig had nothing to do with the myth? What if it meant something else, something else that I was missing?

I pushed myself back from the desk and stared down at the index. I was no closer to finding an answer than I had been after leaving Dickinson. If anything, I was more confused.

In the past, when I was stumped on something, when I couldn't move forward, I'd talk it through with Hank, but that was getting difficult, especially now, after Ardith's death. He'd retreated into silence. He lay prone, unmoving, not by fate but by choice, his blind eyes fixed on the ceiling for hours on end. There was a lost look in his eyes. They were almost cloudy, like a far off storm bank was building up inside of him. His jaw was set hard, and I hardly recognized him, much less had the ability to talk to him.

But it was him or the dog, and so far, Shep hadn't been much help.

I made my way to the bedroom and stopped at the door. It was all I could do not to break into another round of tears as I watched Hank breath. It was a struggle for him on good days, and the doctor had told us both that pneumonia would be our biggest enemy—pneumonia and bed sores.

Before the accident, Hank had been as hale and hearty as any North Dakota farmer. After the accident, Hank was left with nothing but his mind to occupy him. I had never settled myself to the fact that Hank would never recover, never get better. But he wouldn't. That was the truth of it. Hank would never stand up and walk out of the bedroom on his own, and I could distract myself with more indexing work, farm chores, and amateur detective tasks for Hilo, but I was going to have to face the facts of my situation, Hank's situation, whether I wanted to or not. Sooner rather than later, we were both going to have to leave the farm behind and find our glory somewhere else.

"You're fidgeting, Marjorie," Hank said.

His voice was strong, almost normal. The wind seemed to bounce it off the wall behind me, and I turned, just for a second, hopeful that a healthy, seeing Hank had just walked in the door from the back forty after a hard day's work, and all of this—all of the killing and his accident—had been nothing more than a terrible nightmare. But it was just an echo and a wish. Nothing more.

"Just confused is all," I said, turning my attention back to the real Hank lying on the bed, saddened at the loss of the imaginary one that did not exist. "Where do you suppose someone would get a sprig of mistletoe this time of year?"

"Most likely down at the Ben Franklin among the Christmas decorations, I suppose."

"It's July, Hank," I said. "Besides, I mean a real plant, not the plastic kind you chase me all over the house with trying for a kiss."

"Chased," Hank corrected me.

"Chased. Right."

"Maybe they hung onto it." Hank turned his head and stared at me, unblinking, with his blind eyes. "Kept it alive since the holidays. Probably easier to come by then since it doesn't grow around here."

"That'd take some work," I said, "just to hang onto something for such a purpose. They'd had to have planned it out ages ago, knew what they were going to do with it back in the winter."

"Just a thought, Marjorie. Whoever did this horrible deed went to a lot of trouble both times," Hank said. "Don't seem like no animal to me. But a plotting, thinking kind of creature. Somebody's gonna have to outthink 'im to catch him. You need to keep that in mind, Marjorie. You hear?"

Just as I was about to agree with him, tell him that I would, I heard a sound from outside that caused me to jump. Hank heard it, too, and he turned his head to the window.

Someone had started the engine to Hank's combine. There was no mistaking that sound—or the rotation of the thrashers as the gear engaged to move forward.

CHAPTER 22

It didn't occur to me that the rational thing to do was jump into bed next to Hank, pull the covers up over our heads, and hide until the trouble was over. It was Duke Parsons's job to protect us, to see to any shenanigans the curiosity seekers might cause, and track down a killer bold enough to show up in the light of day and announce himself directly with the start of the combine's engine.

Of all the duties that I'd assumed, it certainly had never fallen to me to be the guard and sentry of the land I claimed as my own; at least not directly, literally. Hank, in all of his frustration and inability, could not stand tall and don the armored suit of a knight like he once had. He could no more ready himself to do battle with evil outside the door than wipe the sweat from his forehead. Along with everything else, I had no choice but to protect us both. Whether it was out of fear or anger, I jumped to the task without any obvious hesitation at all.

I grabbed the shotgun from behind the door and rushed outside with Shep close on my heels.

It was a decent trek to the second barn, but one I'd made a million times in my life. I could've walked that path barefoot in the middle of the night with my eyes closed. I'd done that, too, when a sow was in the midst of birthing a litter and having troubles, or when the need of some tool dictated it in the middle of winter, and everyone else's hands were too busy to run and get it. There were certainties that came with living on a piece of land for the whole of your life, things that came easy, void of thought. Then there were things you couldn't see because you'd been staring at them for years, walking the same path. It was Hank's accident that had pried my eyes open to the realities of life. The Knudsens' murders, and Ardith's, too, had shown me something else: Never believe that there is nothing to fear on your own land. You're never safe. Not really.

The roar of the combine was a different, unexpected kind of concern. Funny thing was, my heart was as calm as it could be and beating normal. I'd had enough of death and worry to last a lifetime, and if I was the one to put an end to the current madness, then so be it. I'd be glad to be the one to do it.

Hank could not do much else other than offer a whisper of caution as I leapt from the room. The strain of the last few days was obvious on his face, more frightful than anything my imagination could dream up. I should have worried about leaving him behind, but I didn't, couldn't. I was rushing toward a fight, an angry wet hen set on protecting her brood, the henhouse, and everything beyond. Pity the fox who was looking for an easy meal.

I glanced over to the police car at the head of the drive as I came off the front stoop and saw Duke Parsons running my way, fumbling to get his service revolver out of his stiff holster. I didn't stop, didn't wait for the roly-poly deputy to catch up. I hurried as best as I could, barefooted, to the second barn, holding my skirt down with one hand, my grip firm on the shotgun with the other. Luckily, the grass was cool and moist against my feet.

I made sure a shell was in each barrel as I came around the corner, then flipped off the safety and gripped the shotgun with both hands. I was less concerned about showing my panties to a stranger, and more concerned about staying alive. No matter the result, I was ready to raise it to aim, pull both triggers, and offer any monster I saw a double-barrel hello.

But there was no monster, no apparent killer set on drawing me out of the house to do me in. My breath suddenly stuck in my chest, and I felt like I had fallen underwater at the sight that greeted me.

The two boys before me were the last two people I had expected to see.

I blinked and refocused my eyes as the combine came into clear sight. I stopped dead in my tracks and felt a wave of shame wash away my assumptions and fears.

Duke Parsons made it to my side just as the recognition settled itself in my overactive mind. It wasn't a killer I was staring at. It was Peter and Jaeger Knudsen, up on the combine, giving it a tune up, making sure it was set to go come harvest. For a moment, they looked normal, and I was sure I looked like a woman who had lost her mind—and her way—offering a threat instead of a warm hello.

The combine's engine was loud even though it was only a four cylinder. The front reel wasn't turning, or it would have been even louder. By most standards, our combine was a small machine, an Allis-Chalmers Gleaner Model E, but it was big enough to do the job we needed it to do—and it was all we could afford at the time we bought it—more than we could afford, truth be told. I feared the combine would never be paid off and might be repossessed when I needed it the most.

The Gleaner was clean metal, not painted, so it was mottled gray with red letters noting the manufacturer, but that was all. It was a utilitarian machine and wasn't fancy in the least or made for comfort. The hard perforated iron seat wasn't even enclosed. Hank couldn't afford such an extravagance, nor could he see need of any kind of housing. He'd said it'd be like closing in a tractor. He liked to be out in the elements, see what was below and all around him. But the truth was, he was no different than any other man in our parts. I saw how he had looked at the big fancy combines, showing up at the implement dealer, the ones with enclosures and car radios. He had green envy in his eyes. Those were long days in that uncomfortable seat, out in the weather, no matter how much a man loved it. He'd be stiff and hardly able to walk once the chore of cutting the wheat was done.

"Hey," Duke Parsons, yelled, "what're you two doin' up there?"

Jaeger was on top of the combine, a good twelve feet up, peering into the engine, watching it like a clockmaker intent on finding a flaw in the tick. He didn't flinch at the deputy's question, didn't act like he'd heard a word, and probably hadn't with the engine running like it was. Or he was ignoring Duke, which was just as much a possibility.

Peter, the younger of the two, was standing on the ladder attached to the side of the machine. He looked down to us and nodded, then tapped on Jaeger's shoulder, alerting him to our presence. The dark-headed boy looked up, glanced back to the engine, then shut it off. It sputtered, coughed, and gasped with a loud exhale as it shut down. The whole combine shook like a small explosion had gone off underneath it before it finally went quiet. The timing had been off since the end of last season.

Peter scurried down the ladder and landed on the ground with a two-footed thud. His ever-present smile was missing, and his shoulders sagged like he was carrying invisible buckets in both hands. His eyes were red, and it didn't look like he'd had any sleep in the last few days at all. Peter, the light-haired, smile-prone boy that I'd known since the day he'd come into the world, happy as a lark, looked like a forlorn old man.

"Mrs. Trumaine," he said, with a doff of his faded green John Deere cap. He never would call me Marjorie.

He forced a smile, but it disappeared as quick as a snow bunting landing on the white ground in January. "Deputy? Is there a problem? Ma'am?"

I shook my head no, and watched Jaeger make his way down off the combine. I hadn't released the shotgun or the shame I was holding onto.

Jaeger was the bigger, more muscular, of the two boys. He took after Lida's family, she'd always said. Truth was, the boys looked more like cousins than brothers. They had the same nose and eyes set back on their faces, but their complexions and dispositions were as different as Jupiter and Mars. Jaeger's left eye drooped slightly, and he wore a little scar there, just under his eyebrow, that was hard to miss. It looked like he'd fallen on a broken pop bottle at some point in his life, but Lida'd told me of the scar a long time ago when I was lamenting the fact that I'd never experienced the joy of childbirth.

Lida's first pregnancy had been a difficult one, and the doctor'd had to use forceps to pull Jaeger out of the womb. The way she saw it, he was content to stay there and fought all the way out. Lida thought Jaeger was still angry about that, because unlike his brother he almost never smiled. He seemed perpetually angry at something, though it might have been just the shape of his face, how he held his mouth. I'd always just found him to be focused, diligent, and intense. Good qualities for a man intent on being a farmer on unforgiving land.

"You two are the last people I expected to see here today," I said, resisting the temptation to rush to them both and pull them into the biggest hug I could offer.

Just seeing them lightened my heart, then it sank deeper than it had since I saw Ardith lying dead behind the first barn. "What are you doing?"

Jaeger stepped forward, his face as long as Peter's, his hands drenched in fresh oil, black as dried blood and smelly as old soil. "Told Hank last week we'd see to it that the Gleaner was tuned and ready to roll. Just doin' what we said we'd do, Miss Marjorie."

I nodded. "You two have other things to do," I whispered as I looked to the ground. "You should be at home. Don't you have folks coming?"

Jaeger didn't break eye contact with me. "If it's all the same to you, ma'am, it's easier bein' here than anywhere else." He looked out over the field that led to their house. They'd walked over, taking a familiar and comfortable path that was out of eye sight from the road and the parade of gawkers.

I nodded. "I suppose so," I said. "Are you hungry?"

They shook their heads no in unison, and I felt bad all over again. I didn't imagine they had much of an appetite at the moment, but I was just leaning on the past, remembering them eating through the cupboard like termites after a long day's work.

"You're all right, then, Mrs. Trumaine?" Duke Parsons said, as he started to back away. His service revolver was still in his grip, only down at his side. He looked relieved that the monster killer of my imagination hadn't shown up.

"I'm fine, Duke. Thanks for coming to the rescue."

"Don't look like you needed me much," he said with a quick smile down to the shotgun, then back up to my eyes.

I returned the smile and shrugged. We were all in uncharted territory, finding out things about ourselves we didn't know existed—including me.

Duke nodded and walked away, back to his post. I was, at the very least, calmed by his reaction. I trusted him to come running.

I turned back to Jaeger and Peter. "You'll stay for dinner then?"

They both shrugged.

"I'm going to make lefse and potato sausage. I was planning on taking some over to Hilo." I looked down to the ground, let my words trail off. I couldn't avoid reality, no matter how hard I tried to pretend everything was normal.

Both the Knudsen boys looked up at the mention of lefse and nodded with a familiar, anxious smile.

"Peter'll be glad to stay with Hank, if you need to leave, Miss Marjorie. Won't you, Pete?" Jaeger said.

"Be happy to." Peter said, and glanced back toward his home. The look on his face was clear. He had no desire to return home anytime soon—and I couldn't say that I blamed him.

CHAPTER 23

Lefse was most often thought of as a holiday treat, a potato-based flat-bread that was buttered, sugared, then rolled and eaten with delight. I can't remember a Christmas without it on the table, or when I wasn't in the kitchen at my mother's apron as she mixed the ingredients and then cooked the bread on the same hot iron griddle that I continued to use.

I was twelve when I made lefse on my own for the first time. I had to flip it on the four-hundred-degree griddle with my mother hovering behind me, ready to take over if I got in trouble—she made the task look easy, but it was an orchestra of movement that my young hands were inexperienced at. From then on, the mechanics of cooking the bread was my job. One that I cherished. Though, now, considering lefse as funeral food for Ardith Jenkins, I was less than thrilled with the prospect of all that the process entailed.

The ingredients were easy to keep over the winter, and the recipe was ingrained in my mind, as well worn as the path to the second barn. Boiled, peeled potatoes; mashed, mixed with butter, cream, and salt. Then the flour was folded in until the dough wasn't too sticky to work with.

I rolled the dough out on a board covered with a flour sack and heavily floured, until it was really thin, almost translucent, which is harder than it sounds. The rolling pin was corrugated and had been my great-grandmother's, brought over from Norway. It moved easily across the fragile dough, but would betray me if I pressed too hard. The dough would rip and I'd have to ball it up and start all over again.

After the dough was rolled out, I carried it, piece by piece, to the hot griddle with a lefse stick. The stick was nothing more than a window blind slat with the tip carved to a curve. Mine was worn and oiled with fingerprints from years of use—it was stored back in the blind after use and stood out from all of the rest. To the uninitiated, the slat just looked a little dirty, out of place. Most people never noticed, but our people always did, people who were brought up on lefse.

I fried the first side of the paper-thin bread until it started to bubble, then flipped it—actually, more like rolled it carefully—with the stick, until the bread was done. Then I'd do it all over again until all of the dough was gone.

I usually made a couple of dozen pieces, but since I was feeding the boys and Hank and taking the lefse to Hilo's, I tripled the recipe.

I had just enough potatoes and cream. Baking a cherry pie would have been much easier, but I'd been careless in that effort, wasteful, and didn't have any cherries left.

I liked to eat lefse straight off the griddle, slathered with fresh butter, but in this case I had to cool it—so I layered it in clean dish towels. Some women I knew made cozies to separate and cool the bread, but I'd never gotten around to that sewing project—I had too much to do over the winter the way it was.

Once it cooled, the lefse would travel well and be delicious paired with the potato sausage, another staple recipe of the plains brought over from the old country. Most folks made their own sausage, but since I'd had my hands full in the past months, I got mine at the Red Owl meat counter—most likely made by the butcher, Mills Standish.

The sausage was a mix of pork, ground beef, potatoes, onion, salt, pepper, and a hint of cloves. It aged well over the winter, too, and was a perfect mix with the lefse, when it wasn't used as a treat, but the store-bought sausage paled in comparison to the sausage that came out of my own meat grinder.

I stood in the kitchen warmed by the stove and the sound of Peter and Jaeger tinkering with the Gleaner. Life was far from normal, but I allowed myself to be comforted by the rote movements required to make the lefse, the sound of wrenches turning and men cussing as they busted their knuckles, trying make something run the way it was intended to.

How do you put the world back together when it is so broken? I couldn't even begin to answer that question and tried not to think at all as I continued my work.

Shep was in the bedroom with Hank, lying at the foot of the bed, not allowed in the kitchen while I was cooking. The house was filled with the wonderful aroma of fried flatbread, and it was difficult not to be transported to the holiday season, to the slower days and longer nights of winter when work on the farm sometimes ground to an achingly difficult halt. It was then that indexing filled my hours with pleasure and labor and guaranteed a consistent flow of money—as long as the projects continued to come in. Indexing projects were as dependable as the crops, though less reliant on the weather—as far as I knew.

My ear was tuned to the road, listening for mail truck. It was hard to say when the new set of page proofs for the headhunter book would show up. Once they did, the clock would start ticking again on my deadline, regardless of whether there was a killer on the loose or not.

I almost chuckled out loud at the thought. I had to wonder if anyone had ever used that as an excuse for missing an indexing deadline? How would Richard Rothstein react to such a thing? It was terrible of me to think such a thing, especially with the victims being so close to me—but it crossed my mind, almost made me laugh out loud, and I nearly burned the lefse on the griddle.

I hurried up and flipped the piece that I was cooking and was able to salvage it. That's what I got for allowing my sense of humor to turn morbid. Still, I would've liked to have seen Richard Rothstein's face at the suggestion of missing a deadline because there was killer lurking about.

I sighed out loud, then went back to rolling, flipping, and cooking, glad to be feeding the boys and Hilo, even under the most desperate circumstances.

I packed the last dish of sausage and lefse into the truck, then turned to face Peter. "You're sure you're up to this?" I asked. I couldn't have hid my nervousness if I'd tried.

He stood on the stoop, his hands jammed in his pockets, his head bent down toward the ground. Shep sat at his ankle. "Yes, ma'am," he answered as if he were talking to the grass.

"I'm not convinced."

Peter Knudsen looked up at me, and in that moment I saw the little boy I had always known; accustomed to being second, surrounded by people, mostly his father and brother, telling him what to do and when. Now he was being left alone with the full knowledge of what had happened when I was away last time. Jaeger had gone home to tend to the house, to the well-wishers who were still dropping off food, offering their condolences, and snooping about a bit if they could.

How could Peter not be uncomfortable, scared?

"I'll be fine, Mrs. Trumaine." Peter said. "I hope they do show up. I'd like to get my hands on them for what they did to us. I sure would. I'd offer 'em the same thing in return. A knife across the throat." His bottom lip trembled, then he bit it to make it stop.

Please don't cry, Peter, I silently begged. "I don't have to go," I whispered.

"Yes, you do. Hank and Jaeger said so. It's the right thing to do. You got to go for us all. Sheriff Jenkins' and his wife've been kind to us all my life. My father held them in high regard."

I couldn't argue with Peter. I had to go to Hilo's. I had taken pies to the boys, and taking Hilo lefse was all that I had to offer—but being away from home and being out by myself didn't sit well with me. But what was else was I supposed to do? Hide until the killer was caught? What if that never happened? I would have to leave the house sometime. I couldn't hide under the covers with Hank forever.

I turned to leave, then turned back to Peter as something settled into my mind without a place to file it away. "What about your mother?" I asked directly, wishing I could take the question back as soon as it left my tongue.

Peter looked surprised, flinched. "Ma'am?"

"About Hilo? Did she hold him in high regard?" I couldn't stop myself, because honestly, I couldn't ever remember Lida Knudsen saying a kind word about Hilo Jenkins. I couldn't remember her saying anything about him other than that she always referred to Ardith as "Hilo's long-suffering wife." I'd always assumed it was because Hilo was the sheriff, was gone from home a lot of hours of the day, was used to being in charge, and had a strong personality. But now I wasn't so sure. I wasn't sure of anything.

Peter shrugged. "Can't rightly say." Then he looked to the sky, blinked his eyes, and grew distant. It wasn't clear if he was looking for an angel in heaven or begging me to stop asking questions and leave.

I was missing something. Like there was an important index entry missing, but I couldn't find it even though it was staring me in the face. That happened sometimes when you looked at text for too long and too late into the night.

"Was it because of her cousin?" I pressed.

Peter looked back to me, his cheeks held tight. "I'm not sure what you're gettin' at, Mrs. Trumaine? My mother never said one way or another how she felt about Sheriff Jenkins. And I don't know about no cousin that might change things."

"Hilo's best friend. At least, when they were young, before the war. Herbert Frakes told me about him, that he was wounded on D-Day and then moved to Minneapolis after the war. That cousin. You've never met him?"

"Oh, *him*," Peter said. "Uncle Roy."

I nodded—now I had a name. "So, you do know of him?"

Peter mimicked my nod. "My mother didn't hardly speak of him, or to him. Ever. I only saw Uncle Roy once, and that was at his mother's funeral when Jaeger and me was little boys. He limped and smelled like moth balls drenched in whiskey."

"Lida's aunt?"

Peter nodded again. "My mother didn't speak to Uncle Roy then, either, and corralled Jaeger and me away from him every time he came close."

"Why's that? Do you know why, Peter?"

"It hurts to talk about her, Mrs. Trumaine. I wish you could go ask her these things yourself." Peter's lip trembled again.

"I wish I could go ask her, too, Peter. But if she was still here, I wouldn't need to know the answer to my questions."

"Why do you need to know that?"

"I don't know. It just seems important. There are things going on that none of us understand. I'm just trying to make sense of everything, that's all. I just want to understand what's going on."

"Maybe he'll be here. Maybe Uncle Roy'll come for the funeral. You can ask him these things yourself. That'd be better. The showings are tomorrow. You know that? You can ask Roy at the showings if he has the gall to show up."

I nodded. I hadn't looked at the paper or read Erik and Lida's obituaries, but I knew the timing, two days or three; it was time to start burying them. I had been avoiding the reality of what was to come. "Maybe," I said about Roy. "But I'd like to know what you know. Then I'll go. I promise," I said, looking past Peter to the western horizon as the sun dipped toward the edge of the earth.

He nodded one last time. "She said that he was a thief, that Uncle Roy had taken something really important and really valuable, then lost it. That's all she ever said, but I could tell it really made her mad. Momma wasn't that kind of person, didn't have a mean bone in her body. But she didn't like him, that was for sure. Not at all. She didn't like Uncle Roy."

"What'd he steal, Peter?" I pushed. My spine tightened like a piece of iron had just been inserted in it.

"I don't know, she'd never say." His voice trailed off, and Peter looked the opposite way from me, away from the setting sun, toward his empty home. There was nothing but ghosts there now. Ghosts and specks of blood that shouldn't have been there.

"If you remember, you make sure to tell me, okay?" I said.

"All right, Mrs. Trumaine, I will." And with nothing else to offer, Peter Knudsen walked into the house, set on taking his place as guard and protector over the dominion of Hank and glad, I was sure, to be as far away from me as possible.

CHAPTER 24

I settled into the Studebaker's worn bench seat, closed my eyes, and ran through an imaginary checklist to make sure I had everything that I needed. It was a habitual exercise, an unprovoked response that came as a natural to me as walking and talking. But one that wasn't foolproof. I'd been known to forget things from time to time. I'd lost trust with myself in the last few days.

The lefse and potato sausage were packed up in a basket like it was going to a church picnic. There was no way to rid the cab of the smell of food—of distant pork ground to a pulp, mixed with cloves, and stuffed in a pig's intestine—but I was far from hungry. I had hardly been able to eat since I'd first heard the news about Erik and Lida.

Usually, I found comfort in the aroma of food, the consistency and presence of it, the memories it evoked, but I was less than thrilled with the journey I was about to take. I feared that this memory would be what would return to me in the future when I smelled the flatbread and sausage. Lefse would be associated with the death of Ardith Jenkins from now until the end of time. Instead of a holiday celebration, it would be a reminder of the ugliness of man, of hate, and of bloody murder. Just a whiff of lefse would make me sad as an old woman—if I were lucky enough to live that long.

My purse sat next to me, filled with all of the appropriate necessities and unmentionables to get me through the visit; my reading glasses, multiple handkerchiefs, a fresh compact, my opened pack of Salems, matches, and the amulet, which I planned on returning to the sheriff as soon as it was politely possible.

I didn't know what state I would find Hilo in, but I imagined that at some point he would still remember he was sheriff, that he had asked me to investigate the amulet—without telling me why or that it was possibly stolen. Of all things I would have liked to have forgotten that happened over the last few days, my visit with my cousin Raymond was one of them. He'd put a splinter in my shoe from the moment I walked into his cottage.

I'd just as soon have thrown the amulet out the window or drowned it in the closest duck pond, but I couldn't do that no matter how much I wanted to. It was on loan to me. A secret possession that had brought nothing but bad luck since it had first touched my skin.

In between my purse and the basket of lefse was the .22 rifle, the barrel pointed down to the floorboard, the butt wedged in between the basket and purse, and easy to get to if the need arose. Hank's orders. He wouldn't hear of me leaving the house without a gun. I didn't argue. I took it to make him feel better, so he would worry less, but I took it for me, too, I suppose, though the presence of the rifle was cold comfort.

Of course, Hank himself was the big thing that was missing. It should have been him sitting behind the Studebaker's steering wheel, driving off to Hilo's to offer support and love in a time of grief, and me sitting in the passenger seat, dutifully bereft, sad beyond compare. But that wasn't the case. Instead of me, it was the little Western Auto Remington, sitting in wait, emotionless and unforgiving. I had my doubts that the varmint gun could protect me from whatever it was that was out there, but it was all I had.

I'd thought of dressing up, putting on my one fine black dress and pillbox hat, but I would be wearing it plenty in the next few days. It wasn't like I had a huge wardrobe to choose from. Dress up occasions had always been rare: weddings and funerals, mostly. I had on my best everyday dress, a light shade of gray with a broad white collar, cut below the knee—another McCall's pattern that I'd sewn myself a few years ago. The dress went with my best shoes—the black ones with the thick sensible heels that had been originally bought for Sundays and expected events.

Most of my clothes were utilitarian. Fashion was the least of my worries on the farm. I always wondered if Sir Nigel, or any of the other authors I worked for, for that matter, would have been offended if they'd known that the woman who wrote the index for their books walked around with chicken shit crusted on the soles of her two-dollar Sunday shoes.

I hadn't thought much about church visits recently. They were even rarer than weddings these days. My lack of visible faith was frowned on by some and not considered by others. We'd always toiled far more than we'd worshiped. Hank's parents were stricter than mine about attendance at the Lutheran church up the road, about demanding a true belief in the Lord—prayers before supper and at bedtime, that kind of thing.

The distance from the church came with regrets in certain times, especially when the triumph of good over evil, light over dark, or an invisible savior's gentle touch was in serious demand for the hope of some kind of comfort. Unfortunately, my faith had suffered through a deep drought even before Hank's accident, and the roots of it had never recovered, mostly since the loss of my parents. I had a hard time believing that they were dancing on streets paved of gold, out of sight, up in the clouds joyfully while I was still down here on earth all alone, missing their voices, their direction, their constant presence, especially when a killer was lurking about and slashing peoples' throats.

I'd read far too many books to be able to tell one story apart from the other, which put me on par with most of the academics in town if the truth was to be told. I wasn't quite an atheist, but I was as close to a godless heathen as one could be—and the events of late were doing nothing to change my mind.

I started the truck, checked myself one last time in the rearview mirror, then put the truck in gear. I wanted to be presentable. That hadn't been lost.

There was no avoiding what I had to do, and no avoiding leaving the farm, but that didn't mean that I was looking forward to walking in Hilo Jenkins' front door. I had no choice. I *had* to go to Hilo and Ardith's home on this grim evening. It was the right thing to do.

It didn't take long to arrive at Hilo's house—about ten minutes as the crow flew, fifteen by the road without regard to a speed limit. I slowed about half a mile away to gather myself.

I had to resist the urge to keep on driving, to be just one more truck in the long parade of gawkers on the tour of death. But I couldn't do that. I had to stop, I had to pay my respects to Ardith, to Hilo. I just hoped I could leave my guilt in the truck.

I would forever think it was my fault that Ardith Jenkins had been murdered behind our barn—that it should have been me there, instead of her.

Me there, instead of her.

I trembled at the thought, geared down the Studebaker, and pulled onto the drive that led up to Hilo's house.

A deputy stood beside a brown and tan police car, a familiar Ford, and he waved me through without asking me to stop. It was Guy Reinhardt.

I had to wonder if he'd had any sleep since I'd seen him last, but that wasn't my concern. I didn't stop, just kept on driving with a weak return of a wave of my own, but I watched him disappear in the rearview mirror. He stood stiff and watched after me, his hands stuffed in his pockets.

Guy made me uncomfortable in a way I hadn't felt in a while—not a threatened way but a female way, a distant tingle that suggested betrayal and need. I ignored it the best I could.

The drive was a half-mile stretch that curved up a slight rise, announcing a change in elevation. It was not unusual for the land to roll into a hill, especially when there was a river close, but the incline was unexpected for the most part. At least for me. Our land was as flat as the bottom of a skillet, and there was no need to worry about what was around the next bend of the road, or over the top of a rise. Everything was open, easily seen—with the exception of the shadows behind the barns. Recently, the land had betrayed me more than I ever thought possible, and I dropped the transmission into first gear to climb the hill, nervous that I'd come grill-to-grill with another truck. Or something worse.

I didn't know the drive to Hilo's house as well as I knew the Knud-sens' drive or my own. Visits to the sheriff's house were rare. Hilo came to see us, even when Hank was at his best, standing on two feet, itching to get out into the field to hunt or work. I could hardly remember the last time I was at Hilo's house. I thought it had been to drop something off for Ardith, and then we'd stood on the porch. An invitation inside had never come.

I crested the rise and thankfully found myself on flat land again. A football field's worth of cars and trucks met my vision. I was glad I was in first gear. It looked like everyone who had driven by my house had ended up at Hilo's.

I parked next to a green Ford pickup, straightened my hair one last time, and made my way to the house carrying holiday treats on the saddest day of the year.

CHAPTER 25

Most of the women who populated my life had flour behind their ears, not Chanel No. 5, but Hilo's house smelled of sweet perfume, musty stale bread, and cigarette smoke.

Upon entering the front door, it was immediately apparent why Ardith hadn't invited me inside on that long-ago visit: She was embarrassed, or didn't want me to see how she and Hilo really lived.

Beyond all of the hovering mourners, the house was a wreck: a lifetime collection of newspapers, magazines, skeins of embroidery floss, and knickknacks of all kinds were stuffed wherever they would fit, or left where they were last touched. There wasn't a clear spot on the surface of any shelf or table or anywhere in the room that I could see. Ardith Jenkins was no housekeeper, and the idea of maintenance or upkeep seemed as foreign as a rag devoted to wiping away dust to her.

Honestly, I was taken aback by the deteriorated state of the house. As my eyes scanned the front room, my mind tried to categorize everything that I was seeing, but it was impossible to think, even more difficult than it was to breathe.

It had never occurred to me that Hilo and Ardith lived in such a way, that she wasn't tidy and organized. I was foolish to think that everyone was like me, but the two of them always presented themselves as clean and pressed, though Hilo could look a little rumpled in his uniform—the same uniform he wore day after day. I couldn't remember seeing him dressed in anything else now that I thought about it. But I hadn't expected to see him dressed any other way. He was the sheriff, after all, and his daily wear of the uniform fulfilled my expectations. So did Ardith. She always wore a simple dress, usually flowered in one way or another, but subtle, beautiful in its simplicity. I guess the truth was you didn't know people as well as you thought you did, no matter how many years you'd spent in each other's company.

I had to wonder what else I didn't know, but pushed away that curiosity as soon as it crossed my mind. Maybe I didn't want to know. Just like I could have lived the rest of my life without knowing that Hilo and Ardith had lived like pack rats.

The house was small, most likely four rooms: the front room, two bedrooms, and a kitchen in the back—the standard floor plan for an early twentieth-century North Dakota farmhouse. Along with the lifetime collection of stuff and lack of organization, there were people everywhere: people I recognized from town, from church, and people I couldn't recall ever seeing before.

I stood in the doorway dumbfounded, lost, akin to what Alice must've felt like when she first tumbled down that rabbit hole. I worried that I would encounter the Mad Hatter and the Queen of Hearts, especially when a voice came to my ear. "The food goes in the kitchen, honey," a woman to my right said.

She was tall, leggy, with even taller blond hair, of the likes I'd hardly ever seen before. She looked glittery, polished from head to toe in a bright store-bought orange dress, a big city girl suddenly transplanted into the country directing funeral food. She looked like an expensive lawyer's secretary. It was her perfume that had accosted my nose when I had walked in the door. I preferred the smell of pig shit to Chanel No. 5 to be honest.

I didn't budge. "Do you know where Hilo is?" I asked.

The woman stared down her nose at me with a look that needed slapped off her face. Fortunately, my hands were full.

I was not an idiot for asking the question—which was what her haughty expression voiced silently. I'd come to deliver food and to see Hilo, and that's what I was going to do. I had left Hank once again, and I was worried beyond description about what I would find when I returned home. But here I stood. "I have business to discuss with Hilo," I said with a harsher tone than I'd intended.

"Today's a bad day for that, honey."

"Do tell."

My response flustered the woman even more. She shook her head and looked to the ceiling, exasperated. "Hamish told me to direct food to the kitchen, and that's all I know."

That explained it. She was Hamish Martin's latest go-to girl. The insurance salesman traded in secretaries as often as he traded in convertibles. Once he put a little mileage on them, dinged up their fenders, and eyed a newer, shinier model, they were history. I'd never seen this one before. But we'd stopped buying insurance from Hamish Martin eons ago, after a policy he sold us refused to pay out for some hail damage we'd suffered, so I'd lost track of his conquests a long time ago.

"Thanks," I said, eyeing a path to the kitchen. It was going to be a bump-and-shove journey through all of the people, but the decaying smell of the room, and the realization of where I was and why, was starting to overwhelm me more than I suspected being inside Hilo and Ardith's house ever would.

I said nothing more to the secretary, didn't like her anyway, and pushed my way through the front room, excusing myself as I went.

A soft apology went a long way—if it was heard. The room was as loud as a tavern on a Saturday night. Not that I had much experience with that, but Hilo's front room *was* how I imagined it to be.

I had to wonder if Herbert Frakes was there. Everybody else from town was. Though I hadn't seen Calla, either. I really hadn't expected to see the pair from the library, but it would've been nice to have had the comfort of one of my friends, even though she was annoyed with me for upsetting Herbert. Circumstances had a way of washing away anger. It would've been nice to sneak a cigarette with Calla, but that didn't look like it was going to happen, either.

The kitchen was no more organized, cleaner, or emptier of people than the front room was. The counters were cluttered with tuna-and-noodle hot dishes, platters of fried chicken, cakes, and pies—enough food to feed Hilo for the next twenty-five years. It was a smorgasbord of grief.

On a good day, the kitchen could've handled two or three women accustomed to a ballet of handling pots and pans, frying, boiling, and ultimately cleaning, but to be honest, I couldn't count all of the bodies—mostly men—in the kitchen. It was so foggy with cigarette smoke that I could hardly smell anything else. That might've been a gift, but my lungs didn't seem to think so. I felt like a gasping fish trapped in a shrinking mud hole.

I stopped again, elbow-to-elbow and knee-to-knee with strangers. I didn't know what to do with the lefse and potato sausage, so I sat it on top of a closed sheet cake and wiggled away toward the back door to get a breath of fresh air.

"Excuse me. Hello. Excuse me." A few feigned smiles, and I was outside.

The back porch held two old washing machines, a rusted stove that looked like it was home to a family of raccoons, and another group of men I didn't recognize. After standing and listening for a second, I realized that they were all deputies from other counties. I was surrounded by police officers. That made me feel better and I could breathe again, but they were all smoking, too. Or seemed to be.

I took another deep breath and stared out over Hilo's backyard, glad to be free of the food I'd brought, and even happier to be left alone for a moment. A few of the men doffed their hats, offered a restrained, "Ma'am," then went back to their muted and private conversations.

The land at the back of the house sloped down into a dense line of trees—a few willows, sycamores, and oaks—which explained the presence of the coon nest in the stove. The river cut through the north side of the property, allowing for a yard free of a gopher town but home to other critters that most people didn't have to deal with.

The wind had kept up steadily without any hint that it was going away any time soon, and the sun had traversed down behind us. Delicate pink fingers stretched out overhead, gentle clouds that offered no threat and only reflected the setting sun—no rain, no storm, just the promise of more calm weather. It was a perfect evening for a picnic, or to work late tuning up the combine if that task was required.

I was about to turn back around and go into the house and try to find Hilo, but I spied him walking the tree line away from the house, alone, about fifty yards off.

I clutched my purse tight, thought about taking off my heels to hurry after him, but decided against running barefoot across the unknown yard in my good dress and headed off the porch in pursuit of the sheriff as quickly and carefully as I could.

Hilo turned when I was halfway to him and stopped. I was glad of that. The grass was moist, slippery against my smooth flat soles that hit the ground with purpose, but with very little purchase, even with the heels. I was afraid I was going to tumble the rest of the way down the slope and find my very own rabbit hole.

"I thought that was you, Marjorie," Hilo said. He was still dressed in his uniform: dark brown shirt and dark brown pants with an even darker stripe up the side, wrinkled, of course. But it was easy to notice, even in the declining light, that there was something missing. The five-pointed star that was forever pinned over Hilo's heart was gone. The only thing that was there now was a small empty hole, tattered around the edges. I restrained myself from saying anything about the missing badge.

Hilo's face was puffier than normal, his hatless white hair a muss, even more so than normal, but he was standing on two feet, and his eyes were reasonably clear, more so than I had expected them to be.

I had to catch my breath before I spoke, so we stood there looking at each other for another long moment. The years passed between us and now we shared another tragedy. I had not been able to speak with Hilo when he had responded to the call about Ardith, come onto the property in a rush, then fell to the ground in disbelief as he saw Ardith, murdered and bloody behind the first barn. I was lost in my own hysteria and could hardly bear witness to his. His terror and moan had sounded like a distant train, mournful and lost, about to derail.

"I'm sorry," I whispered. And then the tears came. I couldn't help it. They flooded out of my eyes in rivers, like they'd been building behind an invisible dam. I just couldn't help myself, couldn't hold back my grief, my guilt, my pain, any longer.

Hilo said nothing. He just reached for me as I crumbled into his arms.

CHAPTER 26

I took a deep draw off the Salem and stared past Hilo to the gloaming sky. Dainty pink clouds had stretched out farther to the west, eating into soft yellows, all being chased by a darkening blue that would soon fade to black. Daylight seemed to go on forever in the summer, and mostly that was a wonderful thing for a farmer, but under other circumstances some days seemed to go on far too long. Grief was a heavy, invisible ankle weight that made the easiest step difficult, and the sky was dark no matter the time of day.

A magpie flittered from one fence post to the next, its long feathery tail dragging from lack of wind or enthusiasm. The black-and-white bird eyed us first with suspicion, then with opportunity. We had nothing to offer it that I knew of. The scavenger would have to fend for itself until Hilo rid himself of all the food that was stacking up in the kitchen.

"I brought lefse," I said, exhaling smoke as I spoke. There was little comfort in the act, and Hilo matched the magpie's first gaze. He seemed suspicious of everything, even me. I couldn't blame him.

"Hank thinks you quit smoking," he finally said. Crickets chirped nearby, but there was no music to add from his voice. It looked like it hurt him to speak.

We were a good fifty yards from the house, and the voices from inside floated down to us like vibrations from a grand party that we hadn't been invited to, or were trying to escape.

The mention of lefse didn't give Hilo a reason to flinch or show any enthusiasm at all. I was sure the thought of food turned his stomach as much as it did mine.

"Yes," I said. "But I'm sure he knows I have a cigarette occasionally, he just doesn't say anything. I try not to smoke around him. It's a crutch I need some days more than others."

Hilo stared me directly in the eye and let a thoughtful pause settle in between us. "It's not your fault, Marjorie."

"I left her there, Hilo." It was a broken sigh. The words got tangled up in a bramble of sadness that had lodged itself in the base of my throat from the moment I'd found Ardith. It had never left.

How could I not have regrets? How could it not be my fault?

"How were you to know?" Hilo asked. "I left her there, too." His voice trailed off down the hill to the riparian tree line that hid the sight of the river, but not the smell. The water added a freshness to the air that couldn't be found anywhere else. Without reason, the crickets stopped chirping. Maybe they were listening to us like we were listening to them.

I looked at the hole in Hilo's shirt, where the badge used to be, and he caught my gaze.

"I resigned," he said. "If I can't protect my own wife, keep her safe, then how can I expect to keep the people of Stark County safe? I'm finished. Probably should have quit long before now."

"You told me after Hank's accident not to make any rash decisions, not to rush off and sell the farm. 'Slow down,' you said, 'the storm clouds will clear soon enough.'"

"I was right, too, wasn't I?"

"Mostly, but there are days when a first-floor apartment in town, close to the hospital and the library, would be less work, easier. Some days, an easier way of life would be just fine with me."

"Hank'd never survive the move, the loss of the land. You either, as far as that goes. Be like taking a fish out of a pond and putting it into the ocean. How could you breathe?"

I shrugged and put the Salem's white filter to my lips again. It was already tainted with a light coating of my lipstick, and I suddenly wondered if it needed refreshed. I wore it light to begin with. Then I wondered why I should care.

I took another puff, not so deep. "You're probably right. But I always wonder if a change of scenery would do him good. Especially now."

"And?"

"We haven't talked about it," I said. "Not recently. But he's always said the only way he was leaving that farm was in a pine box stuffed into the McClandon's hearse. And you know Hank ..."

"He means it," Hilo said.

I nodded, exhaled, and didn't want to consider the thought. But it was too late. I'd held that final image of Hank in my mind a million times, tried to ward it off like the coming of the flu, with happy thoughts, cheerful notes, a warm soup, but it never worked. The grim vision of the simple coffin being lifted out of my bedroom never left me, especially when I was there.

I glanced down at my purse, trying to take my mind away from my own personal pain. "I didn't find much," I said.

"About the amulet?" Hilo hadn't moved, just stood before me like he was going to catch me again if I fell, if I crumpled to the ground. He was good at reading me.

"Yes," I said. "Just mythologies that I can't connect anything with— except..." I stopped.

"The mistletoe." Hilo finished my sentence.

"You know about that?"

Hilo shook his head no. A wiry hair spiraled over his ear, and he pushed it away immediately, like it was a mosquito, an insect on the attack. "Not really, not the details. Just makes sense, that's all. First they leave the amulet in Erik's hand, then mistletoe in Ardith's. I don't read much, but I figure I can see a tell as much as the next cop. Whoever done this was leaving a note, telling us that he was there, flipping his nose up at us like he's smarter than all the rest of us."

"Then you think it was the same person who killed them all then?" I asked.

"I do, but that doesn't mean it wasn't somebody else tryin' to follow along with the Knudsens' murders, copying it. I don't really know any-thing for certain, Marjorie. It could be the same person, or it could be two different ones. For the life of me, I can't imagine why anyone would do such a thing. Not here."

"They would have to know, too, Hilo," I said. "They would have to know what the amulet was and the story that's depicted on it. If it was another person, two different ones."

"The detail of the amulet left behind hadn't been released to the press, and the mistletoe won't be, either. Not until we . . ." Hilo paused, looked to the sky, then said, "not until *they* solve this thing."

The cigarette dangled between my fingers, as comfortable there as a red pen was. "I was going to give you the amulet back. I don't want it, don't need it."

Hilo just stared at me, then stuffed both his hands into his pockets.

The crowd in the house roared with laughter, drawing our attention to it for a brief second. I wasn't upset or offended. People dealt with tragedy and pain in a lot of different ways. Somebody probably told a good joke. Besides, it wasn't my place, my house, to be offended.

Hilo didn't seem to mind the distant laughter. "I'd like you to keep it for now, Marjorie, if it's all the same to you," he said. "Probably be best that you give it to the new sheriff, whoever that'll be. I'll let you know when I've told them that you have it. No one knows you have it. You're safe."

I nodded yes, then stopped, and shook my head no. "That's not true," I said.

Hilo leaned into me and examined my face like it was under a microscope. "I told you not to tell anyone."

The sudden change in his tight face and his hard voice startled me and made me feel like a little girl caught in a betrayal. "I showed it to Raymond. My cousin."

Hilo withdrew. It was only a momentary flash of anger. "Right. Hurtibese. The professor," Hilo said. "Raymond Hurtibese. Your cousin. Of course, you would show it to him."

"I'm sorry. I thought he might recognize it. He said another professor had some similar pieces stolen recently. Is this connected to that, Hilo?" It was a question I'd wanted to ask him since I'd talked to

Raymond, but it had seemed as inappropriate as laughter. I hadn't seen him other than when he came to the farm to see to Ardith, the crime scene, and the emotional wreckage.

There was a part of me that was angry with Hilo, especially if the answer was yes and he hadn't told me that I'd had a piece of stolen jewelry in my purse.

"This wasn't from Professor Strand's collection," Hilo said. It was a definitive answer. No argument.

"You're certain?" I couldn't help myself.

"I showed it to him before I brought it to you. He was interested in it, of course, because of his own acquisitions from the original collection, and for field study. But he assured me that the amulet that was left behind at the Knudsens wasn't one stolen from him. He'd never seen it before."

"There's more than one?" I pressed. I felt bad, but I couldn't help myself, even though each word looked to drain Hilo of more energy than he had to start with.

"From what I understand, there were six pieces in the original collection, but they were separated by estate settlements or sold off during years of drought, when the need was great for money, for saving the farm. I'm sure you understand that. Strand has collected them for years. He is distraught that his were stolen, and distraught and deeply upset with the appearance of the new one that was found at the murder scene."

"I went to see him after I left Raymond's, but there was no one home."

"I haven't had any contact with him since I brought it to you," Hilo said. "Other things . . ."

I lowered my head. "Is this amulet one of the original pieces?"

"I don't know, Marjorie. Strand was checking into it for me, too. He was the obvious place to start my investigation. The new sheriff will need to talk to him, and to you, once it all becomes official. I hope you understand."

I nodded. "Of course."

Hilo stepped back and stared down toward the trees, to the hidden river. "I'm sorry," he said.

"For what?"

"For involving you in all of this. I should have never bothered you with it in the first place. Maybe if I hadn't, Ardith would still . . ." Hilo stopped, then looked up at the house. "I'm tired, Marjorie. I just want to get some rest. It looks like I'm going to have to sleep in the truck."

"That's awful," I said.

Hilo forced a smile. "I've been sleeping behind the steering wheel of that truck for years, Marjorie. I guess I should've been paying closer attention to things, that's all."

"This isn't random, is it?"

"No, no, I don't think so. I kind of wish it was. It would make it easier to think that there's nobody from around here that would do such a thing, that a stranger is wandering through town and will move on down the road. But I don't think so. I don't think it's a monster we've never met. We've looked this one in the eye at one time or another. I'm sure of it."

I agreed silently but said nothing. I started to turn away, walk back up to the house, leave Hilo to his grief, what was left of his life, but I stopped. I had one more question that I needed to ask him. "What about Roy?"

That flash of anger I had seen earlier returned with the impact of my question. Only it didn't disappear. It started on Hilo's haggard face and twisted into a mask that was nearly unrecognizable. His chest lurched forward, and if I had been standing close enough it would have knocked me to the ground.

"Roy doesn't have anything to do with this," Hilo growled.

I stepped back and put a broomstick's distance between us. "I'm sorry, Hilo, but I had to ask. Herbert Frakes said . . ."

"I can imagine what Herb said about Roy." Hilo stepped forward with the rage of a father restraining himself against an intransigent child, and pointed his index finger at me. "You leave Roy out of this, you hear me, Marjorie Trumaine. You just leave him alone, goddamn it."

It was a rare cuss word directed my way. Hilo looked like he was about to froth at the mouth. There was nothing more I could think to say. I was shocked by Hilo's reaction. I hadn't expected it.

I clamped my mouth shut, turned, and hurried up the hill toward the Studebaker. I wanted to be as far away from Hilo Jenkins as I could get.

"I'm serious, Marjorie. Leave him be," Hilo yelled from behind me, into the wind, into the coming darkness. "Leave Roy be."

CHAPTER 27

A pair of beady eyes reflected back at me in the darkness as I sped down Hilo's drive. The sudden yellow glow barely caught my attention; an animal alongside the road was not an uncommon night-time sight. There always seemed to be something lurking about at the intersection of light and dark in the summer. The windshield was peppered with splashes of bug parts.

My hands were gripped so tight on the steering wheel that I could hardly feel them. I was numb with an emotion that I couldn't quite define or recall ever experiencing so deeply. It bordered on rage: an unsettled anger, fear, and confusion. I wanted to scream, to pound the dash, lash out, but all I could do instead was swerve and barely miss hitting a shiny-coated female coyote as she bounded across the road inches from the front bumper of the truck.

"Trickster," I whispered aloud, as I watched the wild canine disappear over the berm with a hurried, single leap. "Go away," I said louder, not quite a yell. "Just go away," I added, full-throated, so loud inside the cab of the truck I couldn't hear anything else.

And then there was nothing ahead of me. Nothing but the sharp white light of my headlights cutting into the infinite blackness of night. There was no city glow to pierce the dome of darkness. All there was was me, alone in my truck, so mad I could spit nails.

I straightened the front of the truck from the slight swerve and pressed down on the accelerator. I wanted to be in the comfort of my home as soon as possible.

I just want to be home where I belong, with my Hank.

It was hard to envy Hank in his current condition, blind and bedridden, the world lost to him, but some days I thought he had it far better than anyone else I knew. I would never tell him that I thought that. I'm not sure he'd understand—or ever agree with me. He just wanted to be whole again, or dead. One or the other. There was no in-between for Hank Trumaine.

I wasn't prepared for another coyote to jump in front of the Stude-baker, but one did—in the blink of an eye—an unexpected life fleeing from something or running after something, showing itself in the light. Vulnerable, suddenly afraid, fear in its eyes. I felt a deep kinship with the beast.

Coyotes rarely ran in packs, or even in pairs, especially in mid-summer. A spring sighting like this wouldn't have been so surprising to see: a couple intent on mating, on stalking the night together in search of an easy meal, an easy kill. Maybe they were siblings, hanging on to their youth for as long as they could. I couldn't blame them for that.

Instinct demanded that I swerve again, and I obeyed. This time, the tires slipped out of control on the gravel, and the pickup's bed swung sideways as I slammed on the brakes and overcorrected more aggres-sively than I should have.

This coyote was a big male, as big as Shep or bigger, and he was close enough to hit.

As leery as I was of coyotes, killing a living creature of any kind didn't settle well with me. Especially right now. I fought gravity without the aid of the power steering that came in the newer, fancier, trucks. This task demanded the muscle of a man accustomed to chopping logs and baling hay, not a woman who rolled out delicate potato dough to make lefse or typed indexes on an old Underwood typewriter.

I struggled and slid for another twenty or thirty feet, cringing, waiting for the inevitable thud underneath the truck, but none came. When I finally came to a stop there was no sign of the coyote. It was almost like the animal had never been there at all, had been a figment of my imagination, or had responded to my request to disappear.

If only I had that kind of power, that kind of magic. Hank would be able to see and walk again. I would turn back time. I would save Erik,

Lida, and Ardith from a horrible, unthinkable death—from being murdered in cold blood. It was a silly thought, and I vanquished the idea of supernatural power as quickly as it came. In all of my years on this earth I had never seen an iota of proof that such a thing existed. Goodness was a human invention. So was evil.

I saw nothing in front of me except the dust settling from my slide—earthly glitter, a million tiny stars burning out, going back to sleep, road dust and powdery white limestone falling back to the ground where it belonged. There was nothing behind me but the same darkness I had driven into. My heart beat faster than it should have, and my wrists and shoulders stung from the tension and effort it had taken not to wreck the truck.

The .22 had fallen over to the door, out of reach since the basket of lefse and sausage had been left behind at Hilo's. I reached over for the little Remington, brought the butt back up next to me, then barricaded it to my thigh with my purse.

I squared myself, glad the Studebaker was still running and that I hadn't killed anything in my blind rage and lack of attention to the road. I just wanted to get home as quickly as possible and relieve Peter from his watch over Hank—and be as far away from Hilo Jenkins' house as I could. Tomorrow was going to be a long day for us all. The showing for the Knudsens was in the afternoon and would last well into the evening. Betty Walsh, the girl at the Rexall counter, had said the whole town would turn out, and I fully expected her to be right about that.

I released my foot slowly from the brake, eased the truck forward toward home, and glanced casually into the rearview mirror, hoping to catch sight of the coyote, safe, alive, bouncing off after some kind of trouble or another.

I expected to see nothing, darkness, but I was surprised by a distant pair of headlights growing brighter by the second.

I didn't react for half a second; people came and went all the time. *Maybe it was somebody on their way home from Hilo's.* And then the next thought exploded into the front of my mind and stayed there: *Maybe it's somebody coming for you, Marjorie.*

My throat went dry. I had never felt so alone in my life. I begged the coyotes to come back, but they weren't Shep, they wouldn't protect me—they would wait until I was dead and consider me a feast that they'd had the good fortune to have stumbled upon.

I shoved my sensible-heeled Montgomery Ward's shoe down on the accelerator as hard as I could, wishing the whole time I had boots on, boots with anvils strapped to them so I could make the Studebaker go faster than it ever had.

The tires spun, and the bed fishtailed again, this time with intent, with as much control as I could muscle into the steering wheel.

I glanced up to the rearview mirror again, and the headlights had gained a lot more ground. They were half as far away as they'd been when I'd first spotted them. *Go, go, go* . . . I smacked the steering wheel with the palm of my hand and maintained as much force on the accelerator as I could. It was a good thing that the floorboard wasn't rusted, or my foot would have gone right through it.

The rear tires finally caught and rocketed me down the gravel road. I headed straight for home. My safe place. Where Hank and Peter were waiting for me. Hopefully, a county deputy was at the gate, too. Duke Parsons to the rescue. He had come for me before, when the start of the combine had grabbed our attention.

I didn't know for sure that it was somebody after me. I had thought the same thing coming home from Raymond's, panicked then, and it had turned out to be a false assumption. A green Chevy in a hurry to go somewhere that had blown by me like I was standing still. A lot had happened since then, and I wasn't taking any chances. People drove fast on these roads all the time. Speed limits were more a courtesy than a law. I'd never met a person in my life who'd got a speeding ticket this far out of Dickinson.

The front of the truck was slightly out of alignment, and it shimmied with the constant threat of breaking apart as I sped toward home. I struggled again to hold onto the wheel, and my shoulders ached with foreign pain from the effort. Once more, the lack of maintenance came back to haunt me.

It only took me a couple of seconds to get my bearings. My turn off was three roads up, just past a dead oak that had been struck by lightning years ago. The tree's decay had taken years, encouraged more by the weather than insects. Termites were not a big threat in North Dakota like they were in Africa.

I looked behind me again, and the headlights approached at greater speed, catching up with me even though I had pushed the pickup truck up over seventy miles an hour, its limit.

Hot white light suddenly filled the cab of the truck. Four bright headlights aimed at the back of my head. I could hardly look in the rearview mirror because it was like looking into the sun.

I was hunched forward, urging the truck to go faster. My body was as tense as a matchstick. One wrong moved and I would snap in half. I was sure of it.

I expected the car to go around me, but it didn't. It stayed on my rear bumper and flooded the interior with light, making it nearly impossible to see what was ahead of me.

I was two turns away from my road, but I was starting to rethink my course. *Did I want to lead them to my house?*

And then it rammed me.

Thunder behind lightning. The push was a hard hit, not direct, but on the right corner of the bumper. Along with the shimmy of the front end, the collision at the rear end catapulted the Studebaker into a vulnerable moment of instability. The steering wheel jumped out of my hand, and the truck whirled into a spin.

One of the advantages of living in North Dakota is the experience of driving in difficult situations on a regular basis. I have spun a truck on ice on more than one occasion. It's never fun, there's always panic—but this panic was heightened. I had just been rammed with intention. I had to think that the person who had killed three people that I loved in the last few days was trying to do the same thing to me.

I tried to relax, not overreact, not slam on the brakes. I turned the steering wheel in the same direction as the spin. Luckily there was nothing but open fields on both sides of the road. Then I lifted my foot off the accelerator and downshifted the truck into low gear, all the while trying to keep an eye on the attacking vehicle behind me.

I careened off the road and into the field, leaving the gravel and anything to gain traction on behind me. The truck jumped up and down, and the intensity of the bright headlights grew dimmer, more distant. A quick glance told me that the car had slowed and remained on the road.

The field had been recently cut, and the stubs of wheat stalks were still reasonably stiff. It sounded like I was running over spikes instead of plants intended to provide bread to the world.

I got control of the truck and finally came to a quick stop about twenty-five yards from the road. This time, the Studebaker coughed and died. I immediately tried to start it. I knew I had to get out of there as fast as I could, but the engine ground over and over again, refusing to turn over. Sweat dripped from my forehead, carving canyons in my makeup. My fingers were numb—along with the rest of my body. I had never been so afraid in my life.

I was a sitting duck.

My own headlights cut across a barren field. There was no place to run. I looked over my shoulder, out the back window, and saw the car just sitting there, still running, lights on, patient as a red-tail hawk sitting on top of a telephone pole waiting on a hapless mouse to make a move—a wrong move, any move.

Think, Marjorie, think. And then I looked over at the rifle. "Aim for the head," Hank had said. I had a better idea. I'd aim for the eyes. Just above the headlight. One of them, just to let them know I was armed, that I could hit a target. I wasn't just going to sit there and wait to die. I had to get back to Hank.

I grabbed the rifle, took a breath, and made my way out of the truck, hunkering down alongside the bed to keep myself covered. There I was in a dress and heels, with a rifle, and about to shoot at a car in the darkness of night. Annie Oakley I wasn't, but at that moment, I sure could have used some of her confidence.

My eyes had adjusted to the starry light from the sky. I could see the silhouette of the vehicle, and there was no mistake that it was a car, but I was too far away to see the color, the make. I didn't have that kind of knowledge. The only way I could tell a Ford from a Chevrolet was by what was written on the front of the car. Hank knew every make and model from the time of the horseless carriages to the present. I wished he was with me. He could tell me what I was looking at in pitch dark.

I could hear the constant rotation of the engine as it idled. The droning metallic presence was foreign to the land, unexpected and uninvited.

There was no time to hesitate, to wait. For all I knew, the driver had gotten out the car and was heading my way, a sharp knife in his hand to slit my throat with. I raised the rifle, steadied it on the truck, sighted my target, and pulled the trigger.

The shot echoed in the cool night air like the sudden yip of a hundred coyotes. Then metal crashed into metal, a cold crack, not near as loud, but enough to get the attention of the driver of the car. I'd hit just behind the headlight, but didn't shatter it.

"You're messing with the wrong woman," I said, under my breath.

My strategy worked. The car revved its engine, lurched forward, spun its tires, and tore away like it was running a one-car drag race.

I was tempted to take another shot at the red taillights as they disappeared over the first rise, but I restrained myself. I didn't want to miss and accidently kill someone, the hunted suddenly becoming the hunter. Enough blood had been spilled in the last few days to last a lifetime.

CHAPTER 28

A red flare sizzled at the head of our drive. It glowed on the ground like a star fallen from the sky, struggling to stay alive. My shoulders drooped as I lifted my foot off the accelerator, and started to brake. *Home again. Thank god.*

Duke Parsons stood up out of the brown and tan Ford as I turned in and came to a stop.

"Marjorie," he said with a nod. My window was down, had been since I tore out of the field and hightailed it home, constantly checking behind me for a pair of headlights and listening for a roaring car offering chase. Every fiber of my being was on alert.

I hadn't seen a soul the rest of the way to the house.

"Someone," I gasped. "Someone came after me." I was on the edge of tears, had fought off the bottomless fear I'd felt the best I could, but it was impossible to hold back any longer. I was overwhelmed, more afraid than I had ever been in my life. Any fool could see that I was agitated, about to come unhinged.

Duke stared at me, his always-puffy eyes a little glassy, like he had just stirred from a nap. He still reminded me of a blood-engorged tick with the ability to talk. "You all right, there, Marjorie?" He peered inside, and I could smell mustard and sweet pickles on his breath. He had been eating, not sleeping.

"I left Hilo's, and someone came up on me and rammed into me. Spun me off the road. I nearly rolled the truck, crashed. I could have been killed, Duke."

"Hit you, ya say?"

"Rammed me on purpose is what I said Duke. Came after me. I didn't know what was going to happen."

"What'd ya do?"

"I shot at them." I glanced over to the Remington, then back to Duke. "I took out my varmint rifle and I shot at them. What else was I supposed to do?"

"You probably shouldn't a done that, Marjorie. You coulda killed someone."

"They rammed me, Duke," I said through my teeth. "I just let them know that I wasn't going to wait for them to do anything else. I had to get home to Hank."

Duke Parsons stood back from the truck's window, taking the smell of his dinner with him. He squared his shoulders, pulled the flashlight off of his utility belt, and turned it on. The sudden burst of light caused me to blink and hurt my eyes. When I opened them, the beam of the flashlight was directed to the rear quarter-panel of the truck, away from me. For a moment, I thought he was going to treat me like a criminal. That's the way he looked at me, like I had done something wrong, broken the law.

Duke walked around to the rear bumper, bouncing his head up and down with every thought, and examined it like a doctor seeing a new patient for the first time.

I watched him in the rearview mirror, seething. *What else was I supposed to do? Sit in the field and wait for a killer to come and ask me if I needed help, you idiot?*

"Yup, there's a dent and a scratch all right," Duke said as he turned off the light and walked back to the driver's side window. "Hard to say if it's fresh." He seemed nonchalant.

"What? You think I'm making this up?"

Duke shook his head no. "No, ma'am, not at all. Nothin' that happens these days surprises me. Seems like every day somebody else is comin' up dead around here. Kind of like a plague of locusts has fallen from the sky. Something Biblical has descended on us, if you ask me. People always look for the signs of the end times so they can change their ways, get right with the Lord. Seems to me if you did that every day, you wouldn't have to wait until there was a mad killer on the loose and you was scared to death he was knocking on your door—or bumper in your case."

"I'm sorry? What are you saying?"

"You haven't heard?"

"Heard what, Duke? I haven't heard nothing. I've been over at Hilo's."

"Oh, yeah, right, you have. There's been another one, Marjorie. Sure gonna be a busy few days at the funeral home."

My entire body went cold. "What do you mean *another one*, Duke? Please don't tell me . . ."

He nodded. "Yup. Another murder. Makes four. Can you believe it? Makes a man wonder what set this one off, don't it?"

I gripped the steering wheel as tight as I had when I looked up in the rearview mirror and saw someone coming up on me. The Studebaker's engine idled, but I could smell it getting hot. I glanced down to the gauge on the dash and saw that the temperature was rising. It would only be a matter of minutes before steam starting seeping out from underneath the hood.

"Who?" I asked. "Do they know who was killed?"

Duke nodded yes. I braced myself.

"A professor at the college," he said. "Been dead for a couple of days the way I hear it. House smelled to high heaven," Duke said.

"No," I whispered, looked down to my lap. *Raymond.* I thought about the last time I had talked to Raymond. It could be him. "It wasn't Professor Hurtibese was it?"

Duke shook his head no. "A fella by the name of Strand. Phineas Strand. You know him, Marjorie?"

It was my turn to shake my head no. "That's terrible."

"It is. Same as the rest, too," Duke said. "Throat slit wide open."

The news snapped my head up. "You think it's the same killer?"

"Sure, everybody does, Marjorie. Everybody does."

I let Duke's words settle back to silence, then glanced down at the temperature gauge again. I either needed to turn off the engine or go park the truck. "I need to go see to Hank," I said.

"All right, then. Just lock your doors and windows. Know that I'll be here for you the rest of the night if something comes up."

"I appreciate that, Duke." I eased my foot off the brake and started to roll forward.

"Hey, Marjorie," Duke called out.

I stopped. Looked back. "Yes?"

"Postman came by with a parcel. Hold on, I got it in the car. I got strict orders not to let anyone on your property, not even Wally Howard."

Duke trotted back to the police car, opened the rear door, and pulled out a box big enough to put a pie in. Even in the dark of night, I knew what was inside of it: The properly paginated proofs of Sir Nigel's headhunter book.

The deadline clock had started to click again, and it wouldn't stop until I put the index in the mail, no matter whether there was a tornado or a mad killer on the loose, slitting people's throats as he goes.

Shep started barking as soon as I shut off the engine of the truck. The engine complained, rattled, and groaned, and let out a puff of steam, but I was glad to be home. I didn't feel safe, but I didn't feel alone, either, and that meant something more at the moment than it had a little while ago.

I grabbed up the rifle and made my way to the front door of the house. Shep was on the other side of it, inside, pulling guard duty, watching over the house, Peter, and Hank. It struck me at that moment that we had suddenly all become prisoners in our own homes. We were all like Hank, blind and unable to move. I had tried to understand how he felt, but now I really did, fully, completely. I almost started to cry again, but I steeled myself and pushed inside the house, so happy to see Shep that I didn't shush him one time.

There was a light on in the front room, but no sign of Peter. Shep danced at my feet, barking, both ears up. His bushy tail swished so fast that the black and white transformed into a gray blur. I set down the rifle at the door and sighed, glad to be inside, glad to step behind walls that held books, pictures of my parents, and the lingering smell of lefse.

"All right, that's enough," I said, and Shep, exuberant and happy, understood my tone immediately. Not that it was nuanced, but I wished most people would respond in kind.

I had not quit considering the news that Duke Parsons had given me, though I tried to hold it off, push it away, like I hadn't heard it. I was in no mood to make sense of anything.

I looked to my other hand, felt the weight of the page proofs, stared at the red printing on the top of the brown package: "URGENT!" it said in bold, dramatic writing.

I didn't need to be told that. I knew the delivery of the index was urgent, just as I knew the sun had fallen from the sky and left us all in a cold, unpredictable darkness.

I was tempted to hurl the box out the door, stomp on it, set it on fire, then call Richard Rothstein and give him a piece of my mind. But I wouldn't do that anymore than I would strike a match inside a library. I had made a commitment, I had unknowingly staked my reputation on this index, and if I hoped to continue working in that field with a correspondence course education, I would have to meet that deadline come hell or high water, tornadoes, or a madman on the loose. The repagination wasn't Richard Rothstein's fault. It was just the way it was. Some years, the ground's too wet to plant, and when the time comes every farmer in the county is pushed to get their seed work done before that magic window passes. This was no different, but knowing that didn't make the stress of the deadline any easier.

I sat the box down, and Shep immediately had to investigate it, see if it moved, lived, could be herded. Too bad he couldn't type.

I looked up and Peter appeared in the doorway that led into the bedroom. He stood there, staring at me. It was easy for a light-haired boy to look pale in dim light, but across the room, in the shadows, he looked skeletal, frail. I could hardly see any of his parents' warm features in him at all. It was like all of the life had been sucked out of him, taken by his parents as they'd left this world.

"I was hoping that was you," he said, then leaned back to put the shotgun in its rightful place. It had been at his side, tucked away in the darkness, ready to be hoisted. I hated it that guns had become so prevalent in our lives. Everyone was afraid.

I nodded and stared at him. I heard the regulator clock tick, the wind push at the door, and the roof sigh with a familiar groan as it stood up to the weather. "Are you all right, Peter?"

He looked down to the floor, then back up at me. Peter Knudsen shook his head no, and I swear he looked like a seven-year-old boy who had woken up in the middle of the night from a bad nightmare. "There's been another killing," he whispered.

"Duke told me. A professor in town. I don't think that has anything to do with us," I said. I wasn't sure I believed that, but Peter didn't need to know that that.

He shrugged and stared at me in a way I had never seen before. I shivered and felt like something was wrong. "I need to go," Peter said. "Is that okay?" He started pinching the skin on his wrist quickly.

"Yes, sure."

Peter looked over his shoulder, nodded a good-bye to Hank, then made his way to me, toward the door. I put my hand on his arm to stop him. His skin was clammy, like he was feverish, but he didn't look sick—he looked nervous, like he was about to throw up, stricken.

"You're sure, you're all right?" I asked as warmly as I could. I had a motherly tone that was rare in its use, but Peter had been the most direct and consistent recipient of it.

Peter stopped. His eyes were bloodshot, more tired from the last few days than any unrelenting planting or harvesting stint could have ever made him. He knew the tone.

"Did you know the professor?" I pressed, uncomfortable by the boy's reaction. I felt like I was demanding the truth from a troublesome child, not my sweet Peter. "Did you?"

"Yes, I knew him," Peter said. "I knew that professor. Me and Jaeger did some work for him not too long ago. What's next? What's next now?" He didn't wait for an answer. Peter pulled from my grasp and made his way out the door in more of a hurry to leave my house than I had ever seen before.

I imagined him crying all the way home, a little rabbit lost from its mother for the first time in its life, seeing an owl's wing in every cloud, hearing a coyote's step in every snap of the grass, certain that death was waiting at every turn. And he might have just been right about that. He might have just been right . . .

CHAPTER 29

I watched Hank breathe for a long second before I said anything. His eyes were open, staring blankly at the ceiling, his chest rising up and down steadily, without any struggle. At least he was all right, the same as I had left him. No better, no worse. It was always the "no worse" part of that thought that carried more strength, more worry. The "better" part was a wish, a miracle, a fantasy that would never happen, while the other was a journey into loss that I did not want to consider at that moment. Up until a few days ago, my biggest fear was walking into the bedroom and finding him gone, slipped away on his own without me there to bear witness to his passing, my heart broken, never to be healed again.

I knew it tore Hank up to lie there, not to be in the thick of things. His jaw was set tight, his lips pursed. I was just waiting for him to scream. It wouldn't have been the first time.

"Hilo resigned," I said, standing over Hank, watching his face for a reaction. There was none. He didn't flinch. Even in his withering I recognized the boy I once knew, but even that familiarity was fading, wasting away into a fallow field I feared I would not know.

"He's lost everything then," Hank finally said. There was no edge to his comment, no sadness or judgment, just matter of fact; typical of Hank, even in a weak body and weaker voice.

I nodded. "Everything but the ability to breathe and stand, and I'm not sure how much longer he'll have that. He seemed to be on the verge of collapse."

"Wouldn't want to be Hilo right now." Hank's voice was firm, lucid, the volume low. He licked his lips, and without thinking I picked up the glass of water that always sat near and guided the straw gently to him. He sucked on it like a man who had traversed the desert on the harshest of days.

"You knew about the killing in Dickinson," I said. It wasn't a question.

I pulled the straw away, put the glass back where it belonged, and checked the pitcher. It was half full.

"Duke came in, told me and Peter about an hour ago," Hank said.

"Peter's awfully upset."

"Wouldn't you be?"

"I am."

"Did you know that one?" Hank asked.

"No," I said. "I'm worried about Raymond."

Hank turned his head toward me and flashed a scowl that he reserved for Raymond's name. "He's a stuffy asshole, Marjorie. He does nothing but look down his nose at you. I'm blind and I can see that. Why on earth would you be worried about him?"

A show of Hank's temper had been as rare as a snowy owl sighting in July—or Hilo cussing in front of me. It took a great deal of effort for Hank to physically express any deep emotion, much less speak it. I could count the times he'd cussed in my presence on my right hand since we'd been married. Most of those had been an occasional "shit" or "damn" here or there. He reserved that kind of talk when he was among the men, when they gathered off to themselves, out working in the barn or field, hunting, fishing, and the like. I knew they had their own secret language, their own way of expressing themselves when they thought they were out of earshot of women, but the North Dakota wind was strong. It carried voices farther than most people realized, or cared. Isolation grew to be a comfort. You got used to having no one around, not looking over your shoulder or listening in on your conversations.

"Raymond is family," I said.

"To you," Hank replied, then turned his head away from me so I couldn't see his face.

An old silence settled between us. Hank hated it that Raymond was an academic snob who belittled other people who were not from the same station in life as he was. I had the same issues, but I was accustomed to that tension. It had existed between my father and his sister, Aunt Gilda, Raymond's mother—a constant competition, a one-upmanship about who was smarter, richer, happier. I was so accustomed to the division between Raymond and me in my family that I rarely noticed it, though Raymond never missed an opportunity to remind me that I hadn't finished college and that I was in no way qualified to do the work that I was doing. Imagine, an indexer, educated by the United States Department of Agriculture, not classically schooled in the library sciences at all? I was a joke to Raymond. I knew it, and for the most part I had not cared. Out of sight, out of mind. I was happy to do my work on the farm and not think a wit about Raymond's snobbery.

Hank, on the other hand, had a little Irish in him and was prone to hold a grudge. I stared at the back of his head, and my throat quivered with the words as they rose upward. "He didn't mean to," I whispered.

Hank's face snapped back to me quicker than I'd seen it move since the accident. Fire was blazing in his blind eyes. I knew what he was seeing. I knew the memory, the vision replaying in his mind.

"Yes, he did, and you know it, Marjie. He killed that dog on purpose."

I didn't reply, didn't want to ignite an old argument, an old wound, but it was too late for that. Hank was lost to the past. He was stiff, tense, twisting inside himself the best he could. In my imagination, I saw him fighting to get out of a briar patch. With my eyes, I saw him lying in bed motionless, his eye tooth clamped down on his bottom lip so hard I feared he would draw blood.

Shep, like so many farm dogs, was one of many, a long line of animals brought onto the land to perform a single job, who before long had wormed their way into every aspect of daily life. Including emotional life. It was easy to love a smart dog, a good dog, a dog who knew how to read you better than you could read yourself. It was easy to come to rely on them, to believe they were as invincible as you. And then one day, you found out differently. Dogs were mortal, too, like everything else on the farm, susceptible to pain, illness, accidents, and sudden death.

The knowledge of two things came early to those of us born to the land: Sex and death. A ram jumping a ewe was a common sight growing up—so common that by the time a natural curiosity about sex was supposed to arise, it was already accepted, a known act that seemed as natural and necessary as breathing. If only death were as easy.

Hank had a border collie before we married. The dog was a bit bigger than Shep, and was as wise as any farm dog I'd ever known. Loving, too. Hank's dog was affectionate in a way that broke down a crusty young farmer's walls, made him forget for a time that dogs lived short lives in comparison to humans. The two were inseparable, one always inside the shadow of the other—except, of course, inside the house. Even then, Hank put his foot down, wouldn't let a working animal live inside our four walls.

One day, not long after we were married, Raymond came to visit. He drove his mother out to the farm to deliver a wedding gift, since she'd been on a trip to Rome at the time of our ceremony.

It was an uncomfortable visit from the start. Hank had little tolerance for taking time out of the day to just sit and drink a cup of tea, but he did it for me. He'd always been shy around town folk, but the college people really set him on edge. Hank could read a book well enough, but it was never an exercise he'd sought out for pleasure. He'd rather watch a mushroom rise and bloom out than engage himself in a story.

Raymond and Aunt Gilda were dressed to the nines and not accustomed to soiling their shiny shoes with the mud of a farm. They didn't stay long, and when they went to leave Hank's dog started barking his fool head off. The dog circled Raymond's car, and no matter how hard he tried Hank couldn't call him off. Without regard for the dog, Raymond gunned the engine and drove straight out the drive. He ran over the dog, sent him reeling into the field, and didn't bother to stop.

It broke Hank's heart to see that dog hurt, and it was even harder to watch him hold him in his arms as life slipped away. I learned the depth of Hank's love for months after as he moped around, grieved by the loss. To this day, he couldn't speak the dog's name without tearing up.

Thor. The dog's name was Thor. My mind instantly tried to make a connection between the dog's name and Loki, Balder, and Odin—the Norse mythology described on the amulet. I knew little of the details, but I knew that Thor was Odin's son, and Loki and Odin were blood-brothers. There was a link there. The link of an uncle, but not by blood.

It hadn't occurred to me until that very moment that Raymond had killed Thor a long, long time ago, though it seemed just like yesterday. I was starting to get an uneasy feeling about everything that had happened recently. A feeling that I didn't want to consider possible, but come the light of day, I knew I would have to investigate, whether I wanted to or not.

CHAPTER 30

The night settled in quietly. Hank calmed down, and we both went about the chore of getting ready to end another day. I ignored the box of page proofs and the fact that Duke Parsons was still parked in front of the house, offering as much protection to us as he could. Deep down, I knew if someone really wanted to get inside, to hurt us, they would. Plain and simple. They would. Nothing would stop them. The world had shown me that much in recent days. Safety was just an illusion for us all.

I worried about Peter and Jaeger as I saw to the pigs and chickens. I secured them against predators for the night, with Shep at my heels and the .22 in my possession, always within reach. It was the first time in my life that I was concerned about the location of a gun while I went about my chores.

I was certain, especially knowing that there had been another murder, that I would be more focused in my aim if I had to use the rifle again. I still didn't know if I could shoot to kill a human being, but I was confident that I would shoot to bring a killer to a stop. I'd shoot to maim, at the very least.

I didn't tell Hank about my encounter on the way home from Hilo's. He'd had enough excitement for one day. No use telling him that I'd felt threatened, scared enough to fire a rifle at a car in the dark. He knew I took such a thing seriously. It would only be one more incident to remind him of his inability as a husband to protect me, that he couldn't look out for me, keep me from harm, any more than he could have saved Thor or Ardith from the tragedies that had befallen them.

I had saved a bit of lefse and sausage for our supper, but neither of us could eat much. I think we said two words to each other before the darkness of the night grew deep and impenetrable. Finally, I locked the doors and windows, turned on the fan, and slid into bed next to Hank. He was already fast asleep, or acted like he was.

I was tempted to snuggle up against him, hold him, and pretend that he was holding me, but I couldn't force away the reality of our life, of our current situation.

We both had reason to be unsettled, afraid of what would come next. I had always thought that feeling would go away as an adult, that the unknown would become known, that sadness and pain would become easier to handle, but I was wrong. It grew harder by the day— by the night, to be more honest.

Instead of cuddling, I lay next to Hank, shoulder to shoulder, and stared up at the ceiling, trying to imagine stars and galaxies, but all I could see in my mind was a field of dead, bloody sheep. Silent, and too many to count.

I could only wonder what Lida Knudsen had been thinking about on that last night she went to sleep, the night her life had been taken from her so unmercifully. I could only wonder, because I had no way of knowing, and I knew I never would.

Sleep came in fits and turns. I was used to the window being open, to the caress of the breeze and the comforting sounds that only came alive in the dark; the ubiquitous cricket sawing its legs, a distant owl hooting for its mate, the late train pulling out of Dickinson, the whistle low and sad. Now there was nothing but the whirl of wind generated by a gray metal fan aimed up at the ceiling. I feared Hank would catch a cold if it was pointed directly at the bed. I always feared a cold, pneumonia. It would be the death of him.

Finally, I couldn't take the stuffiness, the rolling thoughts in my head, the forced desire to sleep, to rest, to retreat, to escape. Unable to reach any of it, I got up and made my way quietly to my office.

It was the middle of the night. Shep followed me to the bedroom door, stopped, and lay down, so that he was exactly in the middle of Hank and I. It was a low level of protection, but it came out of instinct, out of love, and that simple act, by our one and only dog, comforted me.

My feet ached from my time in heels. Practice for the coming days, when dress shoes would be required more often than not. I could hardly wear muck boots to a funeral home, but the thought flittered through my mind. Lida wouldn't have minded.

I glanced over at the parcel from New York on my desk, then went straight to the window, and peeked through the curtains. It took a second for my eyes to adjust to the light. The moon was still in its new phase, leaving the sky black and wide, poked with tips of distant silver stars. A thumbnail of light would appear in a few days. The moon would rise and fall in its waxing crescent phase, offering a bit of light to navigate by, but for now, there was nothing. Nothing but the orange glow of Duke Parsons' cigarette against black velvet. I took a little comfort in that, too. At least he was awake, still alive.

I looked over my shoulder and saw that my purse was right where I left it: on my desk next to the box of page proofs. I took another quick look back outside just to make sure everything looked like it was supposed to. Thankfully, it did.

I dug into my purse after my Salems and matches, listening intently as I went. I felt like a teenager sneaking a smoke behind the barn, afraid I was going to be caught by my parents. Hank hated the idea of cigarette smoke inside the house more than he was against the presence of a dog, but there was no way I was stepping out the door in my nightdress. I might wake Hank, or encounter Duke. Either way, it wasn't an option that I wanted to consider. I'd just crack the window and blow smoke out as directly as I could.

It wasn't that I had forgotten that the amulet was stuffed in my purse. I think I had just pushed the possession of it from my mind and didn't want to consider its existence, especially inside my own house. I should have been more insistent with Hilo, shoved it into his hands, but my heart wouldn't allow such an act. I could have no more forced the amulet onto Hilo any more than he would have forced the possession of it on me. I had accepted it, taken on the responsibility and task of finding out what it meant, seeing if I could help find out what had happened to Erik and Lida and why. So far, I had run into dead ends. I no more knew why the killer had left the amulet in Erik's hand than where the moon was hiding in the sky.

I sat the cigarettes down, picked up the amulet, then unwrapped it, keeping the linen over my palm. I didn't want it to touch my skin like it had Erik's.

There was a simple beauty to the amulet that I'd overlooked before. The copper held no patina, showed no age. It was polished, clean, so much so that it glimmered in the dim light of my office. I traced the lightning bolt with my index finger, then over the three runes that rimmed the copper edge.

Each of the runes represented characters—Fenris, the Midgard serpent, and the goddess Hel—but it was the depiction of Thor in the middle of the amulet that captured my attention. I knew the piece of jewelry had nothing to do with Hank's dog, but I couldn't help but connect the two in my mind.

I covered the amulet back up and put it back in my purse, out of my sight, away from my touch. It had felt cold, but warmed quickly like it wanted to be warmer, come alive. My imagination was tempted to outrun rational thought. I knew better. The amulet was nothing more than jewelry, and the marks depicted on it were nothing more than a story. A simple story cast down from the ages that had absolutely nothing to do with the present. Or did they?

I knew Sir Nigel's book was more important, at least to my bank account, to my future and to Hank's, but I had to be alive to see to those tasks. Alive not dead. I had feared for my life out in the dark, on the way back from Hilo's. I was certain that the killer had come for me, was bearing down on me like a hawk swooping after a jackrabbit.

Now that I was home, I knew I had to find him before he found me. Hilo was helpless, and from what I'd seen and heard everyone else around was either unable or too shell-shocked to put two and two together.

Invigorated, I sat down at my desk, put on my reading glasses, pulled out the index I'd started and a pile of cards, and set about my work:

A

amulet
  found in Erik Knudsen's hand.
    See also murder
  Norse mythology. *See also*
    Norse mythology
  purpose of (protection)

Ardith Jenkins
  married to Hilo Jenkins
  mistletoe in hand when
    murdered
  murder #3. *See also* murder
  not housekeeper I thought she
    was
Asgard, gods of

B

Balder
  god of light
  killed by mistletoe
  return to heaven after battle at
    Ragnarök
  second son of Odin. *See also*
    Odin
Betty Walsh (counter girl at the
  Rexall)
Book of Norse Symbols, The, Calla's
  lack of discovery of
Burlene Standish
  gossip (couldn't resist putting in)
  said she heard something
    (what?)
  wife of Red Owl butcher

C

Calla Eltmore
  librarian
  mad because Herbert was at
    Wild Pony
  Carnegie Library
  Calla and Herbert only
    employees
  Norse mythology information
    found at
children of Loki
  Fenris wolf
  Hel, goddess, ruler of realm of
    dead
  Midgard serpent
Curtis Henderson
  new extension agent
  shows up in a green Chevy
  wanted to talk to Hank
  wouldn't talk to me

D

D-Day
Dickinson University
Duke Parsons, deputy sheriff (lacks
  ambition)

E

Erik Knudsen
  amulet found in hand
  did he serve in WW II, age is
    right?
  murder #1

was Hilo's best friend in old
    days
what did he steal? (is it true?)

S

Shep (our border collie)
suspects
    Curtis Henderson?
    Peter and Jaeger?
    Raymond?
    Roy (Lida's cousin)?
    a stranger?

T

Thor (god of thunder, protector of
    mankind)

Thor (Hank's dog), ran over by
    Raymond

W

Walter Hurtibese (uncle by marriage
    to Aunt Gilda). *See also* Raymond
    Hurtibese
Wild Pony (tavern in Dickinson)
World War II
    D-Day
    Erik Knudsen (did he serve, age
        is right?)
    Herbert Frakes
    Hilo Jenkins
    Roy (Lida's cousin)

There was certain criterion that I used for my personal index that I never would have used for an H.P. Howard and Sons index. First off, I indexed everyone by their first name. An academic index would never use that kind of sorting rule, I would have sorted surnames first. I did it this way for myself, for familiarity. I also added in my questions, which most certainly wouldn't be included in an academic text or index, since index entries in a sense were answers to questions in the first place. Nor would personal comments be acceptable. But beyond that I couldn't think of anything that I had missed.

When I looked back over my index, I had more questions than answers, more suspects than most likely were necessary.

I felt bad about including Peter and Jaeger on the suspect list, but I had to. They were there, in the house at the time as far as I knew. I didn't know where they were when Ardith was killed, and Peter had confessed to knowing Professor Strand, so I couldn't rule them out no matter how much I wanted to.

Same with Raymond—I couldn't rule him out. Without regard to how much he annoyed me, I didn't want to believe he could be such a monster, could kill a human being on purpose. I never agreed with Hank that Raymond ran over Thor with intent. It was an accident, though I kept that to myself to keep the peace. I know how much Hank loved that dog.

I didn't know Curtis Henderson or Lida's cousin, Roy, so I guess that made it easier to put them on the list, though I couldn't think of a motive for either one of them, especially the new extension agent. He was only on that list because of his choice in cars—for choosing a green Chevrolet over a black Ford or maroon Chrysler.

My eyes burned, and I was more tired than I realized. It was still dark outside, and I could hear nothing but the whirl of the fan and Hank's easy breathing as he slept.

All I could think to do was lay my head down on the desk. It wasn't the first time I'd slept there, and I hoped it wouldn't be the last.

CHAPTER 31

Summer days in North Dakota can seem exceedingly long, making it easy to take the presence of light for granted and be uncomfortable when the heavy curtain of night finally falls. There are times in the season when dusk is reviled by men working in the field, their bones aching from long hours of toil, their minds weary, and their hearts nearly worn out from all the worry and concern of looking to the sky and then to the ground. Too wet, too dry, never perfect, always fearing a hailstorm, a tornado, or something worse. Just one more minute of light is pleaded for. Other times, darkness is a gift, a reason to stop working, to retreat inside, to rest, even if the rest is short-lived and filled with more worry about the next day's chores. Nightmares and screams were common in my house. Rest was a distant luxury.

I'd slept as soundly as I could with my head on my desk, then woke with a start as the first meadowlark trilled and started to rustle about outside. I was achy, stiff, and felt like I'd planted five hundred acres the day before, but I was glad to be alive, awake, whole in body, but questionable in spirit. I had to pull a strand of hair out of my mouth. It needed cutting. Time for a visit to the beauty parlor for most women, at least town women. I was as comfortable in a beauty parlor as a doctor was inside of a corn silo. I pushed the hair, along with any vanity I might have considered at the moment, out of my way. My concern was public, what people would think, and even though I knew it should have been the least of my worries for the coming day, I couldn't help myself.

Everything looked to be in its place, normal, untouched, as I made my way out of the office to the bedroom, replacing my thoughts about my appearance with my usual concern about Hank.

I girded myself for what I'd find, a habit formed long before the murders started. Even when a known event came straight at you, and you played it over and over again in your mind, you really didn't know how you'd react until said event becomes a reality. I feared Hank's death more than any other.

Shep hadn't moved from his spot in between us. He perked up and swished his tail, happy to see me. I nodded to the dog, certain that he needed let out, grateful that he hadn't found a place inside the house to relieve himself. Hank would've thrown a fit. But that would have to wait.

I stopped cautiously at the door and took stock in the dim morning light. Hank stared at the ceiling, alive, the same as always, waiting for our morning routine to start. It was his habit to wake up before I did. Sometimes, I wondered if he slept at all.

"I'm going with you," he said. His voice was made of steel, a tone that I knew all too well. He might as well have added, "There's no use in arguing with me, Marjie," but he didn't. Really, there was no need, and I knew it.

It wasn't like Hank couldn't be moved, though it was troublesome. For the most part, he didn't want to go anywhere other than where he had to. Hank would only go to the hospital, to see the doctor, and even then he refused to ride in the hearse from McClandon's, which doubled as the county ambulance when the need arose. I would load him, with the help of Jaeger and Peter, in the bed of the truck and take him that way. Which meant the weather would have to cooperate the whole of the ride. If there was a threat of rain, or whatever, it would be a cause for the trip to be cancelled, which most often was just fine with Hank. The doctor could come see him if it was that important. And sometimes he did.

"I talked to Peter yesterday. It's all set up." Hank continued to stare at the ceiling. The steel in his voice cracked, the words sounded rehearsed. He knew what was coming from me.

"Shame on you, Hank Trumaine." I stomped over to our bed, my anger quick, like I'd stepped on a honeybee. Shep cowered out of my way, against the wall. "What were you thinking? Asking those boys to come and see to you on such a day?"

Hank drew in a deep breath, then exhaled slowly, like he was trying to rid himself of all that ailed him. "Those boys are as close to being kin, sons, as we'll ever have, Marjie. I want to be there for them, for you. We got that wheelchair. I'm not dead yet. I'm going with you and that's that. Peter'll be here shortly. Now come on, we got to get things ready."

He was calm as a cucumber, and that made me even madder, but how could I argue with him? "You're something else, Hank. I just don't know what I'm going to do with you sometimes."

He didn't respond. He needed to save his energy. Besides, we'd been married long enough to complete each other's sentences and thoughts. Usually, he would say, "Just cut me up and leave me to the coyotes after it's all said and done," but he passed this time, and I was glad of that. I could barely think of my world without Hank Trumaine in it.

The phone rang just as I slipped on one of my black Montgomery Ward's shoes. I looked up from the opposite side of the bed and waited. I thought about letting it continue to ring, like I was outside seeing to a chore.

"You going to answer that?" Hank asked, annoyed after five or six rings. The sound had shattered the silence of another perfect morning. I'd opened the window to allow the breeze in, the freshness of air moving about. Spending the night with locked windows and doors had been like sleeping in prison.

"Don't want any more bad news," I said, staring out the door, silently willing the phone to stop ringing. It continued just to spite me. I was sure of it.

"Might be the Irish Sweepstakes callin' to tell you that your ship's come in."

"You really need to quit giving out our phone number."

He feigned a smile, and in response I furrowed my brow, shook my head, and got up to answer the phone. Hank'd had his sight long enough, too, to know what the look on my face was.

He was ready to go, lying on top of the bed, uncovered, dressed in his one and only suit, the one I knew I would bury him in. That wasn't hard to imagine on a day like this.

The phone continued to ring. I limped to it with one shoe on and reached it just as the first edge of my nerves was about to fray. "Hello," I snapped.

"Marjorie?" I knew the voice immediately. It was Calla Eltmore.

"Calla, it's good to hear from you." I relaxed as quick as I could, kicked the shoe off, and immediately wished my Salems were close at hand, wished for a moment of normalcy. Our last couple of conversations had been tense, more tense than I could ever remember. I valued Calla's friendship, as well as her professionalism as a librarian, more than I knew. "Is everything all right?"

"Yes, thanks. Look, I wanted to get back with you and apologize. I know you've been going through a lot recently. I was just upset about Herb, that's all. You understand. He doesn't have anyone to look out for him, and well, all of this turmoil has been hard on him. Hard on us all."

"Yes, I think I understand. I'm sorry, too. Is he all right?"

"I think so. He's promised to escort me to the funeral home for the Knudsens' visitation. I was afraid he wouldn't go, but I think he should."

"Good." My shoulders sagged with relief. I wanted to ask why she thought Herbert Frakes should go, but I resisted. She would tell me if she thought it was important. "Maybe we could sneak off for a bit of fresh air," I said with as much lightness as I could muster.

"I'd like that." Calla paused, and the receiver buzzed as the wind bounced the lines between us. "Look, I did some research on Norse headhunters, and it turns out that they engaged in that activity, would take the head of their enemy in defeat as a trophy. Does that help?"

I sighed. I'd nearly forgotten that question and how it related to my own private investigation. I think I was looking for symmetry between the cannibals in Sir Nigel's book and what was happening around me in real life. I honestly didn't think it had anything to do with the murders at all. Hilo had said death had come quick to Erik and Lida. Most likely to Ardith and Professor Strand, too. There was little comfort in that, but I didn't think the killer was after a trophy. To be honest, I didn't know what the killer was after.

"Thanks, Calla. I appreciate your effort." Silence again. Only this time it was prolonged. "Calla?"

"Yes?"

"Is there something else?"

"Yes." It was almost a whisper. "I found out some information about that book you asked me about, too: *The Book of Norse Symbols,* by Larrson. The author's full name is Ithgar Larrson by the way."

It was my turn to say yes. I leaned into the receiver. "Really?"

"Yes," Calla answered, "The university library had one copy, but it was checked out recently."

"Who checked it out? Please tell me it was Raymond Hurtibese."

"No," Calla said, softening the curves of her R's and dropping the volume of her librarian's voice at the same time. "Professor Phineas Strand."

"Oh," I said. My knees shook. "You've heard the latest news then?"

"I have. The professor is dead, has been for a few days."

I nodded. At least that was a secret I didn't have to keep.

"The thing is," Calla continued, "when the library dunned Strand a week ago, he said that he couldn't find it. It was a rare book. The university was mildly concerned but had faith in the professor. I'm sure they're a little more worried about the book now."

"Raymond said his copy was a first edition, valuable" I said. My voice was hollow, and my whole body trembled like it was the middle of winter, even though I tried to make it quit.

"Do you think this means something, Marjorie?"

"I don't know, Calla; I just don't know." Silence again. Shep pushed by me, sat loyally at the front door, and stared straight at the knob, trying to open it on his own with the powers of his exceptional mind.

"I should go, Calla," I said, interrupting the crackles the wind between us caused.

"I'll see you at the visitation, then? Good-bye, Marjorie."

"All right; thanks, Calla." Before I could say my own good-bye, she rang off and hung up. The conversation seemed odd, strained, but familiar and comfortable. Maybe I was being too sensitive to Calla's mood from the conflict we'd had before. I needed her presence at the library. I needed her friendship.

The truth was now that Ardith and Lida were dead, Calla Eltmore was the closest female friend that I had, and even with that I had never felt so alone in my life.

CHAPTER 32

I was about to hang up, but I heard someone breathing on the other end of the line. Truth was, I was listening for it, hoping for it. "Burlene," I whispered, "is that you? Are you there?"

Silence. Breathing; consistent and familiar. Someone *was* there. I was almost certain that it was Burlene. Almost certain, but not one hundred percent. It could have been anyone. Now I was suspicious of everyone, even the wraith on the other end of the line. I knew it to be true, but I couldn't help myself, couldn't find a way to stop my failing lack of trust in every encounter that I faced or participated in.

I was still trembling from the information that Calla had given me. There was no way I couldn't help but wonder if the Larrson book Raymond had cited was the same one that Professor Strand had checked out and then misplaced. But it was in plain sight. On the bookshelf. Raymond had pulled it out from the bookshelf. If it was stolen, wouldn't he have hidden it?

"Burlene, please say something if that's you. I won't be mad, I promise," I whispered into the black plastic mouthpiece.

I looked over my shoulder. Shep was still waiting to be let out. Still no answer. I was getting impatient. "What did you hear, Burlene? What did you hear?"

I didn't even know that it *was* Burlene Standish on the line, but I knew someone was there. The question I just asked had been at the forefront of my mind since the last time Burlene and I had talked, and I had to ask. I had to. Even if it wasn't her. Even if it was the . . .

I gasped at the thought that it might be the killer on the other end of the line. If I had been cold and trembling before, I was frigid now,

about to shatter into a thousand tiny pieces of ice. "Please, Burlene..."
It was a stronger whisper, a demand, a prayer, a plea.

"I heard a scream," Burlene Standish finally answered, her voice
fleeting, shaky.

"It could have been the wind," I said, repeating what Hank had told
me when I'd talked to him about Burlene before.

"It was a scream. I heard her scream." Burlene insisted. And then a
loud click echoed in my ear. The party line went dead—silent, private,
alone, like it should have been all along.

"Burlene!" I yelled, but to no avail. She was gone, sitting on the
other side of the telephone staring at it, I imagined, just like I was: fear-
fully uncertain, afraid to move.

Even in its most basic form, the telephone was a technological
marvel. One like the television that brought the outside world into our
house without regard to emotions, the truth, or what was happening
at that very moment. Sometimes, I thought that Hank and I had been
born in the wrong century.

Shep barked at a car as it pulled onto our land. I was at the front door,
about to check on Hank, ask him again when Jaeger and Peter were
supposed to come by and help load him into the truck. I had the door
half open, expected it to be them, but it wasn't.

The car that had pulled casually past the county police car at the
end of the drive was familiar, unexpected. Just the sight of it shook me
to the bone with a reminder of sudden fear. It was the green Chevy. I
slammed the door shut at the sight of it.

Shep kept barking, which alarmed me further. I marched into the
bedroom, grabbed up the Western Auto Remington, then spun around
to make my way out of the room.

"What is it?" Hank asked.

The tone of his voice stopped me in my tracks. "I don't know," I
said. I looked back at him. He was white, pale in his only suit, which

was loose at the neck, with no tie and a moth hole that I'd failed to see just at the belt loop. "I'll be fine, don't you worry," I said, then headed out of the house with Shep.

I met Curtis Henderson, the new extension agent, on the front stoop with the .22 firmly pasted across my chest and a scowl on my face as hard as the granite blocks that made up the foundation of our house.

Henderson recoiled as shock and surprise registered in his eyes. He gripped his briefcase as tight as he could and focused his attention directly at the Remington in my hand. "Mrs. Trumaine?" he said. His voice cracked. He was a twin to Hank, at least in state of mind and emotion; the plague of fear and uncertainty had infected him, too.

Curtis Henderson still had a boyish face and unruly ironweed hair. The darkness of him stuck out to me, for some reason, even though he was pale with fright. I didn't like him. He frightened me.

"What do you want?" I glared at him, then arched my head to the side, just in time to see Guy Reinhardt ease up out of the police car and look my way.

"I need to speak to Hank, if it's all the same to you, Mrs. Trumaine?" He stuttered on Trumaine. It sounded like he'd said Tru-Tru-Trumaine. I heard a distant train in my memory.

"You can talk to me," I said. "I told you that before. Nothing has changed."

"I'm sorry, it's imperative that I speak with Hank, with Mr. Trumaine."

I shook my head no. "That's not going to happen. Not today. Haven't you been paying attention to what's going on around here?"

"Hard not to notice that, ma'am," Henderson said. It took a concerted effort for the young man to breathe deeply. I bet they didn't teach a class in college that specialized in handling a gun-toting, mad as hell, farmer's wife. "But I still got a job to do," Henderson continued, "and I really need to speak to Mr. Trumaine. It's important, or I wouldn't insist on it. I really wouldn't."

I stared at him, at the sweat beading on his lip. He really was no more than a kid just out of college on some kind of mission that concerned Hank. If it concerned Hank, then it concerned me, no ifs, ands, or buts.

Guy Reinhardt walked our way steadily, making his presence known, but not showing any immediate concern. That in itself allowed me to relax a bit. I was grateful that it was Guy on duty. It gave me confidence, made me feel safe in a way I hadn't felt for a long while.

"You wait right there," I said to Curtis Henderson. "Just stay right where you are."

He nodded and signaled that he would, but a look of curiosity fell across his face, especially when I pushed past him and made my way to his car.

I stopped a couple of inches from the green Chevy, just at the driver's side taillight.

"There a problem here, Marjorie?" Guy asked.

I didn't let my eyes leave the side of the car, and my feet didn't stop moving as I made my way slowly to the headlight. "I was run off the road last night coming back from Hilo's. I told Duke about it, but there was nothing to do since I didn't see the car. But I got a shot off at it. I'm just making sure this wasn't the car."

Guy walked alongside me. I could smell him, fresh and cleanly shaved, splashed with Old Spice aftershave, and dressed in a heavily starched uniform. I tried to ignore him, but it was impossible.

"What do you mean you shot at a car?" he asked, as he came to a sudden stop, put his hands on his hips, and looked at me like he was trying to decide whether to write me a ticket or not.

I had stopped just at the bend of the Chevy's chrome front bumper, just as the silver hunk of metal reached around to the front of the car, where I thought I had aimed in the dark. "They rammed me, tried to wreck me," I said as I craned my neck to look up into his sky-blue eyes. "I wasn't going to sit there and shiver, wait for someone to come for me. I let 'em know that it'd be a mistake to come any closer, to come after me."

Guy sighed, then nodded. "Probably best that you did that, but I wouldn't make a habit out of it, Marjorie."

"No need to worry, Guy. I've had this rifle in my hand more in the last couple of days than I have in the last couple of years. I'd just as soon set it behind the bedroom door and never touch it again. My fingers are more comfortable on typewriter keys, not on a trigger."

I didn't wait for him to say anything else. I made my way to the other side of the car and inspected it as closely as I had the driver's side. When I got to the end of the rear fender, I hadn't seen anything to alarm me. Not a bullet, a scratch, or what might have looked like fresh paint. Unless Curtis Henderson was an expert at body work, it didn't look like this was the car that chased after me, that I'd shot at.

I was only mildly relieved. "Not it," I said as I made my way past Guy Reinhardt.

I'm sure I looked like a crazed moose, dressed in funeral clothes, a .22 clutched in my hand as I made my way back to Curtis Henderson. I didn't care, to be honest.

"Come on," I said, as I passed the extension agent. "Let's go see Hank."

I glanced over my shoulder as I made my way into the house and saw Guy staring at me like it was the first time he'd ever seen me. And he might have been right about that. This was a new side of myself, even to me.

Shep circled around Henderson and barked as the extension agent followed me into the house. To his credit, the new recruit didn't flinch when the border collie nipped at his heels. He wasn't afraid of the farm dog at all.

I was glad to put the Remington back where it belonged. Hank's eyes followed my every move, but he said nothing, just waited. I was sure he had heard most everything through the open windows, and I knew he was tracking the extra set of footsteps with his finely tuned ears—compensation for his blindness that showed itself in the early days after bringing him home from the hospital.

"So," Hank said, "you're Lloyd Gustaffson's replacement?"

Curtis Henderson had stopped at the door. I had cleaned the room of the night's bodily functions, but there was a sterile odor that hung in the room no matter how wide the window was open. I had grown accustomed to the smell of sickness in my house, but judging by the look on Henderson's face, it was much stronger than I thought it was.

"Well, yes, I am, Mr. Trumaine." Henderson stepped forward, and tried to wipe the disgust off his face with a half-hearted smile.

"Call me, Hank."

I stood back, next to the door, and allowed Henderson to approach the side of the bed. He sat his briefcase down and fidgeted with his hands, unsure of what to do with them. One thing was for sure: he had manners, was formal, seemed to have been raised right. It was his natural inclination to want to shake Hank's hand. He stared at it, lying there motionless, then turned to me. I just shook my head no and tried to convey that it was all right with a look, but Henderson didn't seem to understand. I guess he wasn't a mind reader like Lloyd Gustaffson had always seemed to be. Lloyd always seemed to know what we needed before we knew we needed it—like indexing work.

"Sorry, I can't stand up," Hank said. He tried to smile, but it was lost in the discomfort of the moment.

"It's okay," Henderson said.

I let my gaze fall to Hank's face. The tension had not left him; he was as tight as a freshly tuned guitar string.

Henderson looked back at me. "Ma'am?"

"I'm not leaving. I don't care what you have to say. Hank can only do so much now. If Lloyd Gustaffson passed something on to you that concerns this farm, then I'm going to have a say about it, too. I need to know why you're here, Mr. Henderson."

"Marjorie," Hank interjected before the extension agent could say a word.

I knew the tone; it was a directive to leave the business of the farm to the men in the room. The tone was intended to put me in my place, and, after all I had been through in the last few days, I was in no mood to be put there. "No, Hank. I'm sorry, I'm staying to hear what Mr. Henderson has to say, and that's that. Mr. Henderson?"

He looked at me, suddenly sad-eyed. "I hope you'll come to call me Curtis, someday."

"We'll have to see about that, won't we?" I snapped. Hank turned away and cocked his head as far as he could toward the open window.

Henderson sighed, opened the briefcase, and grabbed up an official-looking piece of paper. "I'm sorry to tell you, Hank, that the Air Force is not going to build the new radar station on your land. They have rejected your proposal."

It was like I couldn't process what I had just heard. Along with the missile silos that the Air Force was building, mostly around Fargo and Minot, they also needed radar to track outgoing nuclear bombs. Incoming missiles, too, I supposed. This was a different war than the one that Herbert Frakes and the boys of his generation had fought. I could barely breathe at the revelation. I had never considered a government site on our land. It wouldn't be our land anymore. My house, the only life I had ever known would be changed, gone forever. Anger boiled in the tips of my fingers.

"Hank?"

He turned his head back so that he was staring up at the ceiling, away from my hard, questioning gaze. "It was for you, Marjie. Lloyd and I thought it would be best to get out from underneath the burden of the land. We can't keep up with it. Especially now, without the help of the Knudsen boys. It was all I could do to make sure you'd be all right."

I exhaled deeply as I watched Hank fight off the emotion of loss, of fear, of regret. He didn't have the strength to face the battle. A tear slipped down his cheek and wetted the fresh, white sheet with a brief puddle.

CHAPTER 33

I felt sorry for Curtis Henderson, caught on the edge of more tragedies than he knew how to handle, but I was glad to see him go. A hint of his aftershave—Old Spice, most likely a college graduation gift from his grandfather—lingered after him but didn't last long. One of the pleasures of the constant wind was that it pushed things away quickly—sometimes too fast, other times not fast enough.

I had no time with Hank alone. As the extension agent was leaving, the Knudsens' red International Harvester pulled past the front gate and onto the drive like it had so many times before. An ordinary sight that was forever changed.

I wouldn't have yelled at Hank anyway. Honestly, I didn't know what to say to him at that very moment. It was all too much. I had lost the best parts of him, my two dearest friends, and any feeling of peace and security I might've had, all in a short period of time. I could hardly fathom losing the farm, too, selling it to the government, or otherwise leasing it for an eternity. Just like Hank, I had planned on living on the farm for the rest of my life, dying in our house at a very old age. No matter what happened, I would make do, survive. It was what we did. Or, at least that was what I had always thought and believed—until now.

Regardless of the arrival of the Knudsen boys, I couldn't contain myself. The urge to say my piece was too strong to restrain. I rushed back to the bedroom with words burning on the tip of my tongue. "You had no right, Hank Trumaine. No right, at all."

Hank didn't answer. Didn't flinch, just stared at the ceiling and pretended that he wasn't there. Which might have been the truth of it for all I knew.

A knock came at the door. I waited for an answer from Hank, but none came. "We're not finished with this," I said, then turned to leave. "You just can't . . ." I stopped, conscious of the volume of my voice, of the height of my emotions.

Thunder followed my feet, and Shep opted not to greet the guests; he stayed back, as close to Hank as he was allowed, wagging his tail in short, nervous sweeps. He knew the sound of the red International Truck as well as he knew the sound of Hilo's truck. There was no reason to be alarmed about anything—except my actions, my words.

I opened the door with a hard yank and found myself staring at another sad face.

Distantly, weakly, Hank finally answered—when I was at the very edge of earshot. "Yes, we are," he said.

I heard his words and turned back to the bedroom quickly, riled more than I already was, but unable, or unwilling, to say anything else, to continue the argument in front of one of the Knudsen boys. If they'd ever seen Hank and I cross with each other, it would've been a faint memory. We didn't share our differences with anyone on purpose, and I wasn't going to start now.

Jaeger looked at me, his misshaped face long and dark, reflected by the graying sky overhead. The suit he wore only added to my perception of the heavy cloud that engulfed him. It was a black three-piece outfit that looked a size too small and smelled of mothballs.

Jaeger leaned on the doorjamb, using it to hold himself up. "I came to load up Hank," he said, his words falling, broken before they reached the stoop.

I looked past Jaeger, to the truck, expecting to see Peter making his way toward the house, but my expectations were not met. There was no sign of Peter Knudsen. Instead, a girl sat in the truck, in the middle of the bench seat, next to the steering wheel, like she had been sitting as close to Jaeger as she could.

Jaeger followed my outward gaze. "Betty Walsh," he said. "We got back together last night." Something flickered across his face, and I wasn't sure what that something was until I saw that Jaeger's shirt was buttoned up out of order, his tie thrown around his neck, lipstick smudged on his collar, like someone had tried to wipe it away. There was nothing I could say to him. I didn't blame him for needing comfort of some kind. I just hoped he had been careful—even though careful had probably been the last thing on his mind.

"Hank said he asked Peter to come along," I said, furrowing my brow.

Jaeger nodded. "He had to run a few things into town, to the funeral home. I can handle this. It's the least I can do for you both."

I didn't say anything, just stood there taking in the sky and the sight of Jaeger in the dimming light. The day was off, out of kilter already. I was surrounded by waning light instead of a waxing light. Despair instead of promise. The weather was changing. The string of recent perfect days looked like it was about to break. Clouds had begun to metastasize on the distant horizon, rising tall out of the ground like granite mountains thrust upward from a fiery, angry earth. It was a faraway storm and would either gain speed as it moved east, toward us, or push south, leaving us with nothing but a stronger wind than we had now to deal with. I hadn't listened to the radio to know what to expect for the day. Rain had been the farthest thing from my mind.

"We'll have to prop Hank up in the cab," I said.

Jaeger nodded again, slowly. "Done it before, Miss Marjorie. Hank's no trouble."

"If you say so." I didn't wait for a reply, just spun around and went back inside the house. It was time to go. There was nothing I could do to stop the clock.

I could feel Jaeger's uncertain eyes on the back of my neck, like he didn't know what to say and was surprised by my tone concerning Hank. I guess my ire was the last thing he needed to see, and I felt bad for causing him discomfort, but I was in no mood to explain myself to Jaeger Knudsen, or anyone else for that matter. Hank had left me out of a life-changing decision, and I was put off as much by that as everything else that had happened over the past few days. Maybe more so.

Jaeger secured the wheelchair in the bed of our truck, and Hank was strapped into the front seat tight enough so that he sat up straight as a board. His head was bound with a belt, pinning him in, so it couldn't move from one side to the other willy-nilly. He could just face forward—which was fine by me. I didn't care if he looked at me at all.

He remained quiet on the ride into Dickinson. I didn't push anything; it wasn't the time to sling an arrow into the battle. We had mutually, silently, agreed to a ceasefire, to settle this matter in the privacy of our own home when the time was right. We had other things to do. Sad things.

I looked in the rearview mirror and caught a glimpse of my own pale eyes and makeup too thin to mask the reality of our situation. I had my normal needs stuffed in my purse, along with the index I'd created since the murders started—just in case I needed to add something—and my Salems, of course.

Jaeger followed close behind us—close enough that I could see Betty Walsh nearly sitting in his lap. I wondered how he could drive with her all over him.

I pursed my lips without intention, then sighed as I realized that I was jealous. I was jealous of their youth, of their possibilities, of their future—even under the vile circumstances of the moment, driving to the funeral home to the visitation for both of his dead parents. Jaeger Knudsen and Betty Walsh still had their whole lives in front of them. I couldn't help but envy that.

Beyond Jaeger's truck, I could see the front end of Guy Reinhardt's police car, bringing up the rear of our little caravan. In the end, it had taken both men to get Hank situated in the truck comfortably and safely. Jaeger had been all thumbs.

The moody gray sky followed after Guy. I was still uncertain of what it would unleash, but there was no doubt that the result wasn't going to be butterflies and rainbows. At least not at first. We'd have to go through *something* before that happened. It was just a matter of what that something was.

The parking lot at McClandon's Funeral Home was already full by the time we arrived. Betty Walsh had been right. It looked like the whole town had shown up to see Erik and Lida Knudsen. I barely had enough room to pull the Studebaker up to the canopy that led to the front doors. Luckily, Duke Parsons was there to direct traffic, recognized our truck, and waved me through the throng of onlookers standing about next to their vehicles in small crowds, waiting for something to happen.

"You won't be able to handle the farm, Marjorie," Hank finally said, breaking his vow of silence as I pulled the emergency brake into place. "We are done."

I sighed heavily, looked over at him, at his profile. I barely recognized him. The Hank I knew seemed to be withering away. *Really? Now?* I thought but didn't say. "That's not the point, Hank. You didn't include me in that decision. I have a say. I have a right to be angry about that."

Hank tried to turn his head my way, but the belt across his forehead refused the effort. "It was inevitable. Can't you see that?"

I shook my head no. "It's my house, too, Hank. It will always be my house. I'm not leaving until I have to. You understand that. I know you do." I kept myself from saying anything further, from escalating our disagreement.

A lone raindrop fell on the windshield, and as I looked outward a sea of black umbrellas began to open up; black flowers blooming in unison, like they were celebrating the coming rain instead of warding it off.

"Are you ready for this?" I asked.

"As ready as I'll ever be," Hank said.

McClandon's Funeral Home was an elegant Queen Anne-style house, painted bright yellow and trimmed with pure white shutters. Even in the darkness of night, in the gloom of a storm, or deep in winter, the house glowed with a confident cheerfulness. I'm sure the color choice was made with the full intention to combat the fear and dreariness that existed under the perfectly shingled black roof. No one that I knew of ever looked forward to a visitation or funeral, no matter how beautiful the house was. It held memories of past visits and services, as well as the inevitable that we all had to face. Every mourner from Dickinson shared in the knowledge that they would all end up at McClandon's sooner or later.

I pushed Hank inside, trying my best to adjust to the overwhelming fragrance of a hundred different types of flowers. My mind immediately started organizing lilies, roses, and violets, even though I tried not to. I had never seen so many flowers in my life. Chalices, pots, and vases were stacked full of a myriad of colorful blooms, neatly arranged, organized from floor to ceiling, from the entry way all the way into the main parlor. I had to stop and catch my breath.

"Are you all right?" I leaned down and asked Hank.

"No."

"We can leave," I whispered.

"No," he said again, only firmer, more insistent.

I stood up, and realized that everyone between us and the two oak caskets—parked head to head and thankfully closed—had parted to allow us through.

There had been a murmur on our arrival, and then all of the voices fell silent. The crowd mirrored the flowers; there were too many of them to fit comfortably inside. All I could hear was distant organ music, piped overhead, playing a hymn I knew I should have recognized but didn't.

I looked behind me for Jaeger but didn't see him. He had got lost in the crowd somewhere along the way. I looked ahead of me, back to the caskets, expecting to see Peter standing sentry there, next to them, but he wasn't there either. The two caskets sat there alone, like they were blocking an exit that no one wanted to venture through.

CHAPTER 34

I couldn't remember what Lida Knudsen had been wearing on the last day that I saw her alive, and I was already having trouble hearing her voice inside my head. Three inches of highly polished oak stood between us, preventing me from what I wanted to do most: Give Lida a hug, tell her everything was going to be all right . . . even though I wasn't so sure that it would be.

I knew right then, at that very moment, that I would never see Lida again, and it was all I could do not to break down and howl with grief, scream in pain like I had fallen through black ice—but I held fast and steeled myself with my mother's voice to be strong.

Hank seemed to be unfazed by all of the attention that came his way. We had put a pair of sunglasses on him so folks wouldn't have to see the unsettling gaze that had settled permanently in his eyes. He could nod and talk but kept that to a minimum. Some people touched his shoulder, talked louder to him like he was deaf and perhaps dumb. They all seemed relieved not to be able to look into Hank's eyes. Just like the two caskets, Hank's presence was a not-so-subtle reminder that disabling accidents could happen to anyone, or that death could come calling at any time. Good people were not immune to bad things.

We both put on as comfortable a face as we could as we greeted those who came up to us, but there was a mile between Hank and I, a road that had lost its bridge. I just hoped no one noticed that we needed to take a detour just to touch.

Time slipped away stuffed inside the bowels of the bright yellow Queen Anne house. The weather outside was no longer a worry. But I continually searched the crowd for one face, and I had yet to find it. Peter Knudsen was noticeably absent from the visitation. I had not seen hide nor hair of him since we'd arrived, and I was deeply worried about him.

Hank started to get restless about an hour into the event—that's what it felt like, a grand parade, a showing off of humanity and humility that had no end. I sat next to him, not far from the caskets, just beyond Jaeger, who greeted everyone that came in. The line of mourners snaked out of sight, out of the room, down the hall, and I assumed outside. Some people wore raindrops on their shoulders.

Jaeger noticed Hank's discomfort about the same time that I did. He broke away from the line and made his way to Hank's side. "I need a little break myself, Hank. You need me to take you with me to the men's room?" Jaeger said, quietly.

It was the kind of gesture that I would have expected from the gentler, more attentive, Peter, and as much as it made me proud of Jaeger, it reminded me that something, someone, was missing.

Hank nodded yes.

"You don't mind do you, Miss Marjorie?" Jaeger asked.

"No," I said, "not if Hank doesn't. I could use a bit of fresh air myself."

"If you catch sight of that lughead brother of mine, send him my way, would ya?" Jaeger said to me.

I stood up as he stepped around behind the wheelchair. "I'll do that. Do you have any idea where he might be?"

"I have no idea," Jaeger said, as he started to push Hank toward the hall, "But you can bet on one thing. The next time I see him, he's gonna get the what fors and a foot to his behind for leavin' me here all alone."

As I came out of the women's room, a hand reached out for me and looped inside my arm. The act startled me, but didn't surprise me, considering the circumstances. But I *was* a little surprised when I realized that the hand belonged to Calla Eltmore. Her fingers felt like printed pages against my skin. It was the first bit of comfort I'd had since I'd arrived at McClandon's.

"You look like you need to step outside," she said. Her face was void of any emotion, and her voice was a blank slate. I didn't know if it was an invitation to share a familiar moment, a secret cigarette, or not. I hoped so.

"That would be nice," I said.

"Good," Calla said, pulling me away from the parlor that held the two caskets.

Even more vases of flowers lined the hallway that led to the back door. I was desperate to escape the thick fragrance—it was worse than being in a room full of women wearing Chanel No. 5, but I was worried about Hank. He'd never been alone in Jaeger's care before.

We exited the back door of the funeral home, and I found myself fully protected from a steady downpour of rain by a canopy similar to the one out front. It was like standing under a giant white umbrella that smelled faintly of bleach and flowers. The aroma of blooms seemed to seep through to the exterior of the building.

Two men were standing up against the wall of the house, both smoking cigarettes. One I recognized, was glad to see—Herbert Frakes—but the other, I had never seen before, even though he looked distantly familiar. As glad as I was to be free of the inside of the funeral home, I suddenly had the feeling that I'd been hornswoggled.

I cast a questioning glance to Calla. She sighed. "This is Roy Agard. Lida's cousin. I thought you should meet in private the first time."

I looked back to the unknown man, took him in as completely as I could before I said a word. A rare moment of reflection before my mouth got ahead of me. The surroundings had subdued my mood. All that I knew about Roy was what I had heard, and I was prone to believe that he was a lowlife thief.

Roy Agard kind of looked like Lida, in an odd, sepia-toned picture kind of way. His face was off center, a little like Jaeger's, and he had a similar dark look about him. He was dressed in decent beige slacks and a clean and ironed white Oxford shirt, unbuttoned at the neck, without a tie. His sleeves were rolled up to the elbows, exposing a faded blue tattoo of a ship's anchor on his right forearm. He didn't look like a thief to me. But what did I know? I couldn't ever recall meeting one before.

I instinctively stuck out my hand to shake, and Roy Agard seemed surprised by the gesture but returned it in kind. He had a gentle, confident handshake, and a surprised look on his face that I'd seen before when offering a firm, nice-to-meet-you, grip.

"I'm sorry for your loss," I said to Roy as sincerely as I could. Out of the corner of my eye, I watched Calla dig into her purse for her cigarettes.

"Thank you," he said, staring me in the eye. "I've heard a lot about you."

"Really?" I said. Calla offered me a Salem, and I took it without hesitation.

Roy Agard nodded. "I have to say, I've never met an indexer before."

I flashed a smile as he dug into his pocket, produced a matchbook, struck a match, and offered me a light, all in a practiced, gentlemanly motion. I liked him, even though my sensibility flickered deep in my bones and told me not to. *If Lida didn't trust him, I shouldn't either.*

"I don't imagine you have," I said, after I exhaled the first draw on the cigarette. "Indexers are a rare breed, especially in North Dakota. We winter here."

"It's always winter here," Roy said.

"Which is why I never leave. I like the quiet." I was trying to relax, but it was difficult. Herbert Frakes stood back against the wall silent, staying dry. He never took his eyes off me.

Herbert had on a suit that looked like it had just come off the Salvation Army rack, but it may have been the only one he owned, never having much cause for wearing it.

"Lida's maiden name was Agard?" I asked.

Roy shook his head no. "My mother was her mother's sister."

"Oh," I said, and just stared at the man. Calla had edged over by Herbert, and the two stood there like an old married couple, watching

Roy and I like they expected something to happen, fertilizing my initial feeling of being dragged outside for a *reason*. But the mechanics of my mind overtook that feeling and quickly pushed it away. Curiosity veered toward the familiar, a recognition of similarity and patterns. Agard was precariously close to Asgard. Odin and Frigg were rulers of Asgard. Loki hated the gods of Asgard. Hated them enough to kill Balder. It was an intriguing coincidence. One that was hard to overlook.

A little knowledge was a dangerous thing. I had dipped into several pericopes of Norse mythology—not nearly enough to see a complete picture, but I had enough extracts to digest a bit of foundational knowledge. Agard and Asgard were too close not to ring a bell.

I sighed loudly as I realized that Roy Agard was staring at me anxiously. He suddenly seemed nervous or frustrated, and I matched him in that regard. I had to push away my suspicions of the myth being connected to the murders. It was entirely possible that I was confusing one story with another and they had absolutely nothing to do with each other. Or they had everything to do with each other . . .

"This is difficult for me," Roy said. "I had hoped that Lida and I would be able to clear the air, but that is impossible now."

"I'm sorry; I don't understand." I took a long drag off the Salem, turned my mouth away from him as I waited, and exhaled the smoke from deep within my lungs.

It was his turn to sigh. Roy relaxed, let his shoulders sag, and I worried that he was about to fall over, but he righted himself almost immediately, an expert sailor temporarily thrown off course, pulling in the jib at just the right moment. I was intrigued by his tattoo.

"If a man is lucky in his life, Mrs. Trumaine, he'll grow old and learn from his many mistakes. There are things in my life that I have done, that I'm not proud of, but the past cannot be changed. You knew that Herbert, Hilo, Erik, and I went to war together? Signed up together down at the courthouse the day after Pearl Harbor?"

I shook my head no. I knew that Herbert and Roy had served together, and that was Hilo was in the war, but I didn't know where or what he did. He didn't talk about it. I hadn't been sure about Erik, even though it made sense that they went off together, considering time and circumstance.

"We were all scared to death," Roy continued, "but none of us would admit it out loud. Anyway, they had a sending off party for us all out at Lida's. Her and Erik were tight as glue even then, but that was before they were married. Things got slow, I went wandering, and I came across my aunt's collection of keepsakes that she'd brought over from the old country. And I . . ." He hesitated, looked to the ceiling of the canopy, then to the ground, and then to me. "And I took one. I took one."

"One what?" I asked, even though I was pretty sure I knew.

"A medallion, an old copper thing that I heard my mother say was for protection. I was scared. I wanted protected."

I sighed. "I know," I whispered. "Peter told me, said you'd taken something but wouldn't say what."

"I'm sure he would know. Lida hated me for it. When the thing came up missing, I blamed it on Erik. Her mother never trusted him after that, even after we all came back. *We all came back*—whole, at least physically. I always believed it was that thing that saved us." Roy glanced back at Herbert, then to the canopy as the rain started to come down harder. "I tried to make things right, but Lida and Erik would have none of it. I was shunned, forbidden to step foot on their property or to speak to their children. In the end," Roy said, with a quiver in his voice and a burgeoning waterfall under both eyes, "I gave it to Hilo. He said he'd return it, make sure Erik got it back since they were still on good terms."

I heard Hilo's voice inside of my head. *"This was in Erik's right hand. I was hoping you could tell me what it means."* And my whole body went limp. It felt like all of my blood had rushed to my toes. "When was this?" I asked in a cracked voice.

"Years ago. I moved to Minneapolis not long after. I tried over the years to settle this, but Lida wouldn't hear of it. She was stubborn that way. I guess I didn't try hard enough." He looked to the ground, the defeat old and tired.

My mind was a conflict of ideas, of possibilities, and of sad things that I hadn't even considered—but one thing kept rising above the rest. "Have you seen Peter since you've been back?" I asked Roy.

He shook his head no. "I wish I had," he said, sadly.

Calla stepped forward, away from Herbert, and dropped her Salem to the ground. "I saw him this morning," she said.

"Where?" I demanded.

"Leaving here. It looked like he was heading toward the college," Calla said. "I thought it was odd, all things considered. I thought he should have headed back toward home."

I looked toward the college and thought of one person I knew who I could link with the amulet, with the knowledge of what was going on, who was on my suspect list in the index that I had created, and a shiver shot straight up my back.

"I think Peter might be in trouble," I said. "I just hope I'm not too late in figuring that out. I just hope I'm not too late."

CHAPTER 35

Calla agreed to look after Hank, and without any hesitation at all
I ran out from underneath the canopy into the pouring rain. It
was the kind of downpour that we usually saw early in the spring, long
and drawn out, the grayness like a suffocating blanket pulled all around
you, threatening to wash all of the nutrients out of the soil, a blessing
that quickly turned into a curse.

I was quickly reminded that I had on heels and slick-soled shoes,
instead of my plastic muck boots, as I tried to flee, to get to where I was
going. I nearly fell as I tore around the corner of McClandon's. Luckily,
I was close enough to the yellow wall and bounced off of it with enough
force to restore my balance. Optimism kept me vertical.

My hair quickly became an Aqua Net helmet, and my makeup was
peppered with the pushing rain, streaking it, washing away my feeble
attempt to look presentable for the visitation. I didn't care about anything other than finding Peter Knudsen.

I made my way to the front of the funeral home, shocked to see the
line of mourners had not diminished, but grown, just like the amount
of cars stuffed into the parking lot and beyond. Black umbrellas and
vehicles overflowed into the street for as far as I could see. But I was
only looking for one thing, for one person, and it didn't take long to
find him.

Guy Reinhardt stood taller than everyone else, directing traffic
with a flashlight that bore a tapered orange cone on the end of it.
He stood guard at the funeral home's entrance just like he had protected the gate at our house. It was hard to miss him in his all-weather
gear; Guy was wearing a bright yellow slicker, and his Mountie hat was

covered in the same kind of plastic. He looked like a single blooming flower in a field soaked with black and gray tears.

I rushed to him, avoiding the puddles the best I could, holding my purse over my head with one hand, and trapping my skirt to keep it from flying up with the other.

Guy must have heard me coming, because he turned around when I was about ten yards from him. He stood stoic, as a curious expression washed across his face. "Marjorie?" he said, arching an eyebrow.

I stopped before him, stared at his chest, and tried to catch my breath so I could speak. I kept my purse over my head, but it had failed in the effort to keep me dry and protected. I was soaked to the bone, my best black dress glued to my body.

"You're the last person I expected to see out here," Guy said. "It's rainin' cats and dogs, don't you know?"

"It's Peter," I blurted out. "I think he's in trouble."

A car slowed just as the last of my words tumbled out of my mouth, a long Lincoln Continental the color of blood, the engine quiet, like a miracle machine of some kind. An unknown man rolled down the window and shouted to Guy, "Lot full?"

Guy ignored the man, looked down to me. "What'd you say, Marjorie?"

"I think Peter Knudsen is in trouble. Serious trouble. Nobody's seen him since this morning, and he was heading toward the college at that, not toward home. He's in trouble; I know it."

Guy Reinhardt sighed, then looked away from me, back toward the bright yellow Queen Anne house. The impatient man in the car revved his engine, and Guy snapped his head back to the Lincoln. "Move on, mister, lot's full!" he yelled, motioning the bright orange cone away from him.

The man started to protest, but the look on Guy's face must have been severe enough to stop him. He rolled up the window and drove off in a huff.

"You best go talk to the sheriff," Guy said to me.

"Hilo's here?"

Guy shook his head. "No, I expect to see Hilo later, sometime today. You best go talk to Duke Parsons. He's the acting sheriff now. Will most likely be the one they pick after things settle down here."

The rain had not ceased. Lines of water dropped between us, a curtain that couldn't be crossed. I was glad of that. I could hear the hurt and disappointment in Guy's voice as it fell to the ground with the rain. "I'm sorry."

"It's all right," he said. But it clearly wasn't. Guy Reinhardt looked up questioningly to the sky for a long second, then back to me. "You really think Peter's in trouble?"

I nodded. "I do. I really do. I think he knows more about what's going on than he's let on. I think he might be in real trouble. If we don't go now, it might be too late." I couldn't say that I wanted it to be Guy to go with me, that I had more confidence in him than I had in Duke Parsons. I most likely didn't have to. A light flashed in Guy's forlorn eyes; an opportunity taken that might change things, an open lane on the basketball court that suggested he still had a shot that he could make.

"All right then, I suppose we best look into it. If it was anybody else, Marjorie, I don't know . . ." he said, shaking his head.

"I know, I know. We need to hurry. I'm afraid we're too late the way it is."

"Come on." Guy reached out, touched the back of my shoulder gently, and directed me toward his police car. "Where are we going, Marjorie?"

"To my cousin Raymond's. I'll show you the way."

The inside of the Ford was warm and dry, but I was sopping wet—water quickly filled the plastic floor mat underneath my feet. Guy had taken off his slicker and thrown it in the backseat before climbing in behind the steering wheel. He glanced at me, must of seen a quick shiver, and turned the defrost on as high as it would go. The windows fogged up right away. He wiped the windshield with a dry handkerchief, but it didn't do any good, the moisture returned as quickly as it had vanished.

"We're gonna have to sit here for a minute," Guy said. "I can't see to drive."

"That's all right."

"I don't have a towel."

I shrugged, wiped the rain off my shoulders and dress the best I could. The police radio sat silent, turned off. All I could hear was the pelting rain trying to penetrate the roof of the Ford.

"Why do you think your cousin's caught up in all of this?" Guy asked, as warm air blew out of the vents toward us, drawing moisture away from the windshield.

"I'm not sure. It's just a gut feeling. Raymond's always been a collector. He had a rare book that might've been in Professor Strand's possession before he died, and Peter mentioned that he'd done work for Strand. Maybe he knew Raymond, too. The boy seemed awful upset when he learned the professor had been killed."

"Wouldn't you be if you were in his shoes? His parents being killed like they were?" Guy asked.

"I would be, but he was more upset than normal. Peter is a sweet boy. At least, I've always known him to be. I'm not sure I know anything anymore. But what if Peter was like a relative of his who had made a mistake at a young age, took something for a reason he thought was a good one, but got caught up in something that was out of his league?"

Guy shrugged. "I don't know, Marjorie."

"Look," I said, "I know this won't make much sense to you—I'm not sure it does to me—but I think the amulet that was found in Erik's hand was part of a bigger set and somebody wanted the complete set, the whole collection, because it was worth more. For whatever the reason, Peter might have been tricked into taking it, or letting someone know that it existed, and they were trying to get it—get it anyway they could. Raymond is the most likely person I know who could be Loki."

"What? Who?"

"It doesn't matter. It would take too long to explain. I might be wrong. Honestly, I might be. I'll know when I see what kind of car is in Raymond's garage. I don't know why I didn't think of that before now. I guess when Calla told me that was the direction Peter was heading in, all of the patterns combined, and they all pointed to Raymond. He killed Thor a long time ago. I didn't want to see that then, but I do now. I'm sure he did it on purpose."

"Thor?" Guy asked.

"Hank's dog. He ran over Hank's dog on purpose."

"Oh."

"I'll be embarrassed if I'm wrong, but if I'm right . . . well, we have to find out. We have to find Peter Knudsen. Every answer I come up with says that we should check Raymond's house first."

"What if he's not there?"

"I don't know, Guy. We just have to find him."

The windshield cleared enough for Guy to see, and he put the Ford in gear and looked at me like he was seeing me for the first time but was confused by what he was seeing and hearing.

"Head to the Student Union. Raymond lives across the street," I said, not taking my eyes off of Guy, offering him the directions I was sure he was looking for.

Guy nodded, glanced to the switch on the dash marked SIREN, then to me. "I think I'll leave that off for now, aye?"

"Probably a good idea," I said.

Guy coasted the police car to a stop kitty-corner from the walk that led up to the cottage. "You should probably wait here, Marjorie."

Like hell I will, I wanted to say, but didn't. I knew he was right. I should probably wait in the car. I had no weapon with me other than a pack of cigarettes and an incomplete index stuffed in my purse. The Western Auto Remington was at home, behind the bedroom door, where it belonged.

Guy shifted restlessly in the seat. "Hank would never forgive me if I let anything happen to you, Marjorie."

"He holds a grudge," I said, staring at Raymond's cottage through the rain. We parked even with a big oak tree. It hid us for the most part.

The curtains were open. A Tiffany lamp burned warmly in the front window of the cottage. Across the street, at the Student Union building, people came and went like normal, some with umbrellas, most without, hurrying to dodge the weather.

"We all have our grudges," Guy offered, pulling my attention back to him. He glanced away from me quickly and looked down to his barren ring finger. The impression of a gold band was still there, like a scar that would never go away. Then he looked up, his jaw set hard, his eyes instantly scanning the landscape in front of him, calculating, judging, speculating, planning. I had seen the same look in Hank's eyes just as he set out on a deer hunt. The smell inside the car changed subtly—musky, prehistoric, alive. I had to look away from him. My breath steamed up the window all over again.

"I'm not staying here alone," I finally said.

Guy glanced back to the police radio. It was still off.

I shook my head no. "We don't have time for anyone else to come, for backup. I'm going with you." Hank's voice echoed in my mind when he told me he was going to the visitation. I still didn't think it was good idea. He would be furious with me for not telling him where I was going, what I was up to. But Peter's life was more important.

Guy studied me, recognized my determination, shook his head with frustration, and sighed. "You're something else, Marjorie Trumaine. Just something else. I've never met anybody quite like you."

"You're not the first person to tell me that today, Guy," I said, smiling secretly as I reached for the door handle, pulled it open, and stepped back out into the pouring rain. "I think we should check the garage first," I offered over my shoulder.

Guy Reinhardt acted like he hadn't heard a word I said as he exited the police car, his right hand slipping to the .38 on his hip.

CHAPTER 36

The overhead garage door was locked up tighter than a parent's closet at Christmas time, but that didn't deter Guy. A side-entry door was hidden behind two well-manicured arborvitaes.

I followed after Guy, staying in his shadow. He had his gun out of the holster, barrel pointed to the sky. He jiggled the doorknob with his free hand. It was locked, too.

Instinctively, I searched the ground, spied a rock underneath the nearest shrub, and picked it up. A gold key sat pressed into the soft earth, perfect and dry as the day it had been put there. A darkling beetle scurried away, annoyed by the disruption.

I handed the key to Guy, who had a why-am-I-not-surprised look on his face. He took it, stared me directly in the eye, and said, "Wait until I tell you it's okay to come in." It was his best cop voice. I had no choice but to nod, but if this were a kid's game, I would have crossed my fingers behind my back.

It was no game. Seeing Ardith Jenkins, collapsed and murdered behind the first barn had convinced me that the stakes were high long before today.

Guy pushed inside the garage as stealthily and quietly as he could. A dim, bare light flipped on in the center of the room. He stopped just inside the door and blocked my view—but not all of it. I could see the taillight of a car clear enough to make out the color and model. The sight of it took my breath away.

It was the car that I feared it would be, a green Chevrolet, exactly like the one that had stalked me, then zipped by me on my way back home from town—on the way back from Raymond's, where I stood right now. My knees shook. A gunshot hole behind the driver's-side headlight would confirm that my suspicion of my cousin was true. I was sad that I was right.

Guy Reinhardt had not moved. He stood still, unmoving, like he was afraid to go any farther. "Marjorie," he whispered.

My knees still wobbled. "Yes?" I eased into the garage, accosted by all of the odd, expected storage smells: oil, gas, moisture, and mold, old things long forgotten, like a mouse had died, decomposed. I was close enough to Guy's back to touch him, but I didn't.

"I really think it'd be best if you'd go back to the car right now."

"Why?"

Guy turned to me, preparing to be more forceful with an order, but I glanced around him, saw what had stopped him, and I gasped, threw my hand to my mouth to prevent a scream from coming out of it. A high-pitched aria overflowed through my fingers.

I clamped my lips together, swallowed the scream the best I could, and shut my eyes so tight that there was only darkness, the back of my eyelids. No matter how hard I tried, I couldn't make what I had just seen go away.

A man sat in the front seat of the Chevy, slumped over the steering wheel. His skin was pale white, his eyes wide open. Blood had dried over his chin. July flies peppered the overhead light, then went back for him, revitalized, in squadrons and haste, taking advantage of a new found host. Our presence didn't seem to concern or deter them at all.

It wasn't Peter Knudsen like I'd thought it might be, had feared it would be.

The man behind the steering wheel was Raymond. My cousin, Raymond Hurtibese, and there was no question that he was dead, had been dead for a little while, but not too long. The smell of death hadn't overtaken the normal smells—it was distant, small like that mouse I had thought about seconds before.

Raymond had been taken from this world in the same way as Erik and Lida Knudsen, Ardith Jenkins, and Professor Phineas Strand. Surprised from behind, a sharp knife to the throat, a sudden, seamless slit from one side to the other, an open lapped smile. Quick, fast, and pain-less—I hoped his death, their deaths, had been painless.

Tears burst out of my eyes, forced them open, as I fell forward into Guy's waiting arms. I buried my face in his chest, stricken, afraid, and ashamed. I had thought the worst of Raymond, and I had been *wrong*. Woefully, completely, horribly wrong. I sobbed deeper, more pitifully than I ever had. I wasn't sure that I would ever be able to forgive myself.

"Shhh . . ." Guy offered.

I felt even worse because I found comfort in his embrace. I had longed to feel a pair of strong arms around me in the past few days. I wanted to be held, protected, told that this nightmare would end, that everything would be all right, even though I knew better. Every day brought something worse, more horrible, to life.

It was like I was betraying Hank, but I couldn't pull myself away from Guy. I cried harder, so hard that I didn't hear anything around me. Guy, either. We were lost in a moment.

At first, I thought it was thunder, a loud clap beyond my ears. I thought the rain had stirred up an angry storm overhead. But the sound didn't come from the sky. It came from behind me.

The door slammed shut, and the explosion of sound reverberated inside the small garage, echoed like the door of a tomb closing for the final time—infinite, eternal.

Guy gasped, drew in a deep breath, flinched, then opened his mouth like he was about to say something. But no words came out. I saw fear in his eyes, felt him tense up.

The next sound I heard was a rush of wind, like a tornado spiraling toward me. Only it wasn't a tornado. It was a piece of wood. A straight piece of wood, a two-by-four, aimed directly at Guy Reinhardt's head.

There is no other sound like a hard, fast-moving object smashing into bone and flesh, and I knew that it was something that I would never forget—if I lived to tell about what happened. It was a profane slap, kin to my scream and the slam of the door. Unexpected and still reverberating inside the garage.

Guy's head was an easy target, so much more so than mine. He toppled to the side, was torn instantly away from our embrace by the surprise attack, by the force of physics: energy plus matter equals sudden, intense pain. He fell to the cement floor with a thud, bounced so hard that it forced the .38 out of his hand.

The handgun skidded to the opposite side of the garage, the forward motion stopped by an interior wall full of garden tools. A rake rattled, a tooth tinkled after the gun, and Guy's blood sprayed the rear passenger window of the green Chevy. It was red rain, and I was trapped inside a storm that had obviously been brewing for a very long time.

CHAPTER 37

I blinked my eyes, got my breath, my balance, focused on the man who had slammed the door. "Hilo," I said. "What are you doing?" I was relieved, hoped he had made a mistake, thought, perhaps that Guy was the killer, attacking me. *Hilo had come to save me.* My shoulders relaxed.

Hilo stood there, barricading the door, like the sheriff that he was, holding the two-by-four with purpose, his face blank, staring at me as if I were a gang of strikebreakers, and he was the lone lawman sent to control them, to hold them—me—at bay. I was confused. He didn't look like Hilo. At least the Hilo I had always known. His well-worn uniform was gone, replaced by stiff blue jeans and a thin red and white short-sleeved shirt. His hair was trimmed shorter than I'd ever seen it before. He looked like he was going to a picnic, not a visitation for two dear friends.

"You best just stay right where you are, Marjorie," Hilo said.

"What have you done? Guy is here to help, to find . . ." And then I stopped, grabbed my mouth again, and started shaking my head no. *No. It can't be you. Not you, Hilo. Not you.*

"I was gonna come and see you in a little while, Marjorie," Hilo said. "I guess you saved me the trouble."

"No," I whispered, unable to contain myself.

"You've been a great help."

"Why?" I checked out of the periphery of my vision hoping that Guy was okay, that he was moving, breathing, but he hadn't stirred. His body was as lifeless as Raymond's.

"Now, don't go gettin' any funny ideas, Marjorie." Hilo let the two-by-four slip from his grasp. It bounced off the floor in front of him, and he scooted it to the side with his boot. When I looked back to him, a knife had appeared in his right hand, like magic, out of nowhere. The long, slender blade glinted in the dim light, and I recognized the kind of knife that it was right away: a fillet knife, thin and sharp as a razor.

"It's you," I said. "You're Loki."

Hilo shrugged, didn't respond, but I knew, now that I thought about it, processed what I was seeing. He was a Hilo I barely recognized. I had to dig back into my memory, my research, my index entries, for the keyword *Loki* to access the text, the truth of what I was seeing. *Loki tricked Frigg by wearing a disguise, and asked Frigg directly what could harm Balder—and she told him. She told him, but she didn't know it was Loki that she was speaking to.*

Hilo's disguise was his uniform. He had tricked me into giving him the information he needed.

"Who knows you're here?" Hilo demanded, holding fast in front of the door, the knife gripped tight.

"No one. Once I thought Peter might be here, might be in trouble, I grabbed Guy, and we came straight here." Which was partially the truth. When Calla had agreed to watch after Hank, I told her where we were going, and if she didn't hear back from me in a half an hour, to send help.

"You just left Hank behind?" Hilo said.

"I had no choice," I said.

"Of course you didn't. Looks to me like you stole away to have some time with Guy."

"That's not it, and you know it, Hilo."

Silence settled between us. The rain continued to come down outside. Flies bounced off the light. And blood flowed like a river out of the corner of Guy Reinhardt's mouth.

"Why, Hilo? Why have you done this?"

"I'm not done," he said.

A shiver went up my spine. He meant to kill me, too. He had always meant to kill me and had just said so. *I was gonna come and see you in a little while.* I had to keep him talking—or figure out how to overpower him. I didn't have the Western Auto Remington or Shep to protect me now. He was bigger, stronger, wiser at the ways of wrestling a man to the ground than I was. I had no chance against him, not physically.

"You have something for me. The amulet," Hilo said. "Do you have it, or did you leave it somewhere? Don't lie to me, Marjorie. I've known you long enough to tell when you're holding something back."

He'd believed me when I told him no one knew I was here. He didn't know me that well. "That's what this is all about? The amulets?" I said. "Why'd you bring it to me? Why'd you give it to *me*, Hilo?"

He sighed and shook his head. "I knew you would lead me to the last one. And you did." Hilo nodded at the car, at Raymond. *I gave him the information he needed, just like Frigg.*

I lowered my head. "He still had the one that Aunt Gilda had didn't he?" I whispered in recognition. Raymond had lied to me, said he'd sold all of that costume jewelry, but that wasn't the truth at all. He still had the amulet, and he knew what he had—just like the first edition of the Larsson book. Raymond knew value, worth, when he saw it. Aunt Gilda had taught him that—and it had killed him.

Hilo nodded yes. "With the professor's collection, and the one your cousin had, I finally had the full set. Do you realize how much they're all worth together, Marjorie? Those amulets are museum quality. No one's seen anything like them in years. Not all together. They're my ticket out of here, out of this godforsaken place."

I wanted to throw my purse at Hilo. "You killed Ardith for money! What do you need that kind of money for?" I'd raised my voice, showed my anger more than I'd intended, but I couldn't help it.

"Watch yourself, Marjorie." Hilo raised the knife, twisted his face, stung by the accusation, the truth. "You have no idea how difficult it was living with that woman all these years. Lazy as a sloth . . . She'd ramble on and on. My god, she never shut up. Never. But I took care of that. I killed Ardith so someone else would get the blame."

"Peter," I said.

"My little insurance policy. You can thank him for setting this whole thing in motion. He first sold your cousin a book he'd lifted from Strand."

"And then he stole the professor's amulet collection," I said.

Hilo nodded yes again. "Peter wanted to give one of them to his mother to replace the one that Roy stole from her, and sell the rest. Bad luck for Strand, I guess. I wasn't about to return his stolen property."

"Peter wanted the amulet that you never returned," I hissed. "The one you never really showed to Professor Strand, and the one that was never really in Erik's hand at all. That was just the story you told me . . . You killed Erik and Lida to find the remaining amulet, the one Raymond had, and I led you right to him."

"Yes, you did, much to my relief. Once I had the professor's collection and the one I'd been hanging on to, I knew there was one more out there. I just had to find it." Hilo paused for a brief second. "I see you've talked to Roy."

"Did you think I wouldn't?"

"My mistake, I guess. But here we are, so I guess it doesn't matter much, does it?"

"I never figured you for the type, Hilo," I said, with as much disappointment as I could muster. "I thought your job meant everything to you. You didn't have any worries. I thought you had enough money to get by."

"Enough to get by. You've been in my house. Ardith spent it as quick as it came in, packed that house floor to ceiling with knickknacks and crap. I was stuck there as much as I was in my job. No way out but to die."

I breathed deep, stared at Hilo.

"I always said you were the smartest girl I ever knew, Marjorie." He pointed the tip of the knife at me and stepped forward.

I stepped back, raised my purse to defend myself. "I'm sorry. Stop, please, Hilo. I have Hank to see to, to take care of. You can't do that to him . . ." My mouth went dry as the words came out. They bounced off the walls as loud as the door slam.

"Hank's had some bad luck, hasn't he?" Hilo paused and cocked his ear to the door.

I heard it too, a distant siren. It was too far away to know if it was heading this way or not, but there was no mistaking it for the wind.

"Do you have the amulet?" Hilo demanded.

I hesitated, looked at my purse, then back to Hilo. Fear grew in his eyes, the grip on the fillet knife tighter.

"I do," I said. "You can have it."

Before Hilo could move another step, I reached into my purse, wrapped my index finger around the amulet, and cupped the rest of it in my hand as tight as I could.

Hilo was over six feet from me. The length of Guy's body. I had no choice. The amulet was the only weapon I had. I hurled it as hard as I could at Hilo's head.

Luckily, he wasn't expecting me to defend myself, didn't have time to cower, to cover his face. The amulet hit him square between the eyes, at the bridge of his nose. He screamed in pain, dropped the knife, and staggered backward, to the side door.

The amulet fell to the floor and rolled out of sight.

I had no time to waste. I let go of my purse, and scurried to Guy's .38. It was my only chance. If I stopped, if I hesitated, Hilo would kill me. I was sure of that, as sure as I was that Raymond was dead as a mouse caught in a glue trap.

I grabbed the revolver, pulled the hammer back, and pointed the gun directly at Hilo.

Aim for the head, Marjorie. It was Hank's voice in my memory. But this was no .22. I could taste revenge, hate, in my mouth, and I didn't like it at all.

I hesitated as Hilo staggered upward. His nose was tilted, broken, spewing blood. He rushed me like an injured bull, and I pulled the trigger.

The bullet caught him square in the shoulder and stopped his forward motion. I pulled the trigger again, just to make sure I stopped him. That shot flung him backward, buckled his knees, and he fell to the ground.

The garage smelled like gunpowder and blood. Sirens droned

closer, drowning out the rain. I stood there, the gun pointed at Hilo just in case he stirred, tried to come after me again. My heart raced and sweat dropped across my lips.

I was about to sigh with relief when I heard the thunder. But it wasn't thunder from outside. It was inside the garage, coming from the rear of the Chevy. Someone was trapped inside it, beating on the lid to get out.

I stepped over Guy, kept the gun trained on Hilo, who was nothing but a heap of flesh, groaning in pain, still alive.

The trunk was locked. I hesitated again, then hoped that the keys were inside the car. I didn't want to see Raymond in the state he was in, but I had no choice.

I eased my way along the side of the car, peered in the window, the stench of death growing stronger with each breath, glad to see that the keys were in the ignition. I looked over my shoulder, made sure Hilo hadn't moved, then reached in, grabbed the keys, and made my way back to the trunk. I popped it open as quick as I could.

Peter Knudsen stared up at me, his hands tied together, furnace tape over his mouth, his feet free. I was so relieved that I could have cried, but I didn't. I reached in and pulled the tape off his mouth.

"Boy, Mrs. Trumaine, I sure am glad to see you."

"I'm glad to see you too, Peter. I'm really glad to see you."

CHAPTER 38

I had never been to so many funerals, so close together in my life, and I hoped that such a turn would never come this way again. In our neck of the woods, this would be the crime of the century, a dark cloud in our history.

Thankfully, one of those funerals hadn't been Guy Reinhardt's. He was going to recover, but the doctors still weren't sure whether there would be any lasting effects from the concussion. I hoped not, Guy'd had enough troubles in his life.

Hilo had lived, too, and would have to face the punishment for his crimes. I'm not sure that justice could ever be served, but at least he had been stopped. Hank said I should have shot him in the head when I'd had the chance. I didn't want to live with that.

In between the funerals, I had Hank to see to, of course. I waited a few days before I told him the truth of things. I struggled with that thought. Maybe he would have been better off not knowing, just slipped away with his memory blank. But in the end, I decided that I would want to know if it'd been me. Hank was quieter than normal for days after.

And I had a deadline to face. Reluctantly, I called Richard Rothstein and explained my situation to him. After a long breath of silence, he said, "Well, Miss Trumaine, you may have another ten days. I always pad the indexer's schedule with extra days just in case something like this happens, an act of God, whatever. That line of thinking has served me well. Thank you for the call. Oh, since you called, we have another book that you may be interested in indexing. *A Guide to Shinto Spirits.* Are you interested?" I hesitated. I didn't know what a Shinto spirit was.

Which, of course, was my main reason for saying yes—besides needing the money. There was always that.

I was sure Burlene Standish was listening. But I said nothing as Richard Rothstein rang off, wishing me a good day as he went.

And so, there I sat at my desk two days into Sir Nigel's book, the deadline reachable, the dust settled. Hank was in bed, comfortable, still catching up on his rest, and Shep was at my feet. He perked up at the sound of a truck pulling past the gate, into our drive.

I looked up to see the Knudsens' red and white International Harvester making its way toward the house. Jaeger was driving, Betty Walsh sat in the middle, and Peter sat in the passenger seat, looking out the window. Shep was already out of the room before I could put the lid on my box of index cards. I smiled, eased away from my desk, and made my way past the bedroom. I didn't worry much about the state of my appearance. The Knudsen boys had seen me in worse shape recently, but I was presentable, back to my daily routine of brushing my hair in the morning and putting on a fresh housedress.

"Who is it?" Hank said, his face turned to me with concern.

"Peter and Jaeger. Relax."

"I think that might take a while."

"I suppose you're right." I pushed off, and made my way outside. Shep followed me, circled Jaeger as he got out of the truck. Betty Walsh didn't move, just smiled and waved. I returned the gesture.

"I wasn't expecting to see you boys today," I said. "I would've made some lemonade if I'd known you were coming."

Jaeger stopped before me and nodded. "We won't take too much of your time, Miss Marjorie. I know you're busy."

Peter joined Jaeger, stood shoulder-to-shoulder with his brother. It was like looking at Erik and Lida through binoculars. I could see their profiles, their gaits, hear their voices, but it was all distant. Peter looked me in the eye, smiled, then looked to the ground.

"Peter's going away soon," Jaeger said. "The lawyer and the judge made a deal with the military. He has to pass some tests, a physical, but they don't think it'll be a problem getting him in the Air Force. As long as Peter keeps his nose clean, he won't have a record. But the first foul-up, then off to the clink he goes." Jaeger glanced over to Peter with a hard glare.

"That won't happen," Peter said.

"You're lucky, Peter," I said.

"I know," he answered. Jaeger nudged him with his elbow, and Peter offered me a package.

I stared at his hand, at the little box wrapped in tissue paper, and stared at them questioningly.

"We'll understand if you don't want it," Jaeger said.

Peter nodded. "We both think our mother would like you to have it."

My heart caught in my chest. I knew the amulet was in the box, and I hesitated. I had never wanted to see that thing again, but now I had no choice. I couldn't be rude. I took the box from Peter but didn't open it.

"My mother always believed in the powers that it was supposed to have," Peter said. "All the boys came back from overseas after the war, no matter whether Uncle Roy stole it or not."

Jaeger nodded. "It kept you safe, Miss Marjorie. It protected you from Hilo the whole time you had it."

"Do you really believe that?" I asked.

Jaeger shrugged. "I'm just glad you and Hank are still here, Miss Marjorie, that's all. I'm just glad you didn't get hurt."

"Me, too," Peter said, with a shy smile. "Me, too."

I hugged and thanked them both and watched the three of them drive off, glad that they still had their lives ahead of them, glad that there was still a Knudsen on the next farm over.

I tossed the box from one hand to the other, certain that I would never open it, never look at the amulet again, then glanced down at Shep and patted his head. He wagged his bushy tail, and I was almost certain that the border collie smiled at me.

"Come on, Shep, we've got an index to finish and a deadline to meet. Let's go see what the headhunters are up to now."

Shep barked, circled after me, and followed me into the house, happy to be inside, watching over Hank and I. And I was glad of it, too.

ACKNOWLEDGMENTS

Of all the things that I have learned as an indexer, the most important, I think, is that no two indexers will ever write the same index. The act of indexing is as much a science as it is an art; therefore, the learning never ends. I've had many teachers as an indexer, too many to list here, whether they were true mentors, project editors, copy editors, proofreaders, or readers offering ideas about access points into the varied texts I've had the pleasure of indexing. I thank them all.

I'd also like to thank Mary Beth and Greg Maack for their generosity, hospitality, and encouragement over the years. Our afternoon spent in your kitchen, learning how to make lefse, will not soon be forgotten and is greatly appreciated.

Liz and Chris Hatton and their border collie experience contributed greatly to my understanding of herding dogs. Thank you, Ceilidh and Duffy. I will be happy to be put in my place on Sunday afternoon. It is always a pleasure to thank Cherry Weiner, my longtime agent. She never gave up on Marjorie because she never gives up. Thanks, too, to Dan Mayer for taking a chance on me, and on Marjorie. I've wanted to write this book for a long time. Finally, thanks to Rose. We never knew where this journey would take us, but I'm really happy that you want to continue on to see what happens next.

ABOUT THE AUTHOR

Larry D. Sweazy (www.larrydsweazy.com) has been a freelance indexer for seventeen years. In that time, he has written over eight hundred back-of-the-book indexes for major trade publishers and university presses such as Addison-Wesley, Cengage, American University at Cairo Press, Cisco Press, Pearson Education, Pearson Technology, University of Nebraska Press, Weldon Owen, and many more. He continues to work in the indexing field on a daily basis.

As a writer, Larry is a two-time WWA (Western Writers of America) Spur Award winner, a two-time, back-to-back, winner of the Will Rogers Medallion Award, a Best Books of Indiana Award winner, and the inaugural winner of the 2013 Elmer Kelton Book Award. He was also nominated for a Short Mystery Fiction Society (SMFS) Derringer Award in 2007 (for the short story "See Also Murder"). Larry has published over sixty nonfiction articles and short stories, and is the author of the Josiah Wolfe, Texas Ranger western series (Berkley), the Lucas Fume western series (Berkley), and a thriller set in Indiana, *The Devil's Bones* (Five Star). He currently lives in Indiana with his wife, Rose.